Three extraordinary ladies.
Three extraordinary love stories!

Welcome to Victorian London, where a trio of unconventional widows aren't afraid to take scandalous risks in order to claim their independence...and love on their terms!

In *One Night with the Duchess*

Widowed duchess and virgin Isabelle must prove her marriage was consummated or face losing her title and stepson! Her plan? Seek out notorious rake Lord Ashworth to bed her!

Read Wilhemina's story

After Wilhemina's awful husband is suddenly murdered, she's shocked when long-term friend Leo, Viscount Pemberton, offers to protect her—with a marriage proposal!

And coming soon:

Read Mary's story

Bold Mary Lambert demands that self-made businessman Cameron Sykes offer her a job...but she doesn't count on how tempting working in such close proximity to Cameron will be!

Author Note

Thank you so much for reading *Romancing His Convenient Viscountess*!

In thinking about my three young widows of West End and, specifically, thinking of the types of trauma they might have lived with in Victorian times, I couldn't ignore the opportunity to write one of them as the survivor of an abusive marriage.

In knowing what I do about the Victorian *ton*'s chaperoned, short courtships and the financial and other incentives that went into marriage matches, I couldn't help but ponder how rare it must have been for a Victorian woman, especially a noble one, to find a true love match. Moreover, I couldn't help but think how many of them, girls barely twenty, ended up with men like Windhurst, trapped in situations that, unlike us modern ladies, they could *never* get out of.

Wilhemina was born from those musings. And, although I wanted to focus more on her chance at true love than her past trauma, that was often easier said than done.

But Leo...Leo swooped onto the page with all the love in his heart and about as much knowledge as a Victorian-era man would realistically have had about such things as PTSD (as in, none at all) and, though he made a few mistakes along the way, I think he needed to prove only one thing to both Willa and to me: love *and* the commitment to be there for your partner on their worst days can overcome the worst of suffering.

This story was such a lovely adventure for me, and I hope that you enjoyed reading about Wild Wilhemina and Lovely Leo as much as I enjoyed writing them!

If you enjoyed *Romancing His Convenient Viscountess* and would like to stay in touch with the Widows of West End, Mary and Sykes's book is coming soon! You can also follow along @author.maggie on Instagram for news, promotions and sneak peeks.

ROMANCING HIS CONVENIENT VISCOUNTESS

MAGGIE WESTON

Recycling programs for this product may not exist in your area.

ISBN-13: 978-1-335-54011-9

Romancing His Convenient Viscountess

Harlequin Enterprises ULC
22 Adelaide St. West, 41st Floor
Toronto, Ontario M5H 4E3, Canada
www.Harlequin.com

Printed in U.S.A.

Maggie Weston is a Victorian-era enthusiast. Though she grew up voraciously consuming classical literature, she stumbled upon her first romance novel at age eleven and never looked back. When she's not writing or researching all the weird things our predecessors did, she can be found reading, taking on home improvement projects that she thinks she can handle (but can't) and watching period dramas. Maggie lives with her husband, two dogs and innumerable houseplants in California.

Books by Maggie Weston

Harlequin Historical

One Night with the Duchess

Look out for more books from Maggie Weston coming soon.

Visit the Author Profile page at Harlequin.com.

For my siblings, who are always one call away.

Prologue

London—1843

Wilhemina, Lady Windhurst, stared at her eldest brother Greyson, Viscount Pearson, in silence as his words registered in her tired mind. If she had heard him correctly—and she rather hoped she had—her husband, Earl Windhurst, was dead.

Greyson stood in the centre of her lavishly furnished drawing room, his back straight, his brown eyes staring at her with mild panic. He looked like a foreign prince, she thought. One who'd landed in a country where everything was just a little too quaint for him. His imposing figure looked almost comical against the powder-blue floral background her French wallpaper provided.

There had been a time when she'd truly believed that he was her protector and that he could—*would*—protect her from anything. However, like most things in life, the belief had been a childish fantasy, one that had been swiftly crushed to dust under the booted heel of womanhood.

'Willa,' Greyson urged, coming forward, his hands outstretched as if to calm a wild horse, 'you must leave. Maybe go and stay with Isabelle and Matthew in the country until the worst of the scandal blows over.'

Willa stepped away from her brother's touch, turning her back on him as he had turned his back on her over the last two and a half years of her marriage. 'Thank you for informing me,' she replied, no hint of emotion in her voice save a touch of deliberate uninterest. She wielded it effectively, knowing that it would hurt the man who had once been her favourite person in the entire world. 'You may take your leave.'

But Grey did not go. Instead, he talked to her back, his voice tight with desperation and regret. 'Willa, how long are you going to hate me?'

'Most likely for ever.'

'I did what—'

'I said: get out.'

'And what of your dead husband, Sister?' he asked quietly, reminding her, yet again, of her position in the world. 'If I leave, who is going to help you to arrange everything?' he demanded, his frustration snapping through the room. 'Who is going to organise the funeral and ensure that Windhurst's murderers are brought to justice?' He did not wait for her to reply before continuing. 'Wilhemina, your position in society was hanging by a thread *before* this. And now—'

'I once read a book on Jain karma,' Wilhemina interrupted.

'I hardly see—'

'Do you think my husband's soul will transmigrate as an earl a second time—given the life he led?' She couldn't contain the bitter laugh that crawled up her throat. 'Probably not.' She smiled coldly and, turning to her brother, said, 'Let me tell you one thing I am absolutely certain of: my husband's death was perfectly appropriate considering how he lived his life. A gambler, a womaniser, a brute of a man who was undoubtedly killed by some seedy character he owed money to, in the home he'd bought for his whore.'

'Willa—'

'I do not care what people will say. I will relish the fact that society's last memory of him will be true to his character.'

'Be that as it may, I am thinking about *you* now, Willa. You will be the brunt of society's jokes for years to come. You—'

Wilhemina ignored her brother as he continued to speak. She had been the brunt of society's jokes for over a year, since her husband had taken to town with his mistress in a public display that had left Wilhemina shunned and ashamed. But, so far, she had survived quite well.

She pulled the bell rope in the corner of the room, summoning her maid.

Perhaps realising that he would get nowhere, Grey stopped talking, but the silence that filled the drawing room while they waited for Peggy to get out of bed and dress was cloying and thick, filled with everything they could not take back and, at least on Willa's part, had no desire to.

Peggy knocked on the open door, her eyes still half shut with sleep, her frizzy hair a frightful mess. 'Lady Windhurst?'

'My husband is dead, Peggy,' Willa said with no preamble. She had no need to soften the news.

She and Peggy looked at one another, their silent messages easily interpretable to anyone who had similarly suffered. 'My condolences, milady,' Peggy murmured eventually.

'Please lay out a gown for me. I'll be up to dress momentarily. I have some business to attend to.'

'We have no mourning gowns ready. But I can set out last Season's grey?'

'No.' Willa smiled for the first time in what seemed like years. Aware that her brother was listening, she took an exaggerated moment to mull before deciding. 'I'll want the red silk, Peggy.'

Greyson cursed, which, he should have known, only fuelled Wilhemina's flaming determination.

Although she did not say a word, Peggy's eyes gleamed with vindication and, as she turned away, Willa caught her maid's hell-be-damned grin. There were some things in life, Willa knew, that transcended class and a woman's scorn for cruel men was certainly one of the frontrunners.

'Think before you act, Willa.'

Without moving from the door, she flickered her eyes over her brother. And she felt nothing at all. No sadness over what they'd lost. No regret over the quarrel that had separated them, at least in her mind, for ever.

'Willa,' he begged, his panic breaking through his tone, 'you cannot face this alone. The scandal will destroy you.' He turned his hat in his hands as he looked at her. 'You are going to need my help—whether you want it or not.'

And it was that small word—*help*—issued from his lips that broke her, flooding her with a mingled pain and fury so intense that she could have wept from it.

Still, Willa did not scream as she would have liked.

She opened the door wider and replied quietly, calmly, 'I came to you for help once, Brother, and you turned me away, proving to me exactly where I stood with you: a brood mare that, once sold and proved defective, you did not want returned.' She smiled bitterly at his sharp intake of breath. 'You have been dead to me since.'

She met his shocked gaze even as her forgotten grief started to rise up, clogging her throat. 'Do not come here again.' Her voice was so calm, so quiet, that even she marvelled at her control. 'Do not write me. Do not ever stop me in the street. From this day forward, we are strangers—and you can tell the rest of your family that the same applies to them.'

'Willa,' he urged, growing desperate. 'Rose is with child. She is worried about you—'

Willa's wild laugh rang through the room even as her heart broke with the knowledge that she would never know her young niece or nephew. 'Congratulations, Earl Russell.' She took one step forward and waited until Grey's broken gaze met hers. 'May you be plagued with daughters.' And with that said, she turned and left the room.

Wilhemina did not regret her words—if severing oneself from one's family would typically make a person feel very alone in the world, she felt nothing. Nothing at all.

Leo Vickery, Viscount Pemberton, loved life. And of all the things in life he enjoyed, drinking, screwing and sleeping—typically in that exact order of operations—were at the top of the list. It was no wonder, then, that he woke up angry, the urgent shaking pulling him from a whisky-induced dream involving a specific blonde with the body of a nymph and the mouth of a seasoned dockworker—a mouth he had just been putting to very good use.

He grunted his disapproval once and attempted to roll over, seeking the dream and the fantasies it wrought.

'Leo! For God's sake, you big bastard! Wake up!'

His eyes flew open as he plummeted from the edge of sleep to wide awake. For one perfect second as his brain cleared, he lay still on top of the bed, staring at Wilhemina. She was dressed in a scarlet gown, her long hair haphazardly braided so that it fell in a rope over one shoulder to her waist. She looked so beautiful, so enticingly dishevelled, that Leo momentarily worried he might still be dreaming.

But it was only when she started talking again, saying, 'Do you know that you are naked?' that he realised she was not his dream come to life, but the flesh-and-blood woman.

And she was in his bedchamber.

And he was, as she'd so helpfully pointed out, naked.

Before he could think to behave like the man of thirty-three that he was, he dropped his hands to cover his waking erection and rolled in the opposite direction from where she stood—straight off the bed. He landed on the carpeted floor with a heavy, 'Oomph', as the breath was forced from his lungs.

There was a beat of silence where he could do nothing save close his eyes in mortification.

'Well, now that I've seen you in all your glory, I understand what all the fuss is about,' Wilhemina drawled, no embarrassment in her tone.

Leo exhaled a staggered laugh and banged his head against the carpeted floor as he tried to still his waking body. Willa was here, in his house, dressed in red. And he was naked, face down on the floor. He took a deep, calming breath and prayed his voice was steady. 'Willa, this has gone too far—even for you.'

She laughed and he hated that it sounded so bitter, so different from the wild, joyful laugh he'd grown up with. 'Oh, Leo. I'm only just getting started.'

'What has happened?' he asked, frowning down at the carpet. As his mind cleared, he understood that even Willa would not have sought him out in the middle of the night were the situation not dire.

For a moment she didn't reply, only moved about the room as if searching for something. 'Get dressed.' His dressing gown landed on top of him with a soft thud. 'My husband is dead.'

Leo didn't move. *'Dead,'* he repeated, stunned senseless by the statement.

'Yes—murdered.' And with that she left the room, her footfall quiet on the carpeted floor.

When the door clicked shut behind her Leo pushed to a stand, his typically agile movements made staccato by the blunt statement and the resultant flood of alarm through his system.

Windhurst is dead?

His mind ran ragged as he hurriedly changed, leaving off his waistcoat and cravat in his rush.

He ran down the stairs, his mind working overtime.

Where is the body? Had she tried to dispose of it? Where could he take her?

He hurried through the hall and into his study without stopping to summon a servant. Though he assumed his valet had let Wilhemina into the house, the fewer people who knew she'd come the better.

He pulled up short when he saw her, standing by his bookshelf, staring at the well-cracked spines of titles he'd randomly packed side by side with no thought to genre or title. 'We will leave immediately,' he said, not wasting time with questions. 'I have a cousin in France.'

Willa turned from the books to aim her frown at him. 'I have no intention of leaving, Leo.'

'Willa.' He approached her slowly. He looked into her sad eyes, eyes that used to sparkle with life and mischief. 'You haven't a choice. If you killed him—'

Those sad eyes rounded, momentarily filling with surprised delight. 'You think that *I* killed him?' she asked, not trying to hide her amusement. 'Lord, could you imagine?'

'Are you telling me that you *did not*?' he asked even as his heart settled and his stomach relaxed.

Willa shook her head. 'Leo...' To his absolute horror, her eyes glossed over with tears. 'That your first thought when you assumed I'd killed my husband was to protect me is exactly why I'm here.' She swiped at her eyes in frustration. 'I need your help.'

Her words crushed him, reminding him of all the times in the past year he'd sensed her floundering and asked her if she'd needed him—and all the times she'd said no. He took a step closer, immediately stopping when she shrank back.

He lowered his voice as he might when talking to a scared child or an abused dog. 'What do you need help with, Wild Girl?'

'You are going to escort me.'

He walked to the door by way of answer and held it open, waiting for her to pass before him. 'And where are we going?'

Willa's face was masked with sardonic amusement as she sailed past him. 'Why, to check that the bastard is actually dead, of course.'

He hurried after her, not entirely sure he'd heard her right. 'You...you want to look at the body?'

'Yes.'

Willa pushed open his front door to reveal her carriage. 'My husband's debt collectors have been looking for him. And though Greyson tells me that Miss Pierce witnessed his death, I would not put anything past my husband. He is exactly the type of person who would allow me to celebrate his demise—and then *pop* back up very much alive months from now.' She did not wait for her footman to open the door, merely did it herself and climbed in. 'I intend to confirm that he is deceased with my very own eyes.'

Leo unquestioningly climbed into the carriage and sat down opposite her. Like everything Windhurst had owned, the carriage was ostentatiously finished, with plush red velvet seats and gold brocade trim. Leo found it rather claustrophobic, as if he were Jonah, sitting in the whale's red velvet mouth immediately before it swallowed him whole.

He watched Willa's face in the dark, trying to read her emotions as the wheels rumbled over the cobbled streets. Whatever she had felt towards her late husband had nothing to do with the shock of his murder or the resultant confusion she must be suffering. Leo, who had lost his own mother a year earlier, knew that better than everyone else.

His mother had been like some beautiful, ethereal queen from another world, but she had been cold and elusive as a parent, lacking even the most basic of maternal instincts. In fact, if he truly thought about it, she had been cold and elusive towards everyone save his father. For all her faults, Katherine Vickery had loved her husband.

When she'd died, Leo had been shocked. Not sad. He had not known her well enough to grieve as his father had done. But the surprise of her death and, perhaps, the end of any chance to connect with her had affected him in ways he could not succinctly explain except to say that he had been overwhelmed by his own empty confusion.

So, Leo knew that whatever Wilhemina was feeling just then, even if it was not grief, was not simple. 'Are you all right?'

Willa turned to him, her angular face starkly silhouetted in the shadowed carriage. 'I…' She exhaled a fearful sigh, one that lanced his own heart. 'Leo, I am almost too afraid to believe that I am finally free.' She turned away to look out at the night-darkened streets. 'I had started to believe that it would last an entire lifetime—*my* lifetime.'

Unable to stop himself from comforting her, Leo leaned forward and took her cold hands in his. She flinched at even that small contact, but he did not—could not—let her go. He gently chafed her hands between his bigger palms, trying to warm her even as her bare skin sent a jolt of need careening through his body. 'Where are your gloves, Wilhemina?'

'Hmm? My what?'

'Your gloves,' he repeated. 'Your hands are freezing.'

'Oh.' Willa looked down at their joined hands as if she were outside her body, a stranger watching a magician perform some trick that she was trying to figure out. 'I suppose I forgot them,' she murmured and gently removed her hands from his.

As much as he wanted to touch her, he understood that Wilhemina had been deprived of casual affection for too long to be comfortable with it. 'Once we confirm that he is dead, what will you do first?'

'I will shock the *ton* by forgoing a mourning period,' she stated without hesitation.

'The dress,' he murmured. And even though he tried to be subtle in his perusal of her, it was impossible not to notice how the red silk bodice added curves to her coltish frame, her hidden corset exaggerating a tiny waist that had dwindled past fashionable thinness.

'Do you like it?' She flounced her skirt dramatically, but did not wait for a reply before continuing. 'I will ride my horse in breeches like Isabelle does—except I will ride through Hyde Park at peak promenade hours.' Her grin was wide, flashing white teeth, but to Leo it looked a little untamed. Wild. 'Can you imagine them, Leo? Whispering and gulping like goldfish in their corsets as I ride past with nothing to stay me?'

Leo, though Willa's closest friend besides Isabelle and

Mary, was still a man. His throat tightened at the image her words painted. He could imagine her, long-limbed and slender, wearing fitted trousers—and nothing else. 'What else?' he asked hoarsely, needing a distraction from his own lurid fantasies.

'I want to learn how to fence.' She frowned. 'Though I don't suppose I'll be able to find anyone who will teach me.'

'And you would wear the new trousers, of course.'

Willa nodded eagerly. 'I will sell Windhurst's mistress's house and belongings and use the proceeds to travel Italy.'

'Matthew tells me that one has not lived until they have seen Vatican City,' he encouraged her.

'I will dance at balls again, knowing that my husband cannot stop me any longer.'

'May I have your first dance?'

'Of course you may. I hardly think the rest of the *ton* is going to go along with my plan, Leo. In fact…' she tilted her head in mock consideration '…now that I think about it, I may have to dance *every* dance with you.'

'A dream come true.'

Willa chuckled quietly as if he'd told a joke when, really, he'd spoken the absolute truth. 'But for now…' she murmured.

The carriage came to a gentle stop.

Willa fell completely silent. She did not move. Leo could not even tell if she breathed. 'Wait here one moment.' He clambered out, his hatred for Windhurst growing by degrees when he saw the neo-classical Regent's Park terraced home he'd put his mistress up in.

The home was large and stately, a humiliating fact that Willa had suffered the past two years of Windhurst's overt philandering. Imposing Ionic columns lined the front entrance like fingers, holding up a large, sculptural pediment that housed white statue figures from Greek mythology. Zeus with his royal sceptre, Poseidon with his trident, Demeter with a sheaf of wheat and a naked Aphrodite, among others.

The Metropolitan Police were still at the house, the Peelers' dark blue uniforms merging with the night like spirits in the shadows. The scene—the three or four uniformed men waiting around in the dark outside the grand home—induced a chill to run over Leo's skin.

One of the men approached when he saw the Windhurst carriage. The man's eyes raked over Leo as he tried to put the pieces together. 'May I help you, milord?'

'I have heard that Earl Windhurst has been murdered,' Leo said without wasting any time. If people saw him here, saw *Willa* here…

'Aye, heard right. Shot in t'chest. His dollymop reckons the lads got into it over some debt. The lord made a grab for t'gun, a struggle took place and it misfired.' The bobby leaned in, lowering his voice dramatically. 'The gel ran for our lad on beat, but by the time he got here, it was too late. He'd bled out.'

'Is the Commissioner here?'

'Just missed him. Took the gel to the yard for her witness account.' Having related everything he knew, the man shrugged.

Leo tried not to show his relief. The Commissioner, Sir Charles Rowan, had a moral compass that pointed due north. He had been a war hero prior to his appointment to first Commissioner of the Metropolitan Police, a man whose wartime promotions to lieutenant-colonel in the British Army had been earned in the field, not purchased… All of which to say that he was notoriously straight and unbribable. His officers, on the other hand…

Leo took out a gold sovereign and held it between his thumb and index finger so that it glinted in the moonlight. 'I have Windhurst's wife with me.'

The man grimaced in the direction of the carriage. 'Bloody hell.'

'She wants to confirm that the deceased is her husband.' Leo shook his head, trying to appear morose. 'She's very distressed,' he practically whispered, leaning forward as if imparting a particularly painful confidence. 'She insists it could not be him.'

There was a distinct snort from the direction of the carriage. If the officer heard it, he did not react. His eyes focused on the coin as he considered. 'Ye'd have t'take a man. Can't have you tramplin' about the crime scene.'

Leo passed the coin to the officer. 'Of course. We need only a minute or two to verify that the deceased is, in fact, the Earl.'

The coin disappeared into the man's pocket. He waved his hand, indicating for Leo to follow. 'Come on. Two minutes—' The policeman stopped talking abruptly, his mouth falling open.

Leo did not have to turn around to know that Willa had alighted from the carriage, her red dress catching the moonlight—he could see the stunned appreciation in the officer's eyes. He waited for her to come abreast of him before urging the police officer onwards. 'Lead the way, man.'

The officer removed his hat and bowed theatrically. 'Milady. My condolences.'

Willa nodded and, though Leo saw the mocking gleam in her eye, she did not reply or otherwise contradict his story.

'This way.' The officer led them up the stairs and into the grand hall of the house as if Willa was the Queen of England herself.

Leo marvelled at how quiet the house was—no shocked servants, no grieving friends, not even the ticking of a clock. Beside him, Willa stood tall, her spine straight, her big brown eyes expressionless.

'Are you sure you have to see him, milady?' the bobby asked as he stopped outside a closed door immediately off the hall. 'It's not pretty.'

'Please.'

The officer nodded and pushed open the door before stepping back. 'I'll wait here if it's all the same to ye. Just don't touch anything.'

'Thank you.' When Willa did not move forward, Leo gently took her elbow and guided her into the room.

They entered was what clearly the receiving room, one exorbitantly furnished with extravagant decorations adorning every available surface—plush rose-pink carpets, spindly-legged furniture with pastel upholstery, doilies on every surface, jewelled lampshades and white lace curtains. The warm glow from a single candle added an eerie overtone that made Leo feel positively entombed.

And as if the suffocating furnishings weren't enough, there, sprawled on a dainty sofa, his head thrown back, his eyes and mouth open, his shirt blooming with red blood that contrasted with the soft colours in the room, was Lord Windhurst.

'Are you sure—?'

Willa did not wait for him to finish the question. She marched further into the dim room to stand before her husband. Her red dress, glimmering in the candlelight, appeared strangely harmonic with the fantastical scene. She appeared as a vengeful angel might, standing over the corpse of the man she'd come to judge—and found irredeemable.

Leo stepped quietly to her side as she absorbed the details of Windhurst's face—the breathless mouth and lifeless eyes.

'It is him?' Willa whispered finally, her voice incredulous, as if she still could not believe it even though she stood in front of his corpse to bear witness.

'It is.'

She nodded once and, without looking back at her dead husband or the room, marched for the door.

Leo stayed a moment longer, looking at Windhurst's corpse and damning him to hell. Here was a man who had possessed everything, who could have had it all—wealth, life, happiness, love—if only he'd tried to deserve it instead of taking it all for granted, instead of always wanting more.

He was just about to turn and leave when he saw it: Windhurst's left hand, drooping low off the sofa, his gold wedding band glinting. Before he could think, before he could second-guess himself, Leo reached down and pried the ring off the man's finger. 'You did not deserve to wear this,' he murmured, hoping that Windhurst could hear him in hell. 'You will be buried with nobody to grieve you. And you will go into the ground with no claim on her.'

With that said, Leo stood and quickly left the room before anyone else entered. The ring burned a hole in his pocket, but it did not give him pause. As soon as he stepped outside, he started for where the same officer was helping Willa into the carriage.

'Thank you.' He passed the man another sovereign. The bobby nodded his appreciation and Leo looked up at the driver. 'Mayfair. Windhurst House.' Though they might have escaped notice thus far considering the time of night, he did not want to add to the impending scandal by taking Willa back to his residence.

As the carriage started moving she sank forward in her

seat, head bowed over her legs as she tried to breathe through her panic.

'Willa?'

She started trembling, her entire body visibly shaking in front of him. 'I… I d-don't know w-what's wrong with me.'

He reached for her immediately, cupping his hands under her elbows and lifting her off her seat. He repositioned her on the seat next to him when what he really wanted to do was cradle her on his lap until she stopped shaking.

'W-what are you d-doing?' she managed to say, her teeth chattering.

'I am being here for you,' he replied truthfully. 'Just let it go, sweetheart.' And when she didn't, when she held it in instead, forcing her tremors to become more violent, he whispered, 'I won't tell anyone. I promise.'

Her breath started heaving as soon as the vow left his lips, her sobs filling the confined space, suffocating them both with years of her trapped pain. And as she cried, her body shuddering with emotion, all Leo could do was wrap her in his arms and hold her against him. Though he could not say it to her, he promised himself that she would never ever feel this helpless again.

Chapter One

London—1843,
two months later

Simon Briggs looked at her, his slightly embarrassed expression telling Willa everything she needed to know before the words, 'I'm sorry, my lady, but there is nothing left of your husband's estate', left his mouth.

Still, the word *nothing* fell into the room and Willa was horrified to realise that she was the one who'd said it.

Mr Briggs, Isabelle's kind solicitor, who had stepped in to help her settle her late husband's affairs, shook his head. Everyone else in the room—Isabelle, Mary, Matthew and Leo—remained gravely silent as they digested the news.

'But my dowry was *significant*,' she supplied, struggling to conceive how one man could lose so much in less than three years. 'Even with Windhurst's penchant for excess, his drinking, gaming and whoring, there should have been some of it left.' Her voice fell to a disbelieving whisper. 'Surely?'

'It appears as if your husband was able to mask the true state of his finances from your father and brother at the time of your betrothal.' Mr Briggs cleared his throat gently. 'To be quite blunt, Lady Wilhemina, he probably needed your dowry more than he needed a wife or an heir. Prior to your marriage, his financial ruin was imminent. And as it stands, your dowry, though admittedly substantial, is almost entirely gone.'

Matthew, Lord Ashworth, ran one huge hand through his perpetually unruly hair, his broad shoulders pulling at his tailored jacket with the movement. 'I knew he gambled some—but the *entire* fortune?' he queried.

'It would appear so, my lord,' Briggs replied. 'And the remaining debt that I have uncovered is just his legal debt—to business establishments, his club and several small creditors. My personal interviews with the Commissioner and Miss Pierce suggest that Lord Windhurst had also borrowed a significant sum at an insurmountable interest rate from the Wolfe brothers.' There was a collective intake of breath in the room. 'Though the Commissioner has yet to prove anything, the description of the men who fought with Lord Windhurst on the night he died match two of the Wolfes' bruisers.'

Willa's eyes remained dry, though it cost her to maintain her control. In the two months since her husband had died, she'd been bombarded with bill after bill until, at a loss for what to do, she'd had to ask for Isabelle and Matthew's help.

Her friends had closed ranks quickly, making their first appearance in town since the nasty rumours surrounding their marriage had retired them to the country a year earlier—and they'd come for no other reason than she'd needed help. Even Mary, who was closer to Isabelle than Willa, had closed up her little apartment above her place of work to come and stay in the house with Wilhemina for a few days.

Although Wilhemina had assumed that the situation was dire, she would never have thought Windhurst foolish enough to engage the Wolfes.

The notorious twin brothers had been raised on the

streets of Covent Garden, but their lowborn circumstances had not stopped the duo from clawing their way up the social ladder using nothing but their fists and their remarkable combined intelligence. Though they never actually appeared in society, the rumour mill whispered that they could receive an invitation to any ball or social event using nothing but the information they had garnered in London's darkest corners and dingiest hovels. The fact that her husband had been indebted to them did not bode well—for her and for whatever remained of the Windhurst estate.

'And the house?' she asked. 'The Regent's Park terrace?'

'As you know, this house and the country estate are now the property of the new Earl Windhurst, your late husband's cousin. Even then, the new Earl has inherited a nearly bankrupt estate. It would be a miracle if he could save it.' Briggs took a fortifying breath. 'The Regent's Park terrace house is not entailed, however.'

'So, it could be sold?' A spark of hope flared in Wilhemina's chest. She didn't need much, only enough to humbly live out her days.

Briggs nodded, but there was no comfort in his expression. 'It would need to be,' he clarified. 'To pay off some of the Earl's remaining debt.'

'I see.' Willa steeled herself against the coldness that suffused her the moment all hope was extinguished. She banked her humiliation with little effort; she had, after all, been doing just that for years. 'Well, there goes Italy,' she replied glibly even as a heavy blanket of panic pressed down on her chest, stealing her very breath.

Everything...gone.

Her entire livelihood…

'And what of Miss Pierce?' It was Mary who broke the silence.

'She removed herself from the house immediately upon her return from Scotland Yard. As far as I was able to ascertain, she did not take anything save some of her clothing—no jewellery, no art, no furniture.'

Willa supposed that was something, for at least she would not have to deal with the other woman directly. Still, there was a strange truth that she was only beginning to face: Camilla Pierce, who had come from comparatively humble circumstances to start with, was far better equipped to survive without Windhurst than Willa was. Camilla could, at the very least, find another protector. But Willa... She was widowed and alone in the world and, although her family would take her in, Willa would rather leave the country altogether than become dependent on them again.

As she'd promised Grey, she had refused to see any of them, deliberately turning her brothers away when they had tried to come and talk to her. Though her parents had written, asking to be received, she had not even bothered replying, too betrayed by their participation in her circumstances to forgive them. Even at Windhurst's funeral, which Leo had arranged in her brother's stead, she had pointedly ignored her brothers and any attempt on their part to communicate with her. Though each of them had tried to quietly talk to her, Willa had remained silent and simply pretended they were not there at all.

'Why don't you come and stay with us?' Isabelle asked now, looking to her husband.

Matthew took his wife's hand in his, supporting her request without question. 'Please, Willa. We would love to have you.' He smiled at Isabelle and the look, so unashamedly full of love, caused a strange pang in Willa's chest. 'It's a bit of a selfish request—Isabelle misses you both terribly,'

Matthew added, looking from Willa to Mary, who had taken a job with a powerful businessman, Cameron Sykes, the year before.'The country will give you the privacy you need while Mr Briggs settles what he can here,' Isabelle added.

Wilhemina toyed with the idea for approximately five seconds. 'I can't just live off of you for the rest of my life,' she stated bluntly, pointing out the fact that her friends were so happy to gloss over.

'Why not?' Isabelle demanded. 'We love you. The children adore you. It would be like having extended family always in reach.' To Willa's horror, Isabelle sounded genuinely happy at the possibility.

'You could remarry.' The statement, from Mary, rang through the room.

For anyone else in her situation, remarrying might have been a logical solution. But for Willa, who was still trying to survive the after-effects of her first marriage, the possibility of ever marrying again bordered on nil. She was terrified by the mere suggestion.

'*Excuse* me?' she drawled, unwilling to show just how much the suggestion had affected her. She turned to Mary, her eyebrows raised haughtily. 'I have just rid myself of one husband and you would foist another on me?' She had wanted to sound glib, maybe a touch arrogant. Instead, her words came out timid. *Afraid.*

Mary smiled kindly, her calm demeanour unflinching under Willa's attempt at scorn. 'You are destitute, Willa.' Mary, as usual, cut straight to the heart of the matter. 'You refuse to let your friends and family help. Marriage is your only other option if you do not want to work for pennies.'

'People will talk if she is married so soon after her husband's death,' Isabelle argued immediately. 'It would look indecent. As if she does not respect her husband's memory.'

'I don't,' Willa stated bluntly.

Mary shook her head sadly. 'Izzy, Willa's husband was *murdered* in his *mistress's house*. And Willa has forgone mourning him. People are already talking. The society pages call her *Lady Scarlet*, for heaven's sake! Willa remarrying will be the least scandalous thing to have happened to her in the past three years.' Mary looked across the room at Willa, her expression sympathetic. 'A husband's protection would shelter you financially, Willa.'

The truth of her circumstances washed over her, flooding her with shame and bitterness. How had she fallen so far? There had been a time where she had been welcomed in every ballroom, invited to so many events that she'd had to prioritise her acceptances. But Windhurst had taken even that from her.

'Mary's not wrong,' she said now, deliberately keeping her tone humour-filled. 'Do you know, I didn't actually think that invites were rescinded before this? I had heard of it, of course. But I didn't believe it actually happened and I certainly didn't think it would ever happen to *me*.'

'It happened to us, too, you know.' Isabelle rose from her chair and came to where Willa stood.

'Though we all know Isabelle was rather glad she no longer had an obligation to attend,' Matthew commented from the sofa.

A chorus of chuckles followed the statement. Isabelle was a notorious recluse, someone who would choose to remain home with her little family over going out in society every time. She had been married off to a duke at only eighteen and widowed two short weeks later. But unlike Willa, who had experienced one Season, Isabelle had never come out into society. She didn't know what it was to dance until her feet ached or laugh and flirt until the early hours of the morning.

'True,' Isabelle said now. She took Willa's hands in her own. 'But it passed. We've already received a frightening amount of invitations this Season—'

'Not one of which my wife anticipates accepting.'

Isabelle grinned rather mischievously, her big, near-black eyes glinting. 'I would have thought I was above such petty behaviour, but as it turns out, I rather enjoy declining invitations from all those people who once turned their backs on us.'

'Unlike you, Izzy, I quite deserve to be scorned. I can hardly blame them,' Willa drawled, 'what with choosing not to mourn the bastard.'

'He did not deserve another *second* of your life.'

Everyone assembled turned to look at Leo when he spoke. He had been uncharacteristically silent during the entire conversation, and Willa, valuing his opinion, moved away from Isabelle and went to where he sat. 'Be honest with me,' she said, though the request was unnecessary—he always was. 'What should I do?'

Leo's blue eyes searched her face for a long moment. 'You are not going to like it,' he said, keeping his voice low.

'I want your opinion.'

He nodded slowly as if preparing her for a particularly difficult truth.

Willa could feel her heart thrumming in her chest as her anxiety reared, for if Leo, who was always so optimistic and light-hearted, was this concerned, then she knew her situation was irredeemable.

He shifted suddenly, moving to the edge of his seat as if he wanted to stand or perhaps get up and run away. He was quiet for so long that Willa thought he might have thought better of voicing his opinion after all. But then he reached for her, his large, warm hand closing around hers.

She flinched against the unfamiliar gentle contact, hating that the response was ingrained though she trusted Leo more than any other man in the world. 'Leo?' she questioned, seeing the fear in his eyes. 'Just tell me. Please. The suspense is worse than any dire opinion you could have.'

'I think you should remarry.' He said it calmly, as if he had thought this through before today, as if it were entirely normal, expected even. But then he added, 'Marry *me*, Willa', and the world simply fell away from her.

Wilhemina did not reply. In fact, she thought she had imagined the words until she realised that her friends and the solicitor were making a hasty exit from the room, leaving her and Leo alone together.

The door shut, trapping her with the proposal, with Leo. *'Leo.'* Willa shook her head in denial and tugged her hand from his, even as tears of shame filled her eyes. 'Do not jest—not now. I cannot stand to be the brunt of—'

'I am completely in earnest,' he replied seriously, so seriously that Willa's heart sank.

She spun away from him, growing increasingly embarrassed by the second. 'Did Matthew put you up to this?' she demanded, wanting to know who had coerced him into making such a selfless offer. Even before he had replied, she cursed. 'He had no right!'

'What? No!' He followed her as she moved away, his long legs closing the distance with little effort. 'Of course not!'

'Oh, God.' She closed her eyes. 'Is this what has become of me? Something to be passed on from man to man out of pity.'

'Wilhemina.' Leo's deep voice sounded dangerously through the room.

She looked up at him then and instinctively took a step back when she saw the quiet rage unspooling in his irises. He looked like some fallen angel, a man filled with righteous fury and yearning to do something with it.

He blanked at her movement, his expression cooling instantly, his fists unclenching at his sides. But he did not speak. He only waited for her to gather her thoughts.

'You do not have to save me, Leo,' she whispered as the first tear fell.

He would have, too. He would have married me.

The truth of it hurt far more than she'd ever thought possible, especially coming from Leo. That he, one of her closest friends, would *pity* her enough to offer himself in sacrifice... 'I will make a plan. I will be fine.'

'I am not *only* trying to help you, Willa,' he said, coming closer again. When she did not step away, he gently grasped her upper arms in his hands and tugged her forward. 'I am proposing a trade.'

'A trade?' she queried, growing more confused by the second.

He nodded. 'A deal.'

'What type of deal?' There was nothing she could offer him. She was—apparently—poor. She had severed any family connections he might have benefited from. And, perhaps worst of all, she could not stand the idea of being touched by a man, even one as familiar to her as Leo. It made her feel physically ill. It did not matter that he was sinfully attractive. She couldn't do it. Even now, with his hands loosely circling her arms, she felt trapped, panicked by what he could do to her even as she tried to remind herself that there were people outside she could call for help and that this was Leo and that he would never hurt her.

'I am thirty-three,' he said simply. 'I am *tired* of the

marriage mart. I am tired of being foisted on every young, available woman at every opportunity.'

'Then *pick someone*, Leo!' she said, raising her voice. 'For heaven's sake, you are handsome and rich and titled and an altogether decent man. You could have anyone!'

'I don't want to spend the rest of my life with a woman I picked out of a ballroom like a prime pastry.'

The low tone of his voice, the warmth from his big hands, the proximity to his body, all worked together to confuse her senses. Willa felt fear and anxiety, but also...something that was vaguely resonant of curiosity. She had the strangest urge to lean into him, to press herself against the strong lines of his body and let him carry some of her bone-deep fatigue.

'I could not in good conscience marry someone who irritates me—which eradicates nearly every society lady I've met in ten years,' Leo continued, unaware of her thoughts. 'Willa... If there was ever a woman who I could bear to be saddled to for life, it would be you. We are friends, which means we already have an advantage over our peers. We will give each other the freedom to live our lives without judgement or censure. I will look after you and protect you. I will value and honour your ideas and opinions, already knowing that they are often better than my own.'

'Leo—'

'I will never hurt you,' he continued quietly. 'In fact, I'm certain I would kill anyone who did.'

'Leo,' she interrupted again, hating the picture that he painted, hating that she *liked* the picture he painted. 'If there was ever a man I could marry, it would be you. But...' To her mortification, her tears fell rapidly now. 'I *can't*. I want to remain a widow. I want to be *free*.'

'I will never stop you from doing the things you want to do.' His hands tightened around her arms, pulling her even closer, and Willa was surprised that she did not push him away. In fact, her hands came to lie on his chest, her palms spread open, keeping him at a distance even as the heat of him beneath his waistcoat reached out to warm her.

It took every power Leo possessed to keep from kissing her. She was so close, her big brown eyes round with sadness and fear and, if he read correctly, consideration. Her vanilla scent flooded his senses, drawing him like a bee to pollen. Her upper arms in his hands were *so thin* and it was that that gave him the power to resist her. It was the reminder he needed. Willa was vulnerable.

He released her arms slowly and, even though it physically pained him, he took a large step back, depriving himself of her. 'I will not touch you again,' he promised, 'unless you want me to and until you ask.'

'Leo…' Willa wrapped her arms around herself as if she was chilled through to her very bones. 'I *can't*.'

Though her refusal did not surprise him, it still filled him with a panic that was new in its intensity. He had loved her for so long, yearned for her so frequently, but Willa could choose *anyone*. 'You don't ever have to be afraid of me, Willa. If you marry me, I will do everything in my power to make you happy.'

'There are innumerable reasons why us getting married is a terrible idea.'

'List them,' he demanded, knowing that he would do anything, promise her anything.

'First and foremost, I can't give you heirs.' She said the words quickly, as if she couldn't stand the weight of them in her throat. 'I… I don't know… My courses…' She flushed red, her eyelashes fluttering down in shame. 'They do not come.'

Leo considered her even as he digested the new information. Wilhemina couldn't even look at him. She stood there in silence, her eyes downcast, and it broke his heart. Even as a young girl, she'd always talked of having children in that off-hand way most women did, as if it were a certainty.

Leo himself had assumed he'd have children, too. He was an heir. It was expected he'd have at least one son to pass on his title to. But the thought had never truly excited him. Instead, it had left him reeling with indifference, confusion, and guilt. He had no notion of how to be a good father. Not like Matthew, who had taken to the task with ease and no self-consciousness.

And if the thought of *Willa* pregnant with *his* child made Leo feel uniquely off centre, he couldn't dwell on it. Just then, he was too conscious of the fact that his entire future seemed to be hanging on whether or not he could convince Wilhemina to be his at all.

He would have agreed to anything. So, it was an easy decision. He wanted Wilhemina and certainly more than any hypothetical children.

'How long?' he asked, knowing that he needed to tread with caution.

Willa flushed red with embarrassment. 'Over a year,' she replied, trying for matter of fact, although her voice wavered, and she could still not meet his eyes. 'The doctor does not know if the condition is permanent.'

'Willa…' He wasn't a doctor, but Leo was also not an idiot, and he did not think that her body's recent ailments had just happened to coincide with her marriage to Windhurst and the ensuing misery. She needed to be loved and nurtured. Christ, the woman needed to be fed! Anyone could see that. 'I would rather you without heirs than any other woman with them.'

Willa threw up her arms. 'You cannot possibly know that.'

'None of them has caught my interest—and not for lack of trying.'

'But *I* have?'

He thought over the question, sorting through his thoughts for a half-truth that would not scare her. 'Of course you have caught my interest, Willa. Long ago. You are beautiful and intelligent and interesting. And I, for one, think that any man would be lucky to marry a woman he already considered among his friends.'

She reared back in surprise. 'You are not just offering because you pity me?' Before he could reply, she added, 'Because I know you, Leo. And beneath the rakish façade, you are far too gentlemanly. And if you took me on only as a kindness...'

Leo hated the uncertainty in her voice, hated that she would ever doubt how deserving she was even as he understood that he was using her vulnerability to his advantage. She would never have accepted him otherwise. 'No. Helping you is a noteworthy side benefit. But marrying you is not something I would offer had I not thought it through already and thought it through considerably.'

'And what of love, Leo? What if, years from now, you meet someone and you fall in love? What of me then?' she asked. 'I will not be another man's cross to bear while he spends his nights with his mistress. And you...' She shook her head. 'Leo, your affinity for your mistress—Elaine, is it?—is well known.'

Leo's mouth quirked at the irony despite the serious topic of conversation. For only a moment, he wondered what she'd say if he told her that *she* was the only woman in the world he'd ever loved—and that he'd loved her for quite some time already.

Elaine had been a good friend and a ready lover, but Leo had never been able to give her more—and not for lack of trying. It probably would have been a relief to him if, when Wilhemina had married, he'd been able to move on from her. But he hadn't—*couldn't.* Elaine had known it and she had not cared that Leo's affections were engaged elsewhere.

As a boy, he supposed he had loved his mother, but only in the way of childish desperation born of an instinctual knowledge of what her role in his life was *supposed* to have been. But even that confused attachment had faded by the time he'd been old enough to understand that, for whatever shortcomings she'd seen in him, his mother could not love him in return.

For a moment, Leo's insecurities rose. He wasn't entirely sure Willa could ever find anything to love in him either.

But even if she didn't, even if all they ever stayed was friends, Leo had to take the chance. Because he'd told the truth when he'd said that nobody else had caught his attention—at least not like she had. 'I no longer have a mistress,' he stated. 'Elaine and I have amicably parted ways.'

She raised her eyebrows at that. 'Since when?'

'Since the day after your husband died.'

She paled. 'Why?'

'Call it foresight.'

'Leo…'

'Willa?'

'There is one more rather large problem…'

'Tell me; I'll fix it.' He would, too. He would do anything to put her mind at rest.

'I do not like to be touched,' she said quickly. 'How… That is to say, *if* I were to marry you, how would we get around that?'

Finally, a question he could answer. 'I would work to earn

your trust every day, until one day you asked me to kiss you.' He watched her eyes round with surprise, noted that, though they did not heat, they filled with curiosity. 'I would worship you with my kisses, until one day, you asked me to touch you. And then I would touch you slowly, stopping when you asked, showing you what is it to be loved by a man who knows what he's doing and cares that he's doing it right.'

Despite the absolute truth of his words, Leo still flushed with long-suppressed desire. He had flirted harmlessly with Willa when she'd been younger and he'd distanced himself out of decency when she had married Windhurst. But now, he wanted her to know what he *could* offer. And despite all the things Leo did not bring to the table, he knew, with a confidence bordering on arrogance, that he could show her pleasure. In fact, he *longed* to.

'Oh.' The single word slipped from between Wilhemina's lips. Her brown eyes glazed over. Her brow furrowed with thought.

Leo did not interrupt. She needed to decide for herself and, despite what Willa had been through, she *did* know her own mind. Leo absolutely knew that to be true.

'Leo,' she said after a long, tense moment.

Everything stilled as he waited for her reply. Even his heart didn't seem to beat, instead lying still as he replied, 'Willa?'

'I have one condition.'

'Name it.'

'If we do this, you cannot school me. Ever. And even if you think something I plan on doing is stupid. I will not be told no. I have dreamed of my freedom for too long to give it up to another man now.' She looked into his eyes and he saw her resolve. 'I want to wear breeches and curse and forgo society invitations altogether.'

'Done.' It was an easy promise. Leo was desperate; he would have promised her anything in that moment.

'All right.' She took a deep breath as if she were preparing for some horrible task. 'Yes. I'll do it,' she said, sounding rather alarmed by her acceptance.

His heart lurched pathetically in his chest. For a long moment he only stared at her in shock, almost not believing that she had actually said yes. He took one deep, calming breath. 'That's good.' And though his impulse was to pull her to him and crush his mouth to hers, though his fingers burned with the need to touch her, Leo resisted. As much as it pained him to keep his distance, it was going to take him time to earn Willa's trust.

Willa stuck her bare hand in his direction, in what they both knew was that first gesture of trust. 'We have a deal.'

Leo reached out and returned the shake without hesitation, knowing that, whatever trials might come, he'd just made the exchange of a lifetime.

Chapter Two

They were married a week later at Leo's town house, with only Matthew, Isabelle, their two children and Mary in attendance as guests. The wedding, which had only been allowed due to a special licence received from the archbishop, was not advertised—but that did not stop the *ton* from finding out.

The rarity of a special licence was overlooked as a favour to Matthew's father, who happened to be a dear friend of the archbishop's. But even that favour did not stop the archbishop from completing his duty and looking into Wilhemina's unconventional circumstances. And it was this, confirmation from the senior archbishop of the Church of England himself, that told the rest of society what they had only surmised to that point: Wilhemina was destitute and, given that she insisted on not becoming a burden to her family—a half-truth she'd told the archbishop and thought God might forgive her for—she had no choice but to remarry.

The licence was given. The wedding was arranged, largely by Isabelle and Mary, as Willa did not particularly care if there were flowers or bows, and she and Leo exchanged their vows with little fuss and clear voices. And if Willa couldn't help but compare their small ceremony to Matthew and Isabelle's the year before, which, though also hasty, had been full of love and passion, she did so unself-consciously, with the practicality of a woman who knew that not everyone was lucky enough to have a love match, but that she was lucky enough to have a second husband who was far superior than her first.

It was only after the ceremony, as they all sat in Leo's receiving room, celebrating with champagne, that the situation fully dawned on her. She had *remarried*—to *Leo.*

She looked across the room to where he—her *husband*—sat in a chair next to Matthew, his long legs stretched out in front of him, his golden hair catching the firelight. Next to him, Matthew was his contrast, dark where Leo was fair, large and muscular where Leo, though tall, was lean with ropey muscle.

As she watched, Matthew's daughter, Seraphina, toddled to where the men sat, a crystal ashtray she had picked up off a nearby table in her hand. Without stopping his conversation, Matthew reached out and accepted the unusual gift from his daughter. He thanked her as if she'd given him the very moon, discreetly handed the ashtray to Leo and, removing a handkerchief from his pocket, cleaned Seraphina's little hand, never once breaking stride in the conversation.

Willa felt that familiar pang as she watched the exchange. Though she could not quite think of it just then, she was very aware that the possibility of her ever having children now involved her and *Leo.* Though he was handsome and gentle and kind, the mere thought of being touched again was enough to flood her with anxiety.

But through her nerves, Leo's words resounded.

'I would touch you slowly, stopping when you asked, showing you what is it to be loved by a man who knows what he's doing and cares that he's doing it right.'

And for some reason that she could not explain, it wasn't the shocking bluntness of the statement, or the entirely inappropriate subject matter. It was that when she remembered the words, she realised that she *believed* him.

Leo had been in her life for years. Though there had been a time when she had wondered if he saw her as a woman at all, that time had passed. Her marriage had killed any of the youthful, foolish fantasies she'd once had.

So, it was altogether strange to be the subject of Leo's romantic attentions. Because she believed he would care and, in believing him, she found herself, if not *eager* to be touched, then…curious.

And if the notion that she would ever *enjoy* being kissed or touched or bedded seemed too far away to consider seriously, Willa did not fret over it. Of the many hard truths her marriage to Lord Windhurst had taught her, how to endure might have been top of the list. She could comfort herself with the fact that, even if it was still terrible, she would—nay, *had*—lived through worse. There was nothing Leo could do to her that would be worse than the feeling of Windhurst's strangely soft hands on her skin or his brandy-tinged breath wafting over her face.

On the sofa next to her, Isabelle, who had also been watching her husband and child, sighed. 'I did not know a person could be so happy,' she said quietly. 'It seems rather unfair that I have been allowed so much.'

'Nonsense,' Wilhemina replied, grateful for the distraction. 'There is nobody who deserves to be happy more than you—' she turned to Mary, who sat on her other side '—except maybe Mary and only by virtue alone.'

There was a brief pause where they all remembered that Isabelle had met Matthew under rather scandalous circumstances. Isabelle started laughing first, losing herself in a reminiscent giggle, followed by Mary and Willa, who had been her co-conspirators in the strange circumstances that had followed.

They laughed for a full minute, repeatedly falling back into hysterics every time they made eye contact, until both children and both men were looking at them from across the room as if they'd gone quite mad.

'Is everything all right over there?' Leo asked eventually, his concerned expression forcing a slightly wild cackle up Willa's throat.

Willa waved one hand as she tried to compose herself. 'We were just reminding Isabelle of her and Matthew's rather...*auspicious* introduction,' she stated, careful not to give away her meaning to the couple's twelve-year-old ward, Luke, the young Duke of Everett.

Matthew looked across the room at Isabelle, his love for her there for everyone to see. 'Auspicious indeed,' he said quietly, his sincere tone making Isabelle redden further.

Conscious of the intimate moment between the two, Willa looked away—and inadvertently straight at Leo. He was watching her, his blue eyes focused on her face as if he wanted to divine the emotions there, or maybe see if she felt anything at all.

She smiled brashly in response. She did not want him to think that she was one of those women who needed love. Any illusions she'd had about such things had long since passed. Now all she wanted was to live her life without a man tracking and critiquing her every movement and Leo... Leo had promised her that.

He returned her easy smile, almost as if he knew what she was thinking.

'Aunt Willa?' Luke, the young Duke of Everett, stood

in front of her with a beautiful Jacques of London chessboard in his hands.

'What have you found?' she asked, extending her hands for the box.

'Lord Pemberton says that I may use it,' Luke replied.

'Let's see, shall we?' She rose from the sofa and carried the oak box to a nearby table. As was their custom, Willa knelt with no self-consciousness on the floor on one side of the table, Luke on the other. She opened the box slowly, mindful of any loose pieces, and unfolded the hinged wings. Inside, the bone chess pieces, stained in traditional red and white, were waiting to be placed.

Willa looked across the table at Luke. 'Would you like to start, Your Grace?'

He rested his elbows on the corner of the table and bowed his mop of blond hair in a gentlemanly gesture that Willa had not seen him make before. 'Ladies first.'

Willa barely refrained from smiling, knowing that the twelve-year-old was being completely sincere. She turned the board so that the white chess pieces were on her side and moved her king pawn forward two spaces.

Luke did not need to consider his countermove so early in the game, choosing immediately to move his own king pawn forward one space to confront hers.

Willa advanced her queen pawn and Luke immediately mirrored the move. 'Ah, the French Defence,' Willa noted.

Luke frowned, considering. 'Why do they call it that?'

Willa advanced on the opposite side of the board, giving herself a moment to swallow down the thickness in her throat. 'You know, that is a fantastic question. I have absolutely no idea. It's what my father always called it.'

Luke nodded as if all fathers were perfectly reliable sources of information. He sat back on his heels, his green eyes absorbing the game and assessing the multitude of plays still open to him.

Willa watched, amused by the infallible seriousness inherent to his personality. Whereas Willa's circumstances had made her overtly brash and volatile, Luke's had turned him into a quiet, austere young man. Willa would have worried over the boy's seriousness had Matthew and Isabelle not been such good guardians. Luke would thrive with them—even if it took a while for him to settle with Matthew as his stepfather.

Luke made his move, charging forth with another pawn and interrupting Willa's rambling thoughts. But just as she was about to counter with her rook, a loud knock sounded on the door.

Everyone turned to face it as if expecting a clown or a circus elephant to burst through and start performing. And, Leo, who'd had no need for a butler prior to their marriage, started to rise to see who it was himself, only stopping when his valet precipitously entered the room, bowed and said, 'Her Ladyship's brother is here to see you, my lord.'

'Which one?' Leo asked, conscious that each different Russell brother would require different handling.

'Mr. Jameson Russell.'

Willa visibly tensed, her spine stiffening, her shoulders pressing back as if she were an angry cat, preparing to go on the defensive. But Leo couldn't quite find the same anger. Jameson had been his closest childhood friend besides Matthew and he knew that Jameson would be hurt that he had not been included in their plans.

The only time Leo had asked Willa if she would want any family at the wedding, she had vehemently rejected the notion. Leo had chosen Willa's side without question—and he always would. Despite two decades of friendship, he had not even spoken to Jameson over the past week, knowing that Willa would see it as a betrayal.

Still, he steeled himself against the fact that he had inadvertently betrayed one of his closest friends and held out one hand for his wife, giving her the option to come or stay.

Willa paused only to tell Luke, 'Mull deeply over your next move, Your Grace, for I shall have no mercy.' Luke smiled and nodded, but Leo did not miss the adoring look on the boy's face as he watched Willa.

She took Leo's outstretched hand cautiously, but—for the first time—without flinching. Her long, slender fingers linked through his so that their palms pressed together and he tried not to marvel at how soft her skin was, tried not to ponder how much he enjoyed just holding her hand and tried not to imagine how soft the rest of her would be. 'What would you like to do?'

'I want to hear what he has to say,' she admitted after a long pause, her big, brown eyes filled with cautious resignation. 'Jameson was the only one of my brothers who actually sided with me when I said I did not want to marry Windhurst.' She laughed bitterly. 'Though he did not put up much of a fight when confronted with my father and Grey.'

'We shall leave you.' Isabelle rose from where she'd been sitting, effectively ending the wedding celebration. 'You need some privacy on your wedding night anyway.'

Willa opened her mouth to object, but there was no point. Everyone stood en masse and made for the door at the Isabelle's suggestion.

'Luke,' Isabelle urged when the boy did not follow, but hovered by the chess set.

Willa looked at Luke who, at twelve, was only a few inches shorter than she was. She smiled kindly. 'I suppose we have no choice but to resume our game at another time.'

Luke bowed. 'The pleasure would be mine,' he replied quietly and, with one last adoring look at Willa, followed his stepmother from the room.

The door shut softly behind them, leaving them alone with his valet. 'If you could show Mr. Russell in, Wiggs,' Leo said. He waited for Wiggs to leave the room before adding, 'Willa, if you do not want to speak to him—'

'No. Jameson will not relent unless I put an end to this myself. It is time.'

Leo gave her hand one reassuring squeeze even as his stomach sank with dread. 'I'm going to have to hire more staff,' he offered, providing them both with a distraction while they waited.

'You have a housekeeper, a valet and footmen,' Willa replied. 'I've brought Peggy with me. Who else would we need?'

'A butler for one. I can't have my wife answering her own door.'

Willa's hand jerked in his at the casual reference to her as his wife, but she did not comment on it or otherwise break the contact. Instead, she said, 'I'd like to find someone like Gordy.'

He frowned. 'Gordy?'

'The young Duke's butler, Gordon,' she clarified. 'He's a veritable jewel.'

Leo vaguely remembered the elderly man. 'He works for Matthew and Isabelle?'

Willa shook her head. 'I believe he's managing the Duke's empty residences since Isabelle and the children moved to Matthew's family estate. He—'

Willa did not finish her sentence as the door opened, cutting her off.

Jameson was admitted.

There was a long, stretched-out silence as the siblings looked one another over, each with a look of righteous fury so similar that it would have been comical in any other circumstance.

Jameson, like all the Russell offspring, was blond-haired and brown-eyed. He was larger than Leo, but the two were equally matched at both their boxing and fencing clubs, a fact that Leo did not forget should he have to defend himself against the infamous Russell temper now. For it did not take a close friend to see that Jameson was furious. His typical wry humour was gone, replaced with a quiet rage that Leo knew could only stem from a sense of deep betrayal.

'Willa… Tell me it's not true?' her brother whispered gravely.

Leo himself felt a moment of intense regret over the way things had unravelled. He and Jameson had been through everything together from the age of thirteen. They had fought in the way of young boys, they had rallied against anyone else who had tried to offend or hurt the other and, most keenly for Leo, Jameson had been there for him along with Matthew when his own parents had not.

But even knowing how hurt Jameson must be, his friend's blatant disbelief still wounded deeply. Leo tensed against Jameson's rage and his hand, linked with Wilhemina's, transferred the mutual offence.

Willa flinched. 'Oh, but it is,' she said with a damning smile. 'I have taken a husband. One of *my* choosing this time.'

Leo's pride bloomed through his dread.

Jameson gripped both of his hands in his hair as if he could simply rip it all from the roots. His eyes rounded with shock. 'You do not know him,' he insisted. His eyes found Leo's for the first time, and in them Leo saw everything his friend felt. 'And *you*. My *friend*. You couldn't even be bothered to let me know that you were marrying my *sister*. Using her for your own selfish purposes.'

'What selfish purposes?' Willa's eyes tracked to Leo and, though she did not release his hand, he felt her brace against whatever truth she thought she was about to learn. Her slender hand went brittle in his. 'Leo,' she fairly whispered, 'what selfish purposes?'

'The Earl is dying,' Jameson said coldly before Leo could reply. 'Leo is going to inherit the Vickery earldom, probably in weeks.'

Leo felt nothing at the reminder that his father was at death's door. The man was a biological contribution at best, a stranger in every other way.

Willa frowned. 'I'm confused as to why that would prove a selfish purpose.'

'Isn't it obvious? He needs an heir!' Jameson practically shouted.

Leo, who could see that Jameson was shocked by their marriage and hurt that he'd been excluded from their plans, remained silent, unsure of what he could say that would reassure his friend, but not hurt his wife further. He gently circled his thumb over the back of Willa's hand, trying to calm her.

And though Leo craved even that small contact, Wilhemina clearly didn't even feel it. 'I hate to be the one to inform you of this, *Jameson*,' she drawled, 'but most people who marry do so with the intention of begetting children.'

'But *he*—' Jameson pointed at Leo '—is a replica of Windhurst.'

Leo took the blow in his stride, but he could not help but release Willa's hand, afraid that he might hurt her when his grip turned to steel and his fists curled as he tried to contain his rage. Of all the accusations Jameson could have made, *that* one hit hardest. If only because it was not true.

'He keeps a mistress!' Jameson continued.

He tried to keep calm, reminding himself that Jameson was allowed to be hurt by the fact that he'd married Wilhemina behind his back.

He had cared for Elaine as much as he was able, and had treated her well. They had parted amicably, Elaine with enough money to live independently for the rest of her life should she choose.

'Actually,' it was Willa who interjected, 'Leo and Elaine parted ways the day after my husband died.' She informed her brother of this fact with a small, worldly-wise smirk that made Leo's own lips quirk.

Jameson paled, mortified by the conversation even as he exclaimed, 'You *knew*! And still, you chose to bind yourself to him for life.'

'And what of your whores, Brother?' Wilhemina snapped out. 'Are you telling me that the same applies to you? That because you have enjoyed *numerous* women's company in your bachelorhood, you will never be fit for marriage? Or that because *I* myself have known one lover—albeit a notoriously subpar one—I should never be free to take another?'

Leo could see his friend reassessing. His eyes flickered from Willa to Leo and back again. 'I don't understand what is happening here. You refuse to speak to any of us. Mother says you have not even replied to her letters.' He shook his head. 'Willa, why didn't you come home? If things were that bad, we could have helped...'

'She does not owe you an explanation,' Leo said quietly, knowing that Willa deserved to hold her secrets close should she choose to.

But he risked a glance at her and was horrified to see

that she was crying, her enormous eyes glassy with a grief that he had never seen in her before. The Willa he knew would rather die than show her true emotions and the fact that she could not control herself now told him exactly how much Jameson—her entire family—had hurt her.

'Would you like to know why?' she asked, staring at her brother.

'Willa…' Jameson shook his head, clearly overwhelmed by Willa's tears.

'Because I did not want to humiliate the family I loved so much. Even when I went to Grey and asked him for his help, I only wanted him to speak to Windhurst about Miss Pierce. I thought if Windhurst knew that I was supported by my family, he would staunch some of the physical abuse because…' She took a brave breath. 'I thought the fear was what was preventing me from carrying a child.'

Jameson went bone white. 'He…' He took a step towards her, stopped when Willa took an obvious one back. 'You told Grey that he…'

'Not implicitly, no. I did not think I should have to.'

Leo's entire body raged, his blood burned white hot with fury. Like Jameson, he hadn't known.

'Willa—'

But she wouldn't—or couldn't—hear it. She turned and left the room, leaving Leo and Jameson alone together.

Jameson moved as if he wanted to go after her.

'No.' Leo stepped in front of the door, blocking Jameson's pursuit. 'You have come here, interrupted a wedding celebration that you were not invited to and not only insulted me, but insulted and hurt my wife—your own sister.'

'I did not know. And Grey couldn't have either. He never would have stood for it if he had—'

'Even if you had not known about the physical abuse,

as her brother, you should have intervened long before it got to that point.'

'I didn't know,' Jameson repeated. He stared at Leo as if he were as stranger. 'And even if I had known, what would you have had me do?' he asked tiredly. 'She was Windhurst's *wife*. She was legally his.'

Leo didn't have a good answer. 'Until such a time as Willa chooses to forgive you, you are not welcome in my house. Do not visit us. Do not write to her,' he said, staving off his own pain at cutting off his friend.

'So, this is what twenty years of friendship is worth to you?' Jameson asked quietly. 'After everything…'

Leo used the last of his energy to summon a reply, though it came out sounding as exhausted as he felt. 'Trust me, Friend, as I will only say this once: to me, Wilhemina's happiness is worth far more than twenty years of friendship. It always has been.' He did not let Jameson voice a reply, merely started for the door.

'Do you honestly think that you can make her happy?' Jameson, too, sounded tired rather than scathing, but they both knew it was a barb deliberately designed to hit Leo where he would feel it most.

All of Leo's buried insecurities rose to the surface, filling him with panic, suffocating him. *Could* he make Willa happy? He had not even been able to stir affection in his parents—and they were supposed to love him by biological default. Still, Leo replied with the one thing he knew to be true. 'I cannot do worse than Windhurst—and I certainly cannot do worse than you and your brothers.'

'Leo,' Jameson begged, seeing that any opportunity he had to make amends was leaving.

But Leo did not relent. 'My valet will show you out,' he said and went in search of his wife.

Chapter Three

He found her in her bedroom, the one adjoining his that his staff had spent the week cleaning and her maid had spent the day adding Willa's personal effects to in preparation for her. Though the door was open, showing Willa sitting in a chair by the fire, Leo knocked anyway and watched as she hurriedly swiped her tears.

'I'm sorry, Willa.' He advanced into the warm room and took a seat in the chair next to hers. 'I knew they would come—just not tonight. I thought I'd have time to prepare.'

She smoothed the skirts of her dress, her hands running along the beautiful blue fabric nervously. 'Don't apologise for him, Leo. My brothers are grown men, fully capable of taking responsibility for their actions.'

'I'm not apologising for him. I'm apologising that he hurt you and ruined our wedding day.'

'It's fine.'

'No,' he countered. 'It's not. But it is done now,' he ceded, 'and all there is to do is try to salvage what remains of the night.'

He hadn't meant for the words to sound suggestive, but they flooded the room—her *bedroom*—with innuendo, leaving an awkward silence in their wake. 'Chess?' he blurted, mortified. 'Or supper? My cook did have a full meal prepared for everyone,' he hurriedly added.

'I could eat,' Willa replied hastily, her own voice coming out breathy with nerves. 'Leo…' Willa was watching him, a sad smile on her lips. 'I'm sorry you had to hear…' She swallowed deeply, averting his gaze. 'About the…'

That same rage he had felt when she'd first lost her secret to the room flickered through him. Leo rose from his chair, unable to sit as he fought for composure. 'If I had known he hurt you, I would have come for you—and I would not have given you a choice in leaving him. I would have… Christ, Willa, I would have tied you up and abducted you if you'd refused.'

'I know.' She sniffled delicately. 'It is why I never told you—why I never told *anyone*.'

'Willa, did he ever…' Leo wasn't even sure how to ask her such a personal question '…force himself on you? In the bedroom?' Though he would always be gentle with her, he wanted to know the extent of what she'd suffered so that he could think over how to touch her without scaring her.

But Willa only frowned. 'Leo… I was his *wife*. It was my duty to meet him in the marital bed, even if I did not want to.'

'Willa…' Leo didn't even know how to reply to that, except to say, 'No.' When she only looked at him, her eyes wide with confusion, he softened his tone. 'That is not how our marriage will work. If you ever do not want to be touched, you have only to say so. Do you understand?'

Whether she did or not, Willa nodded. 'Even the physical abuse… He only ever hurt me a few times and only when we were having a row,' she murmured, her eyes glazing over as she thought back. 'But it was as though my body was afraid of being near him even before that. He would enter the room and…' She shook her head sadly. 'And even then, I wonder…'

'What do you wonder?'

'I wonder if God knew that I did not want his children and punished me for it.'

Though he knew she was not aware of doing it, she moved slightly, her reed-thin body rocking back and forth, and it took everything Leo had in him to stop himself from going to her and taking her in his arms. He wanted to comfort her. He wanted to shelter her body with his and promise her that she would never feel like that again. 'Perhaps God saw what you suffered and chose to spare you the additional burden of having his children.'

She slowly sat upright and fought for composure, and Leo wished she wouldn't. He wished she would rage and scream, maybe throw something. He wished she would just let it out so that they could both acknowledge what had been done and rail at the injustice of it. As it were, Leo himself wanted to sink his fists into something hard and unyielding, something that would hurt him enough to balm over the pain he experienced every time he thought of Willa, so slight, cowering under her husband's fists.

'I want to bring the bastard back just so that I can kill him myself. I wish you'd told me, Willa. I wish I'd done more…'

Leo blamed himself for that. It had been so hard to ask her anything about her marriage because it was a reminder that she was not his. So, when he'd asked her if she was all right and she'd lied, he hadn't pushed though some part of him, even then, knew that she wasn't being completely honest. Like her father and her brothers, he should have tried harder.

He moved closer slowly and held out the handkerchief he'd fished from his pocket. 'Seeing as I can't go back, all I can do is promise that you'll never live through that again.'

'I know.' Willa took the handkerchief, but she never used it. She fisted it in her hand and lowered it to her lap. 'Leo… My brother is hurt,' she said, effectively changing the topic of conversation, 'and he is feeling guilty for not interceding with Windhurst, but you know that he did not mean what he said. For all their faults, my brothers, including Grey, never knew the true extent of it. I couldn't… Today…'

'Today was the first time you've ever spoken of it.' Leo's entire body yearned to go to her. Even his palms physically itched with the need to reach out and touch her, to comfort her. But, still, he held his ground, remembering the promise he'd made.

'Yes.'

'I promise that I will never raise a hand to you in anger.'

'Leo—'

'I'm not saying I won't get angry—God knows I have a temper and we both know that you are capable of provoking it.'

Wilhemina did not try to deny it. She smiled knowingly, undoubtedly remembering a few of their epic arguments over the years. Her eyes glistened with humour.

'But I would never hurt you.'

'I know.'

Leo drew closer and, although he did not touch her, he *longed* to take his wife in his arms. 'Tell me what I can do to make you feel safe?'

Willa's eyes softened. 'Leo…' She shook her head, halting his rambling. 'I do—feel safe. Just being here with you now…' her lips curled into a wry smile '…I am not afraid at all. I am merely…confused, I suppose. And if there is any fear, it is fear of…what is to come.'

Leo's heart pounded in his chest. The admission was more than he could have hoped for so soon. He and Willa had known each other a long time, they had been friends for years, but now that he knew the extent of what she had suffered, he was humbled by her trust in him. 'I'm glad,' he said lamely. 'Not that you feel confused, of course. But that you feel safe.'

Good God, man, stop bumbling.

Willa stood, coming to where he floundered, her silver-blue dress glinting in the firelight. She looked him over for a long time, her lips quirking in that way that told him she was thinking something outrageous. 'You know, you are indecently handsome.'

Leo, who had used his looks unashamedly to his advantage for years, had never felt so self-conscious. Now he shook his head, unsure of what to say as his blood thinned with heat.

'In fact,' Willa continued, her small smile telling him she saw his awkwardness and enjoyed it immensely, 'were this not a marriage of convenience, I would be quite concerned.'

'Concerned?'

'Well, it is rather a trial to have such a handsome husband, don't you think?'

'Only as big a trial as it is to have such a beautiful wife,' he countered sincerely. 'Less so, if you think how much more forward men are in their advances.' The thought of other men vying for her attention actually made him jealous. It dawned on him. 'I'm going to have to live with every Tom, Dick and Harry flirting with you for the rest of my life.'

Willa laughed loudly, humour snapping through her eyes and eradicating some of the sadness there. 'I doubt that will be a problem for quite a while, given my scandalous situation.'

Leo, who had been exposed to the avarice of the world in a different way than Willa, knew that the exact opposite was true. But it did not worry him. Willa was not the type of woman to share herself lightly. She was loyal to a fault—the fact that she had been faithful to the undeserving Windhurst was proof of that. And now she was his, would only *ever* be his.

'I was wondering…' she said.

'Yes?'

'Do you think I could…?' She flushed and lowered her eyes in an uncharacteristic display of shyness.

'Willa?' He waited for her to look at him again. 'Tell me what you want. Always.'

'Do you think I could touch you?' she asked. Her hands fluttered anxiously between them. 'What I mean to say is—'

'Yes.'

'If we're going to do this, then I want to get it over with—'

'Willa—' He interrupted her rambling. He took a step closer, coming right up to her without making contact. '*I* am your husband now. You do not ever have to ask to touch me.' Still, he kept his own hands from reaching for her.

She took a deep breath as if she was about to submerge herself in an icy pond and then, so slowly that he tensed in anticipation, she raised her hands to his chest, placing her palms flat against his silk waistcoat. She stood still for a long minute before asking, 'How is it possible that I can feel your body heat through your clothes? I am cold all the time.'

'I have five or six stone on you,' he replied quietly. But it was a half-truth. His blood blazed for her. So much so that he was perspiring beneath his clothes. He wondered how she could be cold when her hands seemed to sear through his layers, scorching his skin beneath.

Her palms brushed over him, spreading beneath his coat to run over his chest, and Leo, feeling his body begin to stir, clenched his fists and sang 'God Save the Queen' in his head.

Willa sensed his discomfort immediately. Her hands slowed. 'You…you do not like it?'

He shook his head rapidly. 'The opposite,' he rasped. 'I like it too much and am trying not to scare you.'

'Oh.' But she did not remove her hands. She slid them up and over his shoulders, lifting his coat slightly.

Leo let his head fall back. He stared at the ceiling for a long moment as he tried to get himself under control. But this was *Willa* and she was touching him as *his wife*.

'Leo?'

He managed a strangled, 'Hmm?'

'Will you kiss me?'

His heart lurched in his chest as his confused mind made sense of the words. His eyes slowly lowered to hers. He saw how much the words cost her, saw that it was not what she wanted and that she was trying to be brave for him on this, the last wedding night they'd both ever have. Still, he was powerless to say no. For all his shortcomings, pleasure was something he was confident he could give her.

'May I touch you instead?' He waited for her to nod, then slowly reached down and lifted her slight weight in his arms.

Willa braced in his arms. 'What are you doing?'

'Holding my wife,' he replied and carried her to the seat she'd vacated. He sat down, positioning her over his lap and stringing her legs over the arm of the huge chair.

Willa was tense and alert on his lap, her entire body brittle against the strange new position he'd put her in. 'Relax, Willa.' He leaned back in the chair, keeping both hands gripped on the armrests, though he longed to touch her now that he finally had her in his arms for the first time.

It took her over five minutes, but she eventually settled, placing her head on his shoulder and relaxing enough that he felt her muscles slacken as she draped over him. 'This is quite pleasant,' she murmured, sounding surprised.

'Over the years we are married, I'm going to show you many pleasant things,' he promised. He would, too. For all the things he could not guarantee, Leo knew he could show her what it was to worship a person's body. The mere thought made him hard as iron. 'But there is no rush.' He slowly brought one hand up to stroke his fingers down her bare arm.

Willa trembled and, because he could not sense if her response had been in fear or pleasure, he stopped immediately.

'No,' she whispered. 'Don't stop. I—I like that.'

His heart gave one pathetic lurch in his chest, one he was sure Willa felt by the way her lips curved in a small smile, but he raised his hand again and repeated the gentle caress, tracing nonsensical patterns over her smooth skin and imagining what it would be like for his lips to follow, wandering that same path.

They sat like that for what seemed an age, basking in the firelight until Willa was no longer self-conscious and Leo was fighting his lust with every ounce of energy he possessed. Willa shivered, her skin prickling with awareness beneath the pads of his fingers. She closed her eyes and he couldn't help but notice the hollows of her eyes and cheeks and the way her long, sandy lashes fluttered.

'Tell me what Jameson meant?' she asked quietly. 'About the Earl dying?'

The words were possibly the only thing she could have said that could have doused his lust immediately.

'My father has been ill this past year. The doctors are not

unified in any one diagnosis; in fact, most of the ones I've sent for insist that there's nothing wrong with him. Yet he does not eat or sleep. He barely talks any more and when he does it's only to threaten to die, which he never does.'

She opened her eyes and tilted her head back to look at him, surprised by his bitter candour. 'You do not get along?'

'You do not know this?' Leo asked. Despite their fall-out, the Russell siblings had always been close. Leo had assumed they all knew about his upbringing.

'No. My brother, for all his faults, is a loyal friend. He would never betray your confidence.'

Leo nodded and though he felt some remorse for how he'd left things with Jameson, he pushed it to the back of his mind. 'My parents…' He floundered, not knowing how much to tell her.

Willa raised her hand to his cheek, only long enough to direct his gaze back to hers. 'Tell me. If we're going to do this, be *married*, I want no secrets between us. Leo, I would rather be hurt by the truth than lied to—always.'

Though he had always avoided talking about his childhood—for what would he say? He had no fond memories or connections to it—her words prompted him to complete honesty. 'I did not know them growing up. Though I never wanted for anything material, they were not present most of the time. They left me permanently in the country with my nurse and came to live in London.'

'For how long?'

'I don't know exactly. I have some memories of them at home when I was very small. More memories of receiving the occasional letter—for Christmas or my birthday—as I grew older. But, until I went to school at thirteen, I was largely alone.'

Her brown eyes darkened with sympathy. 'So that is why

you spent so much time with my brother during the holidays.'

'Yes. Matthew and Jameson alternated who would take me home with them. Though it certainly started out of pity, they became my closest friends because of it. The Blakes and your family…they saved me from myself in many ways. And trust me when I say it was no easy feat. I was basically a lost cause until I went to school. But after that first year…'

He could still remember what it had been like to be dropped off at a strange school by a family footman. Sometimes, when he was on the verge of sleep, he still felt that fearful loneliness in his own house. Now, as a man, he could easily rationalise it away or go to his club and drown it, but as a boy, respite had not been so easily found. 'I was small for my age—much like Luke is now.'

'You were bullied?'

'Only once. By a duke's son—Lambford. But the moment he gripped my collar, I went into an unholy rage. I wasn't used to being touched at all, let alone in any vindictive way. I lashed out and ended by breaking his nose. I probably would have been expelled for no other reason than Lambford's family name, but Matthew and Jameson, who were already friends, had witnessed what happened and came forward to defend me.'

'And your parents?'

Leo shrugged. Though the childish pain was still there, he felt no hesitation speaking to Willa. In fact, this might have been the most he'd admitted to anyone—ever. 'They never responded to the headmaster's summons or asked after me. To be honest, I'm not sure they thought of me at all…'

'What is it?' Willa asked, sensing his hesitation.

'Last year, when my mother died…'

She waited quietly as he sorted his thoughts, not pushing him or prompting him for more.

'I didn't feel anything,' he admitted finally and, instead of the private guilt and shame he had felt then, all that suffused him, with Willa in his arms, was relief. 'It was like hearing of a stranger's passing. Every time somebody would give their condolences, I'd have to pretend to be sad. I felt like a bad actor, one who'd forgotten his lines on stage.'

Willa nestled her head against his shoulder. 'And your father?'

'He was devastated,' he said quietly, still confused by his father's grief a year later. 'He started to decline around the same time that she died and all I remember thinking was…'

'How could two people who loved each other so much be so indifferent to their only child,' Willa said, speaking his mind.

'Yes.'

Willa levered up on his lap so that she could look at him when she added, 'Leo, I am sorry for the child you were.' He shook his head, not wanting her pity, but Willa talked over his denial. 'But I am—for entirely selfish reasons—happy that the child you were shaped the man you've become.' Her eyes searched his face. 'I would not change a single thing about you.' She shook her head. 'Well, maybe I'd make you *slightly* less attractive.'

Leo laughed quietly, feeling freer than he had in a very long time. He shouldn't be surprised really—it had always been like this with Willa. Though she was not ready to hear it, or, perhaps, he was not ready to tell her, she was the one person he had always sought out when he needed lightness and laughter.

Until her marriage to Windhurst, he'd often found himself visiting the Russells even when he knew Jameson wasn't there—because he'd wanted an excuse to stumble upon Wilhemina. He loved being near her. He loved listening to her talk, knowing that he could never guess what she'd say next, no matter how much he tried. 'Willa, I want to tell you something, and I don't want you to panic.'

She tensed, but, after a small pause, nodded.

'Right now, I'm perfectly happy,' he said simply.

Chapter Four

Willa did not laugh at the declaration; instead, she felt the truth of it resound in the depths of her stomach. 'I feel the same way… It's only…'

'Tell me,' he urged quietly. And when she still did not reply, he reminded her, 'No secrets.'

'It is so strange,' she said slowly, thinking through her words, 'to be married to one of my closest friends. I feel as if there is this…*wall* that we must climb over. Even sitting on you like this—' she blushed '—it feels *odd* and my past experience is only a small part of it. The other part is…'

'Self-awareness?' he supplied. 'For the friendship and associated boundaries that we had prior.'

'Exactly.' She thumped her hand on his chest.

'I understand.'

Still, Willa rested back against him, enjoying the way his large body cradled hers. Being close to Leo was strange and familiar at the same time; it felt new even as some primitive part of her understood that this closeness was natural, something that human beings were supposed to experience and, perhaps, even enjoy.

The sound of a throat clearing at the door turned both their attention to Wiggs and Peggy, who stood with supper trays crammed with domed silver dish covers. Wiggs did not seem surprised at all and Willa supposed he had attended Leo in far more scandalous circumstances. Peggy, on the other hand, couldn't quite keep her expression neutral. She stared in open shock.

Willa tried, unsuccessfully, to extricate herself from Leo's lap.

Leo clearly did not share her panic. He slowly moved her offending hand away from his upper thigh and helped her up, waving in their hovering servants as soon as they were both standing. 'Thank you,' he said, addressing them both and with none of Willa's embarrassment.

'Will that be all, milady?' Peggy asked, her eyes darting back and forth between her and Leo.

'Yes, thank you, Peggy.' Though she was not in the habit of undressing herself, Willa found that she *wanted* to stay up and eat and talk with Leo. And while Peggy would have remained awake to assist her, it hardly seemed fair to the poor maid, who had already been run ragged by Isabelle and Mary with the week's wedding preparations. 'Goodnight, Peggy,' Willa said, dismissing her.

Peggy dipped into a hurried curtsy. 'Goodnight, milady.' She repeated the performance for Leo, adding a breathy, 'Milord', before turning and practically running away.

Wilhemina closed the door after them, smiling at her maid's newfound shyness. 'Peggy is not usually so bashful.' She watched as Leo took off his coat and moved to where Wiggs had placed the wine and two glasses.

'There will undoubtedly be an adjustment period for everyone,' he said and handed her a glass. 'Though I think Peggy will have an easier time of it when she realises I'm not like Windhurst.'

'Yes.' Willa sipped her wine. Though she stayed standing by the chair they'd vacated as Leo uncovered the food, she couldn't help but feel slightly forlorn. She desperately wanted to get the wedding night out of the way.

While she did not have the courage to tell him that much, it had taken every morsel she'd had to ask for the kiss and every morsel of strength she'd possessed to remain sitting on his lap as she'd waited for it—or, at least that's what she *thought* she'd been waiting for. And, yes, the awkward position had become quite pleasurable after a while as her body had warmed from the contact with his, but that did not change the fact that Leo had not done what she'd asked. 'Leo,' she asked uncertainly, 'you do not want to kiss me?'

Leo did not look alarmed or surprised by her question. He smiled, almost as if he'd been waiting for her to ask. 'You did not want me to.'

'Well, maybe not at first. But the waiting is terrible,' she admitted. 'I want to get it over with.'

Leo angled his face away from her, but she saw the small indent in his cheek, as if he were trying to bite back his laugh. That he would find her situation amusing filled Wilhemina with indignation. 'Am I amusing you?'

He tipped his head. 'Maybe a little.'

'Why?'

'When I kiss you, Willa, you're not going to want to *get it over with.*'

He said the words with such arrogant self-assurance that Willa couldn't help but raise one eyebrow haughtily. 'Shouldn't *I* be the judge of that, my lord?'

'By all means.' He watched her face closely, his gaze so intent that Willa resisted the urge to squirm. 'You want to play judge?' he asked quietly. *'Now?'*

Though Willa's stomach sank with dread and her palms slicked with nervous sweat, she nodded firmly, knowing that he would not touch her if she seemed anything but certain. 'If I don't do it now, I'm afraid I never will.'

Leo's grin was sudden and devilish. His teeth flashed. That single dimple that rarely made an appearance popped in his right cheek, adding charm to what would have been an otherwise roguish picture. He placed his wine glass down and came to take hers from her. His footsteps, slow and measured as he crossed the room, reminded her of a tomcat stalking something delectable.

He gently unclasped her tense hand from around the delicate stem of the glass and raised her knuckles to his lips. His mouth whispered across her skin, barely touching her, yet eliciting a reluctant pull from deep within her womb.

And when he released her to place her glass down on the nearby table Willa, who had been observing his deliberateness, had half a mind to ask why on earth they would need their hands for kissing.

But then he was back, his large body close, crowding her.

His hands rose to cradle her face, his touch impossibly light yet strangely possessive, too, as if he *wanted* to touch her, but knew to leave her the option to break away if she needed to. He made a deep grumbling sound in the back of his throat, as if he were pleased with only that—touching her face.

Her stomach kicked at the contact, at that faint, possessive touch. Willa's breath rushed out in one long whoosh that she might have been embarrassed by if she'd had the clarity of mind to hear it.

'Don't be nervous.'

'I've never enjoyed this part,' she admitted breathlessly.

Her anxious hands rose between them and Willa, not knowing what to do with them, floundered until Leo took charge, gently grasping them in his own hands and bringing them to rest on his shoulders.

'Look at me, sweetheart,' Leo demanded, his typically sky-blue eyes stormy and wild.

Willa forced her gaze back to his despite the way her nerves reared.

'Any time you want me to stop, you say "Stop".'

She swallowed nervously.

'All right?'

She nodded.

'I need to hear you say it.'

'If I want you to stop, I'll tell you to stop.'

'Okay.' He lowered his head, bringing his lips close to hers, and still he did not kiss her. He whispered, 'Can I tell you another secret?'

His quiet words brushed against her skin, pulling a shiver that originated from somewhere deep within her body, somewhere that was foreign and unfamiliar to her.

'Yes.' Willa's voice was clear despite her rioting senses. Everything seemed amplified: the sound of her breathing, the slight friction of his thumbs brushing her cheekbones, even his *smell*, starched linen and shaving soap, seemed intensified somehow.

'I have thought of this long before now,' Leo said softly, his thumbs never pausing in their gentle strokes. 'I have dreamed of what it would be like to taste you.'

Willa heated with a blush that was equal parts pleasure and embarrassment. That he had thought of her—of kissing her—was scandalous and inappropriate, especially considering she had been married to someone else. It was also strangely enticing to think about…

He dropped his head lower and Willa instinctively tilted her own to the side, giving him unfettered access to her throat. Leo groaned with pleasure at the small, trusting gesture.

Willa tensed against the strange sensations consuming her, but she did not ask him to stop. In fact, she rather felt like telling him to hurry up. The anticipation was unbearable. 'Leo—'

But then his lips were on her skin, gliding over her neck with the faintest touch of pressure. Willa trembled at the odd sensation, which felt rather like several dainty butterflies dancing on her skin. Her hands found the sides of his waistcoat and gripped as if she could stabilise herself against the onslaught.

One of Leo's hands dropped to her waist to pull her closer; the other remained on her cheek, gently tilting her head as his lips moved up her neck and across her jaw. 'God, Willa,' he murmured, 'you're so soft.' He nipped playfully at the side of her jaw. 'You smell so good.'

His words caught in *her* chest and expanded some foreign feeling there. Her breaths felt incomplete, each irritated inhale constrained by her tight corset. Willa inhaled audibly to try to counteract the suffocating panic.

'Relax,' Leo coaxed gently when he heard the sound.

'I can't breathe,' she tried to explain. 'I need...'

'I'll take care of you,' he promised quietly and placed his lips on hers.

Willa did not move. She did not return the kiss. She stopped breathing altogether. And Leo, sensing her growing fear, shifted slightly, pulling back to rub his lips even more gently against hers. The friction was slight, barely perceptible, but each slide of his mouth ricocheted through her. Molten pleasure warmed her body from the inside out.

Her lips sighed open in unconscious welcome.

Leo's tongue swept into her mouth. Before she could

move or break the kiss, he gently slid his tongue against hers, encouraging her to do the same—and Willa *did*. Hesitantly at first, her movements made awkward by her nerves and comparative inexperience, then boldly as she felt his responding urgency.

Her hands moved from his waist to rope around his neck and pull him closer. And, though she was not aware of doing it, she plastered her body against his. Emboldened by the novel sensations flooding her, she sank deeper into the kiss, her tongue lapping eagerly at Leo's.

He groaned against her mouth as he broke away and, even though he stopped and rested his forehead on hers as they both caught their breath, his big hands fell to her bottom, kneading her through her heavy skirts with soft, rounding strokes that had a moan gathering in her throat.

'Leo,' she rasped, 'I want…'

'What do you want?' he asked, his hands moving to her waist and holding her close—close enough that she could feel the hard weight of him through the skirts of her dress, just beneath her hip.

Willa froze, unsure of the answer. She wasn't sure if she was ready to be undressed yet; however, she suddenly found herself rather…well, *aching*. There was an odd heaviness collecting between her thighs, one that felt as if it needed to be dispelled, and her breasts felt heavy and sensitive beneath her tight corset. But Willa, who had never been pleasured by her husband, had not learned how to ask for such things, or even, what *exactly* she was supposed to be asking for.

'What if I go first?' Leo asked and Willa nodded, relieved to have been spared from having to answer the question.

'I need to take your hair down. I've wanted to see it for

so long.' His blue eyes, made a shade darker by his lust, found hers. 'I want it in my hands.'

He did not move until she nodded. But the moment she did, he turned her and started expertly removing her hair-pins, his nimble fingers snatching at the metal clasps, his chest rising and falling rapidly as if he were struggling with intense excitement.

Willa's long, honey-gold locks fell by degrees. She felt each strand as it unravelled to fall down her back, past her waist. Leo murmured something unintelligible as his hands ran through the silky mass, his fingers massaging her head, searching for any remaining pins.

She sighed as the tension left her scalp.

'That good?' Leo teased.

'There are few greater pleasures in life for a woman than the first few seconds after taking her hair down,' Willa confirmed, being deliberately obtuse.

Leo gently turned her to face him again. He held her hands in his as he looked at her. The teasing glint in his blue eyes was slowly replaced with an emotion that Willa couldn't identify. 'Leo? What is it?'

'I'm the luckiest bastard alive,' he said, his earnest tone broaching no argument. 'You are beautiful, Wilhemina.' In a gesture that undid her, he leaned his forehead against hers and exhaled deeply. 'You are clever and funny and brave. You are kind and loyal.' He kissed her again, a quick press of his lips that left her reeling, before he finished with, 'And you are mine.'

The statement was one her late husband had said quite often. But where Windhurst had used the words during arguments to remind her of her helplessness and his legal ownership of her, Leo wielded them in an entirely different way. She could *hear* the reverence in his tone.

He said the words as if to remind himself that his wildest dreams had come true, as if to remind *her* that she would always have one person who would always come for her if only for the fact that he had promised, before God himself, to do so. And it was the strangest realisation that possession and ownership could be *good*, could be *mutual*. For wouldn't she do the same for him, based on their past alone?

As if he'd read her very thoughts, Leo wrapped his arms around her, pulling her close against his chest, and whispered, 'As I am yours.'

The words, though whispered, hurtled through her like a blast from a ship's cannon, crashing through her carefully honed defences—defences she'd spent years building and solidifying. A violent shiver passed through her and, feeling her control begin to break, she used both hands to push at Leo. She could not cry—not in front of him, not on their wedding night.

But he did not let her go. If anything, he held her tighter, pulled her closer, sheltered her with his own body. 'Let it go, love.'

'Leo—' She tried to break free as her tears began to fall.

'Give them to me, Wilhemina. Give them only to me.'

And it was that request that broke her.

The cry that tore through the room was loud and wild, an animalistic keening filled with pain and desperation. And, still, Leo did not tense or flinch against her tears or otherwise release her. He held her as the pieced-together parts of herself refractured and scattered, leaving her adrift and disconnected from herself, from the woman she had painstakingly built to survive.

Willa was not aware that she lashed out, her fists pounding against her husband's hard chest, nor was she aware that he did not try to restrain her; instead, he shifted slightly so that she had more space to rail.

And when she finally collapsed, exhausted from her own outburst, drained after years of trying to be unaffected, it was Leo who did not let her fall, Leo who lifted her and carried her to the chair. It was Leo who cradled her, holding her long after she had fallen asleep in his arms, whispering promises to her in the hope that she'd hear him in her dreams and know that she was finally safe.

Chapter Five

In the first week following her marriage, the truth that Wilhemina had realised in the face of her late husband's cavorting was reaffirmed: a woman could not break society's rules and expect no consequences. The combined effects of her forgoing her mourning period and then remarrying so soon after her husband's murder were dire—perhaps made more so by the fact that she had snatched a *second* coveted bachelor off the marriage mart.

It did not matter that very few people had liked her late husband in the first place, or that he had died due to a scandal of his own making—every invitation she'd received as Lady Windhurst had been revoked, save for those few sent by her own family and one invitation from the Countess of Heather to her annual masquerade ball.

Those letters and requests sent by her family, Willa did not reply to. She did not even open them, knowing that their current impasse would not be resolved by teas, pleas and bargains, but by the passage of a significant period of time in which she hoped the sting of their betrayal would dampen.

The invitation from Matthew's mother, the Countess of Heather, she had accepted on her and Leo's behalf, but only because she would not insult the woman whose own husband had helped them obtain their special marriage licence in the first place. Even then, and though the ball was still a week away, Willa dreaded the event with every fibre of her being.

Her only consolation was that Leo would be there to help her through it. He had saved her, offering himself up in a deal that was completely in her favour. And, instead of marrying her and then abandoning her to a separate life, he had surpassed her expectations as a husband, though, admittedly, her previous experience in marriage had brought those expectations rather low to begin with.

She and Leo had fallen into a quiet routine. His family estate and independent ventures kept him from home for large portions of the day; however, he always sought her out the minute he got home. He asked after her and not because it was the polite thing to do, but because he actually seemed interested in what she'd kept herself busy with.

He dined with her every night and, although Wilhemina had not had the courage to ask him for another kiss since their first had ended so disastrously, their quiet evenings and long conversations were threaded with a weighty anticipation that she had never experienced before.

If he sat down near her, she wanted to crawl into his lap like a kitten as she had done on their wedding night. If he came close, she wanted to lean against him, or, worse, reach up and guide his lips to hers. And, several times, she'd lain awake at night, thinking of him and listening for movement in his adjoining bedroom, confused by her warring desire to go to him and her awareness that she was not quite ready for what came next.

And all this to realise that, in many ways, it was easier to hate one's husband than it was to actually like him. With Windhurst, she'd had one sole objective: avoid him until he sought her out. But with Leo… With Leo she had the embarrassing urge to be wherever he was. She'd even taken to waking up at six o'clock in the morning so that she could breakfast with him before he left promptly at seven each day, a feat which took a momentous amount of effort considering she did not sleep well and, resultantly, had never liked the cheerful disposition of morning.

This morning, she had beaten him to the table by a few minutes, her new habit of wearing trousers at home making her dressing ritual significantly swifter. Adorned in fitted black breeches, tall riding boots, a white linen shirt and a red silk jacket that was surprisingly like a waistcoat, Willa could almost have passed for a young man. Though her slender frame and tall height aided the illusion, her impossibly long, thick hair did not. In the absence of Peggy's help in the early morning, it fell down her back in the loose plait she had slept in, wild tendrils escaping around her neck and face.

Willa placed some lightly buttered toast on her plate and nibbled at it uninterestedly. She yawned tiredly, freezing mid-act as Leo opened the door and strode in, his head bent intently over some correspondence. He was fully dressed and cut a striking image in steel-grey trousers and a matching waistcoat.

'Good morning,' she mumbled.

His gaze snapped up, blue eyes flickering over her, taking in her now-familiar clothing without comment. 'Good morning.' He blinked, seeming to struggle with his thoughts for a moment. 'Forgive me.' He ran one large palm over his freshly brushed hair. 'My brain is still waking up.'

'Mine, too.' Willa yawned again, this time politely covering her mouth. 'I have not been sleeping well.'

Leo frowned at her as he moved to pour himself some coffee at the sideboard. 'Is anything the matter?'

She briefly considered lying to him. She even said, 'I have never been a good sleeper.' After all, it was true. During her marriage to Windhurst, she had lain awake, dreading the moment he would arrive home, listening for any sound of him approaching before finally falling into a fitfully alert slumber after she'd heard him climb drunkenly into his bed.

Leo sat down next to her and took a deep sip of his coffee, his eyes closed as he relished the first taste of the bitter brew. Willa had the strangest urge to reach across the small space between them and brush her fingers through his beautiful hair. She stopped herself, clasping her hands together under the table just as he opened his eyes to look at her. 'Is there anything I can do to help?'

'I keep thinking about the Wolfe brothers,' she admitted quietly after a long pause. She gnawed on her bottom lip, only releasing it when she realised that Leo was staring at the anxious movement. 'If Windhurst owed them as much as Briggs thought, surely they would not let it go so easily?'

He did not placate her or tell her not to worry. He nodded sombrely. 'I have thought about it, too,' he admitted.

'And?'

'The way I see it, they must know by now that Windhurst had nothing left and that everything of value has been sold to pay off his debt. Furthermore, they've been linked with his murder. They would have to be fools to try to pursue the matter.'

'But… You don't think they would come after you?'

'Is that what is keeping you up, Willa?' he asked, his demeanour softening perceptibly.

'Of course,' she said quickly, trying for light-heartedness.

'It would be suspicious if I were to lose another husband so soon after the first.'

She tried for glib, but the truth was that Willa had taken to staring at her bedroom ceiling, worrying. While she was quite independently destitute and completely reliant on the generous account Leo had set up for her upon their marriage, he was a wealthy man. Thoughts of his safety had kept her tossing and turning all week, too anxious to sleep, too tired to get up out of bed and go in search of a book or something else to occupy her midnights.

He looked at her for a long moment. 'If they have any hope of regaining their money, they will not hurt me—at least not without approaching me first.'

'And if they do—approach you?'

'If and when,' he replied. At her blank expression, he explained, 'It's something James—Matthew's father—always said to us growing up. "If and when." We'll worry about it *if* and *when* we have to. But for now, don't let it occupy your thoughts. The Wolfes are certainly dangerous. But they are not stupid. And if they do approach me, I am not going to try to fight them off like Windhurst did.'

'I suppose that much is true.' She considered her next words, knowing that she would need to be tactful.

But Leo must have sensed her need to say more. He drummed his fingers on the table, his eyes never leaving her face. 'Tell me.'

'Will you promise to inform me if they approach you?'

'Why?' Leo seemed genuinely concerned. 'Why would I endanger you, too?'

'It is my responsibility.'

'No, it is not.'

'I *could help*,' she insisted, closing her eyes in her frustration.

'Willa—look at me.'

She forced her gaze back to his.

'If they come to me, I will pay them what is owed them and be done with it. My safety is not something I take lightly and *your safety* is something I would beggar my own title to ensure.' He reached for her hand, which was curled into a fist by her plate, but seemed to catch himself at the last moment, pressing his palm flat on the table and flexing his fingers instead.

Willa wished he hadn't stopped; her own palm itched from the broken promise of contact with him.

'Do you understand?' he asked.

She nodded, but she was helpless to stop the fury that lashed through her. 'I'm so angry that he is still haunting me from the grave. I hate him more now than I ever could while he was alive and—' She bit off the words.

'And what?'

She blinked rapidly, refusing to cry. 'I hate myself for dragging you down with me,' she admitted quietly. 'I didn't think through the consequences when you proposed. If I had, I would have said no.'

'I don't need to be protected, Willa. I fully intend on spending the next fifty years as your husband.'

'Why?' she asked. 'You have gained no advantage by marrying me!' Willa pounded her fist on the table. She was confused by his calmness. She was irked by the fact that he wasn't taking this seriously. And, perhaps worst of all, she was afraid that something might happen to him—because of *her*. And Wilhemina did not like to be afraid.

'Willa…' Leo's quiet voice punctured the silence. 'May I touch you?'

She chanced a glance at him, surprised by the request. She saw the raw need in his eyes. But too confused, afraid and lonely, she did not reply. She could not. All she could manage was a small nod.

Leo pushed his chair back immediately, his haste belied by the way it simply toppled backwards and landed on the carpeted floor with a quiet thud. He didn't even stop to pick it up, merely came to her and crouched at her feet.

He took both her hands in his and chafed them as if he could warm her perpetually cold body with that contact alone. He didn't speak for a long time, only frowned at her jacket buttons as if he was sorting through his thoughts, trying to find the right words.

It was Willa who spoke first. 'I couldn't bear if something happened to you—because of me.' Before he could reply, she hurried to add, 'You have donc nothing to deserve this.'

He did not deny it. He looked up into her eyes and replied, 'I know that, Wilhemina. But neither have you.'

Willa seemed taken back by the statement, as if it had not occurred to her that her late husband's diabolical habits were not her sins to carry. 'I…' Her brow pinched in thought. 'I am *more* to blame than you,' she said finally.

Leo knew that arguing with Willa when she was feeling vulnerable was pointless. She was a dog with a bone if ever he'd met one. So, he didn't. Instead, he curled his hands around hers, stroking his thumbs over her cold, slender fingers, soaking up every second that he could touch her. 'If they approach me,' he said finally, 'I will tell you. But—' she tensed, waiting as he added, '—I will deal with them as I see fit. That is my compromise.'

Her big brown eyes were wide with sadness. 'What do I bring to our marriage except embarrassment and shame?' she whispered. 'And now potential danger, too.'

Leo's heart thudded in his chest—not from pain, he realised. From *anger*. How could she not see herself as he saw her? As strong and fierce and *vital*.

When he spoke, his voice was calm and clear despite the furious hurtling of his blood through his cantering heart. 'The other morning, I was sitting in my study, slogging my way through my accounts, and I heard you laughing with Peggy.' Willa tilted her head like a confused puppy, clearly failing to see where he was going. 'And then Wiggs said something that I couldn't catch and you all laughed again, and I realised that I couldn't remember anyone in my house *laughing*. Ever.'

'Laughter?' she asked drily. 'That is what I bring to our marriage?'

'No, that is what you bring to my house,' he said. 'Joy is what you bring to me and to our marriage.' It was a gross understatement. It didn't matter to Leo that they'd had a rough start. He was the happiest he'd ever been, if only because he knew that he was coming home to her each night. Even the scandal that their marriage had caused, though it had affected him keenly, was bearable when he reminded himself that Wilhemina was his wife.

'You make it impossible to argue when you say things like that.' She pulled a face at him. 'Here I am, trying to be practical, and you completely undermine my reasoning by being romantic.'

He didn't laugh as he knew she was hoping. 'Are you not? Happy?' His eyes searched her face. 'Sometimes I feel as if you are. And then other times, when you are not aware I'm looking, you seem so sad that I can't help but feel your sadness myself.'

Willa considered his question for some time. When she replied, her voice wavered. 'I think that I have been sad for so long that it is hard to break the habit. It feels like re-learning a language, one I used to know but haven't practised in years.'

She raised one shaky hand and touched his hair, her movements shy and unsure. Leo held impossibly still, not wanting to spook her, but not wanting her to stop either.

In the past week, he had taken to working away from home and working more hours than he'd thought possible to try to avoid his insatiable desire to reach out and touch his wife. He'd made a point to keep away all day and then come home to her at night, helplessly torturing himself with a few hours of her proximity each evening even as he fought his urge to reach for her each time she was close.

'Sometimes I wake up, and for just a moment I forget that it's over, and…' She rubbed her hand over her heart as if to relieve the pressure there. 'There's this suffocating heaviness that I can't dispel.'

Leo didn't interrupt, understanding that what she was telling him was important, but his throat tightened with rage, with the need to pummel something in her defence.

'But then I remember that he's gone and you are with me instead. And this impossible relief spreads through me and it's so consuming that I feel like weeping.' She knocked her fisted hand gently against his solid chest, trying to lighten the heavy mood her words had conjured. 'And you know I loathe weeping,' she said glibly. 'It's so pointless.'

'You can cry with me.'

'You hate when women cry,' she pointed out. 'I've heard you tell Jameson that on more than one occasion.'

'You are not any woman. You are my wife.'

She nodded, but Leo didn't miss her rapid blinks as she tried to stop her tears.

'Will you do something for me?'

'Yes,' Willa rasped.

'When you can't sleep at night, or when you want to cry, promise me you will come and find me? Wake me up if you have to.'

She gave a watery laugh. 'And what will you do if I cry?'

'I will hold you in my arms until the grief passes.' He paused as the urge to do just that coursed through him and when he continued his voice was notably strained. 'And then I will read my estate manager's report to you until you fall asleep just to escape it.'

As he'd intended, Willa laughed. But she didn't defer or jest as he'd expected. Instead, she leaned forward and kissed his forehead, her soft lips making contact for only a second. 'I promise.'

Leo held his breath as she drew back, steeling himself against the desire that blazed through his entire body.

A pink blush sat high on her cheekbones, but she still smiled. 'Do you have a busy day today?' she asked, effectively charging forth into a new topic of conversation. 'I don't want to keep you.'

Leo actually did have several imminent business matters he needed to tend to, but for some reason, none of them seemed important enough to drag him away from Wilhemina just then. He pushed to his feet, only groaning slightly when his legs stretched from their confines. 'Nothing pressing,' he lied. And, needing a distraction from his body's awareness of Willa's proximity, added, 'Why don't we cross something off your list?'

Wilhemina's list of scandalous things she wanted to do had plagued Leo. When she wore trousers, as she did this morning, he was overcome by a pagan need to peel them off and touch the slender legs so clearly defined beneath.

And when she wore red, he felt like a bull might when seeing a matador's flag—out of control.

Although he knew the remaining items on her list would prove harder to stomach, he wanted to support her. He had promised to.

Willa frowned. 'Do you know, I ran into Tabitha Horsley—a friend I've known for twenty years—in the modiste yesterday and she completely ignored me. She pretended as if she could not hear me talking to her. It was mortifying. I repeated myself three times before I realised that she was doing it deliberately.'

Leo considered her; though her tone had been light, almost humorous, he could see the glazed hurt in her doe-brown eyes. He understood it, too. Though he would never tell her the extent of it, life had not been easy for him since their marriage either.

Business partners had pulled out of a steel manufacturing venture he'd been pursuing, leaving him dangerously short of capital for what he'd planned. Several friends, some of whom he'd known his entire life, had, like Willa's Tabitha, given him the cold shoulder. Even his own father had managed to pull himself out of his stupor for long enough to write him and condemn him for his choice of bride.

But Leo didn't tell Willa any of that. She had chosen to damn anyone who judged her and he would help her do it. He would do anything to make her happy. 'Do you miss having Tabitha in your life?'

'Not at all. She was always so conceited. No,' she repeated more firmly, as if she had only just then realised the truth. 'My scandal has been a test of true friendship. Only the important people have remained.'

'I have found that a person only needs a few true friends to be happy in life.'

Willa smiled and took a small bite from her toast. 'Out of curiosity's sake, what scandalous activity did you have in mind?'

'I was hoping you would take a ride with me through Hyde Park. It's early yet, so it'll mostly be horsemen and men of business passing through, but those trousers…' Leo couldn't help but look at her legs, his eyes following her shape beneath the black fabric.

'I know!' she said gleefully, running her hands over the soft fabric that covered her thighs. 'Madame Tremblay designed them especially for me.'

'It would be a waste to not show them off really,' he pointed out. 'You could miss your chance to flame the next fashion revolution.'

'You wouldn't…'

'Wouldn't what?'

'You wouldn't be embarrassed? These are completely indecent,' she pointed out.

'Not in the slightest. Though, maybe I should bring my gun—just in case anyone gets any ideas.'

'Ideas?'

'Why, of stealing my beautiful, scandalous wife from right beneath my nose.'

Willa waved away the roundabout compliment, but Leo could not miss the pink blush that flushed her face. He wanted to kiss it away, use his lips and tongue to assure her that he was being entirely genuine. For a long moment, he even considered doing just that.

His gaze dropped to her mouth.

Willa tugged her bottom lip between her teeth and, although he knew that she was unaware of the temptation she presented and that she had not done it to tease him, he braced against the corresponding lust as it punched through his system.

'Come on then.' He held out his hand for hers and Willa took it without hesitation. He pulled her to her feet and, when he would have released her, she changed the position of their hands, linking their fingers together as they exited the room.

Warmth flooded Leo's body. He felt like a green lad again, something as simple as holding his wife's hand close to destroying him completely. Her slender fingers were cold, her palm impossibly smooth where it touched his own. Leo wanted her with an intensity that terrified him. He longed to touch her, to taste her. And more than anything, he wanted to make her his. He wanted to brand her from the inside out.

Disconcerted by the rush of desire that passed through him, Leo refocused his attention on Willa. 'What *were* you all laughing about the other day?'

She leaned forward, her eyes suddenly twinkling. 'I've taken to experimenting my new range of motion now that I can wear trousers… I tried to slide down the staircase banister,' she admitted in a whisper, her head tilted towards his. 'Peggy and Wiggs caught me in the act, so naturally I had to extract a vow of silence from each of them.'

Leo listened to her, fascinated, even as his mind painted lurid images of her, dressed in those damned fitted trousers, sliding arse-first towards him down the banister. 'What did Wiggs say?'

'He said that was fine as nobody would believe him if he told them anyway.'

Leo laughed loudly, the unfamiliar sound travelling through the cavernous hall and pealing through the house. To him, his echoing laughter proved exactly what he'd told Willa: he was happy.

Chapter Six

'Leo, you really must tell me where we are going,' Wilhemina complained from the interior of the carriage two days later. 'This is all very unusual.'

'You used to love surprises,' he commented.

All he'd said when he'd come home early in the afternoon was that he was taking her out and that she should wear her trousers and a pair of comfortable shoes. Willa had momentarily thought it was horseback riding. But the horses had not been saddled. Then, when they'd got into the barouche, she'd thought perhaps he was taking her for a walk in Hyde Park. Except, they had passed the park without slowing.

'I don't know whether or not I like surprises,' she informed him. 'The last few have been either so terrible or so incredible that the discrepancy has left me unsure of them in general.' She wagged a finger at him in mock-reproach. 'It is a dangerous game you are playing, my lord.'

Leo leaned back in his seat, his blue eyes never leaving her face. 'Tell me about your last few surprises.'

'Well, the worst one in recent memory was when my father told me I was to marry Windhurst.' She shook her head slightly, trying to dispel the instant sadness that rolled through her like some great, big wave. 'I had met him before, of course. But I never in my wildest nightmares would have thought that my father and brother would pause to consider him.

'I...' She swallowed down the dry lump in her throat. 'I was so upset. I fought them on it for weeks. If it hadn't been for Mary and Isabelle's friendship, I don't know what I would have done.'

When Leo spoke his voice was cold, almost completely devoid of emotion. 'They were fools.' His hand curled into a tight fist on his thigh.

'It will be a long time before I can forgive them.' The mere mention of Grey, who had once been her favourite man in the world, had anger and despair colliding in her stomach, one swift and anxious, the other heavy and deep. The contrast always made her feel ill with regret.

Leo moved from his side of the carriage to come and sit next to her. He did not touch her or otherwise comfort her, merely lent the support of his frame should she need it. And Willa, who had slowly come to rely on being able to touch him, leaned her head on his shoulder.

Leo relaxed beneath her at the small contact, like a big cat who had been lying around, waiting to be petted. 'Tell me about your other surprises.'

Willa took a moment to think it through. 'The next big one was when Grey told me that Windhurst had died.'

'A good surprise.'

'Yes—does that make me a bad person?'

'No. It makes you human.'

Willa blinked rapidly, but she did not let her tears fall. After weeks of being caught up in some strange emotional back and forth, momentarily happy and then only minutes later scared or sad, she was resolute to not spend any more time wallowing in self-pity. She needed to move on, to forget her life with Windhurst. 'The next one was also a good surprise. In fact, it was perhaps the best surprise of my life.' She sat up and turned to look at her husband.

'I find that hard to believe,' Leo teased gently. 'I know for a fact that you were given a pure-bred Spanish Andalusian for your seventeenth birthday.'

'You remember that?'

The light coming in the carriage window filtered over him, casting his face in an angelic glow that made her breath catch. 'Of course.' He grinned, letting a little bit of the devil into his smile. 'It was the happiest I'd ever seen you.'

'It seems like so long ago. Like the time separating then from now was ten years longer than it really was.'

'What happened to her?'

'The girl or the horse?'

'The horse,' Leo replied instantly. 'The girl is slowly coming back to me.'

'Oh.' The single word slipped through her lips in a moment of surprise. Willa flushed and turned to face the window. 'I called her Atalanta.'

'The huntress?'

'I was *seventeen*.' She laughed. 'It seemed like a fitting name at the time.' She sobered. 'The mare is at my family's country estate. Windhurst didn't like the country and he couldn't ride well.'

'So, he deprived you of it, too.'

'It no longer matters.' She had long ago stopped missing the freedom that had come with being in the saddle, her powerful mare's hooves pounding the ground beneath her. She turned, knowing that it was important she look him in the eye when she whispered, 'Your proposal was a better surprise.'

Leo pressed his lips to her forehead in a kiss that was so

brief she almost thought she might have imagined it, except the moment he pulled away she wished that he hadn't. She wished he had taken her mouth instead, as he had on their wedding night. But too confused, too embarrassed to ask him for what she wanted, she simply smiled and said nothing at all.

They were silent the rest of the drive, both of them lost in the peace of sitting side by side. But in minutes the carriage started to slow. 'We're here.' Leo moved around her to push the door open himself.

He climbed out of the carriage and held out a hand to help her down. Conscious of her attire, Willa peeked out of the carriage—and stopped moving. She was moderately horrified to see that they were in Cleveland Row. 'Leo,' she said uncertainly, refusing to come out, 'we're in *St James's*.'

'I know.' He did not lower his hand, merely cocked his head, smiled and waited for her to take it.

'But… I'm wearing trousers!' she hissed. This was not wearing trousers while sitting astride a horse in Hyde Park at six-thirty in the morning with barely anyone about. Or home. They were in St James's—in broad daylight. Such things were not done—ever. In fact, Wilhemina wasn't entirely sure a lady couldn't be arrested for such an indecent display.

'Willa.' Leo crowded into the carriage's entrance, his broad shoulders momentarily blocking her from view. 'We had a list,' he said. 'Or do you not remember?'

'The list,' she repeated distractedly as she tried to look past him.

'The list of scandalous things you wanted to do,' he replied and, when she just stared out of the carriage, he began counting off his fingers. 'Forgo mourning. Ride in breeches through Hyde Park. Learn how to fence. Sell Windhurst's mistress's house and use the proceeds to travel Italy. Dance at balls again, knowing that Windhurst cannot stop you any longer.' He paused to look up at her.

Willa's heart ratcheted up, beating frantically in her chest when she realised that he had not only been listening to her, but that he had remembered everything she'd said. 'You remembered all that?'

'Of course. And by my calculation, we only have Italy and dancing left.'

'And fencing.'

Leo shook his head, but he didn't argue. He passed her his long coat. 'Wear this if you're shy. But don't do it for me; I love watching men stare at you in those trousers.'

'You *do*?' she enquired with genuine surprise.

Windhurst had hated when other men had looked at her or spoken to her. And when it had happened, he'd always punished her for it by accusing her of flirting or being loose. It had eventually come to a point where she had tried not to speak to anyone in public settings save her family, Isabelle and Mary.

'Why wouldn't I?' Leo's eyes flickered over her even as his grin turned devilish. 'They all know you're coming home with me.'

Wilhemina's mouth gaped at the bold statement. But after a slight hesitation, she stepped from the carriage and past his offered coat, entering the bright daylight wearing nothing but her black trousers, boots, a linen shirt and a fitted black jacket. The truth was that she felt quite naked, but she did it. And she did it for no other reason than to please her husband.

Leo's eyes raked over her appreciatively and in them she saw his hunger and felt the resounding pulls of it whisper through her.

He held out his hand and she took it, loving how his big, gloved palm completely enveloped her bare one. He led her to the doors of the impressive building, ignoring all the turned heads and muttered comments that chased them down the street. The white stone façade of the building glistened brilliantly in the afternoon sunlight. Above the door, a set of crossed foils gave away Leo's surprise. 'Fencing?'

Leo pushed open the door to lead her inside. 'I booked you a private lesson with the master himself.'

'He did not mind?' she enquired through the fist of emotion that lodged in her throat. 'Teaching a woman?'

Leo leaned in conspiratorially. 'He's French.'

'Ah.' Though she had not been to France, her brothers all had. And they had told her that every whispered stereotype surrounding the French was pleasantly true—in this case, that they did not suffer the same prudishness that the English did.

'This way.' Leo easily guided her down a series of corridors, only pausing once or twice to introduce her to a friend on the way to the private room.

Willa slowly relaxed despite the curious stares they attracted. And although some of the stares were bordering on hostile, she comforted herself with the fact that Leo did not seem to notice at all.

Leo watched Wilhemina and the fencing master, Jacques Joubert, for almost thirty minutes before the sight of his wife in her black breeches and his own side-buttoned white fencing jacket became too much to bear.

Joubert had started slowly, talking through a brief history and the basics of the sport—the rules, footwork and grips. But when the master had worked through the riposte and feint and started leading Willa into a series of lunges to test and correct her form, Leo had quickly excused himself. He'd rather get some exercise than torture himself by watching the glossy black fabric stretching tightly over his wife's slight curves. It was too much given how long he'd spent pining for her.

He changed into his white breeches, a linen shirt and the sport-specific flat-soled shoes. Foil in hand, he found a private room and began to practise, efficiently running through a series of quick offensive moves against an invisible enemy. He thrust, feinted and lunged until his muscles trembled from use and his breathing billowed out in great exhales. Sweat slicked his back and chest, soaking through his linen shirt and, still, the exertion only partially helped him forget his wife's long legs bending and gliding gracefully.

Leo, who had never gone long without sexual gratification before, had spent the better part of his short marriage trying to avoid unbridling his lust whenever his wife was in proximity. It was no easy feat. If he heard her voice in the house, he could not sit still any longer, but had to go and seek her out. If she entered a room he happened to be occupying, he had to physically plant his feet and link his hands to avoid going to her and dragging her to the floor so that he could finally have her.

He had never pined for a woman with such fevered, unholy intent. And even though he had found tepid comfort in his own hand, it did little to assuage his growing need to make love to his own wife.

'Tell me you didn't bring my sister here.'

Leo spun around at the familiar voice, all thoughts of his wife's nimble body dying when he beheld his friend. Jameson was dressed all in white, the unrumpled state of his uniform making it clear that he had yet to begin his practice.

Leo dropped the tip of his foil. 'Why would I do that when we both know that I did?'

Jameson seemed genuinely surprised. His eyes widened with shock. 'And she is dressed in men's clothing!' he roared, having clearly heard the whispers spreading like a bawdyhouse disease through the fencing club.

Jameson took a confrontational step forward.

Leo relaxed his body, preparing for the real fight he'd been aching for. 'Your sister has been steeped in scandal not of her own making for years,' Leo accused, showing no mercy. 'She has withstood it without any help or sympathy from you and your family. And now, though she cannot escape it completely, at least she can tell you all to go to hell on her own terms. And, yes, I am prepared to help her do it!'

'My sister is ruining her life by courting such scand—'

'She is trying to be free!' Leo shouted, cutting off Jameson. He threw his foil unceremoniously to the ground and advanced, his fists deceptively loose by his sides. His heart raced in his chest, pumping blood and rage through his entire body until he was boiling with fury. 'She does not need to be reined in like some ill-trained horse. She needs to be loved exactly the way she is!'

Jameson raised his hands, the grim look in his eyes telling Leo that he welcomed the chance to brawl, too. 'You think that now,' he cautioned, spreading his legs in a boxer's stance, 'but by letting her have her way, you will destroy her reputation completely.'

Leo stopped five feet away. 'When I win this fight, I want Atalanta sent to me in London.'

Jameson's eyebrows dipped in confusion. *'What?'*

'Your sister's horse,' Leo reminded him, adding a filthy insult that even Jameson flinched against. 'The Andalusian. I want her.'

Jameson nodded—and then he threw the first punch. The heavy fist came fast, too fast for Leo to dodge completely. It caught the edge of his jaw as he ducked to avoid it, but it did not fell him. He countered with a series of jabs and crosses, forcing Jameson to backstep quickly to avoid them.

Whether the open door or the ruckus attracted attention, the room was soon filled with men dressed in fencing whites, talking and laughing loudly as they made bets on the bout. 'Five pounds on Russell!' someone shouted. 'He has his sister's honour to defend.'

'Ten pounds on Pemberton,' another man countered, 'for allowing us the honour of gawking at his lovely wife!'

A chorus of laughter followed the statement, but Leo didn't let it bother him as he circled his childhood friend. Wilhemina had told him she wanted to be shocking, as free as a widow. And he would damn well give her anything she wanted—he'd give her the world if he could.

'You think this is appropriate?' Jameson demanded, pointing out the ribald statement that had been made.

'I can suffer it as long as she's happy,' Leo countered. He lunged forward, throwing his entire weight behind a right hook; the punch connected with Jameson's cheek, snapping his head back sharply.

But Jameson recovered immediately and countered with a wildly thrown jab that landed on Leo's jaw. His vision wavered momentarily, blackening around the edges, but he kept his feet moving, edging away from his opponent until the world came back into clarity.

The two circled each other warily, each on guard, aware of the damage the other could do if given half the chance.

The spectators clamoured. Leo's and Jameson's ragged breaths sawed through the room, sounding pained. Leo could hear his own heart, beating frantically in his ears, but through the noise, another voice sounded, calm and clear. 'What the devil is going on in here?'

The gentlemen in the room fell silent, immediately falling into their manners despite the reputation of the woman demanding answers from them. 'It would seem as if there is a brawl in your honour, Lady Pemberton,' Lord Whittemore offered sheepishly as a bright red flush spread over his bald head.

A few awkward coughs and barely masked laughs followed this statement.

Leo tried desperately to block out her cool, 'I see', as he kept his eyes fixed on Jameson.

Jameson, too, seemed to be having trouble maintaining his rage now that the sister he hadn't seen in so long was standing in the room. His shoulders dropped, his fists lowered. Leo advanced immediately, his fists raised and ready to finish it, if not for the goddamn horse, then for his wife, who had been hurt beyond repair by her family.

Jameson didn't try to defend against the blow that was so clearly coming. It was Willa who spoke up, her gentle, 'Leo', calling his attention to her.

He spared her a glance. She stood in front of the gathered men, her black breeches and black silk vest startling against all the white uniforms behind her. She would have looked like a general with her army of loyal warriors had her face not been bone-white with fear.

The fight left Leo so suddenly that he had to brace himself as the vigour left his body. Willa had literally been physically abused and here he was using his fists to prove a point. What must she think of him? He stopped only three feet from Jameson and slowly lowered his fists to his sides.

'Why stop now?' Jameson asked tiredly.

Leo opened his mouth to reply, his scathing response

ready. But then Willa was in front of him, her cool palm against his bruised face, her back pointedly to her older brother. She looked at him for a long time, her eyes glossy with emotion. Her fingers traced gently over the smarting spot on his jaw where he knew a bruise would already be blooming. 'It's not worth it,' she whispered, her quiet words travelling in the silent room. 'I don't want you to get hurt.'

'I'm fine, Willa,' he assured her.

But she wasn't having it. She rested her forehead on his chest and closed her eyes, her hand coming to lie over his heart. 'Please take me home now.'

Leo fell into action immediately. He shifted Willa, placing her at his side as he pushed through the crowd of men and started for the club's exit. Nobody spoke as they exited the room. Nobody followed them either.

If Leo had paid more attention to Jameson, he would have seen his friend's defeated posture and regretful look as he watched them leave.

But he did not have eyes for anyone but Willa. He walked her outside, sheltering her with his body while they waited for the carriage to come around, one arm slung possessively over her slender shoulders. 'I'm sorry,' he said, realising he had genuinely frightened her.

Willa looked up at him, her eyes huge beneath her long, sandy lashes. 'I couldn't bear if you were hurt.'

'Neither of us would have been that badly injured,' he replied quietly. 'Willa… What happened to you… It was different. I would never—'

'I know,' she insisted.

'Sometimes, men just need to work things out between each other with our fists. It's stupid and juvenile. But it's also the quickest, least painful way for us to resolve an argument. And we're almost always guaranteed to be friends afterwards.'

Willa crinkled her nose. 'That makes absolutely no sense.'

'Probably not.' He kissed the side of her head, his body tightening when he tasted the sweetly salted sweat from her exercise. 'But it's worked for hundreds of years.'

Willa took a deep breath and shook her head, clearly confused. 'What did he say to make you so angry? It's not like you to brawl…'

Her hand rose to his chest and Leo held his breath for a long moment, suddenly conscious that she could probably feel that he was breathing too fast, his body charged by her proximity. 'He said I would destroy you by letting you have your freedom.'

Willa laughed suddenly, but instead of making him smile, the bitter sound of it terrified him. She was still so hurt, so angry. 'It is strange, is it not, that the very traits they found endearing in me as a child made them shame me as a grown woman? They think I am wild and incorrigible.'

'Willa—' he smiled '—you *are* wild and incorrigible.' She tensed at his side and Leo gently tipped her chin so that she met his gaze. 'But I wouldn't change a single thing about you.'

She sniffed delicately as if she were offended. 'I suppose you think I am rather feral.'

'Barely domesticated,' he affirmed, earning a solid thwack on the chest, one that made his lips twitch. But he leaned down, bringing his lips close to his wife's ear. 'What now, my wildling?'

Willa's hand stroked over his jaw, eliciting a visceral shiver from him. 'Home to ice this, I think.'

He nodded, flinching slightly when the movement resulted in rivulets of tension down both sides of his neck. 'That's probably wise.'

'I have some bay oil. We'll clean you off, ice your poor face, then apply some to help with the pain.'

Leo should have told her that he wasn't that sore and that he'd seen much worse—and probably would again. But he couldn't give life to the words. The idea of her sitting by his head, cleaning the sweat off his face with a damp rag before she applied oil to his bruises was too much to refuse.

He wanted her with such an unholy intent he'd taken to allowing her to nurse superficial wounds—but he didn't care. He wanted every touch she would give him, every second of her cool fingertips on his face. Unable to speak past the lump in his throat and the weight in his groin, he simply nodded.

And Willa, misinterpreting the gesture as pain rather than lust, stood on her toes and kissed the side of his jaw. A primitive flood of greed flamed through him at the dainty touch of her lips, but he did not succumb to his need to turn and crush his mouth to hers. Instead, he exhaled deeply and prayed for the carriage to arrive before he ravished his wife in broad daylight in St. James's.

And if, once they were home, Leo decided that the mutual pounding had been worth every second of his wife's sweet ministrations to his bruised face, he realised he would have quite gladly faced all three of her brothers for another chance to see the way she smiled when, two days later, her horse was delivered to their London home with a note from Jameson that simply read:

I hope one day you will both forgive me.

Chapter Seven

Wilhemina did not *want* to go to the masquerade ball. Though she acted as though the *ton*'s censure did not affect her, she felt the humiliation of each snub, of each flapping fan and wagging tongue that she encountered each time she left the house. If they'd been only directed at her she could have lived with it—she already had for a long time. But now they were directed at Leo, too, and he had done nothing to deserve such scorn.

Willa turned to her looking glass and assessed Peggy's skilful hand with her coiffure. Her maid had expertly woven the ribbons of her mask through her hair, securing them in plaits before collecting the rest of her locks in a massive chignon at the back of her head. The silk mask was blood red, made from the same fabric as the new gown Willa had ordered for this very occasion. If she was going to be the brunt of society's censure, then by God she was going to do it fashionably dressed. 'You are a magician, Peggy.'

'Agreed.'

They both started, but, while Peggy turned to bob into a quick curtsy in Leo's direction, Willa merely met his eyes in her looking glass.

Peggy beamed, her initial awkwardness around Leo having diminished over the weeks that Willa and Leo had been married. 'I'm happy you like it, milady. Is there anything else you need?'

'No, thank you.'

Her maid curtsied again and left the room.

'You look beautiful, Willa,' Leo observed as soon as they were alone.

'So do you,' she replied honestly. Leo, leaning casually against the doorframe, looked impeccably handsome in his all-black attire. Even his black mask, which was expertly fitted over one half of his face, did nothing to detract from him. If anything, it added mystery and danger to his obnoxious good looks.

'May I ask you a question?'

Leo came into her room by way of answer. Instead of sitting in one of the chairs by the fire, he came to where she sat on her long vanity bench and positioned himself next to her on the seat, their arms touching though they were facing in opposite directions. 'What's worrying you?'

She frowned, hating that her distress was so obvious to him. 'Has your life—your *business*—been affected by our marriage?'

'No,' he replied hastily—too hastily. As if he'd sensed it, too, he slowly corrected with, 'Not in any material way.'

'But?'

He looked at her for a long moment before replying, 'Why do you care so much when I so clearly do not?'

'It was easy not to care when it was only me,' she said honestly. 'But now every time I want to do something scandalous or properly rebuff someone, I think of you and the consequences to you.' She sifted through her thoughts. 'I care for you a great deal. I don't want to be responsible for any hardship befalling you—not after everything you've done for me.' She shook her head sadly.

'You are not responsible for my decisions, Willa.'

'Leo,' she urged, growing genuinely frustrated. 'Don't placate me. I want to know how our marriage has affected you.'

He considered her, his handsome face silhouetted in the candlelit room. 'Well, my ability to concentrate on business for any length of time has diminished greatly, especially when you wear those breeches.'

'Leo…' she nudged him with her shoulder '…be serious.'

'A few men pulled out of a venture I was backing,' he admitted cautiously.

'What type of venture?'

'Steel manufacturing.'

'They withdrew their finances?'

Leo nodded, but he did not seem upset. In fact, he grinned. 'Luckily, Mary convinced Sykes to invest the shortfall. I don't know how she even knew my investors had withdrawn—'

'Mary always knows everything—though I have no idea how she does it.' Willa made a note to ask her friend about it, then turned back to her husband. 'What else?'

'Nothing of importance.'

Willa only raised her brows.

'Nothing that I wouldn't lose a hundred times over again if I was given the option to make the same decision.'

'You're impossibly happy about our circumstances when you shouldn't be. You're quite ruined, you know.'

'Do not paint me a hero.' He looked at her, his blue eyes searching her face intently. 'I was prepared, Willa. Do you think I would have tied myself to you for life if I had not considered it from every angle? And, though I shouldn't have to remind you, I am quite happy to be ruined.' His quiet chuckle skittered over her skin. 'Though whoever could have guessed that it would be *marriage* that would be my downfall?'

'Certainly not me,' Willa affirmed. 'My only consolation is that, short of getting married a *third* time, there is nothing I could do that would make things worse than they already are.'

'I wouldn't say that's your *only* consolation.' Leo linked his hand with hers and helped her rise from the bench. He led her around to where he stood.

'Oh?'

'Well, every time you feel ostracised or shunned tonight, all you have to do is think that every woman in the room is most certainly jealous of you—save a few. You will be a countess—a *second* time. Your new husband is far better looking than your last and you did not even have to pursue him.' He stopped at the door and brought her bare hand to his lips, kissing her knuckles gently. 'I snatched you up at the first opportunity.'

Willa ceded his point with a small nod as she tried to calm her errant pulse. She loved that he did not try to pretend that the upcoming ball would be anything but a disaster. She loved that he had no regrets when it came to their marriage—as she did not either. But most of all, and perhaps a bit alarmingly, she loved that he did not release her hand as they left her bedroom and descended the stairs together.

In just a few short weeks, she had come to enjoy his small touches. Although Leo himself rarely touched her first, if Willa reached out and touched him, it seemed to signal to him that she was consenting. His fingers would instantly start tracing lazy patterns on her arm, or fiddle with a stray lock of her hair, or gently brush against her face in a tightly constrained pattern that hinted at his caged desperation. It had become like some torturous game of chess for both of them, one where she had to brave her caution and make the first move in order to get what she wanted—*his* hands on *her*.

She opened her mouth to tell him something to that effect, but snapped it shut when she saw a familiar face at the bottom of the stairs. *'Gordy!'* she gasped, momentarily forgetting herself.

Gordon, for all his infallible formality, could not quite contain his smile at her exuberant exclamation. He tipped into a bow. 'My lady.'

Willa barely refrained from throwing her arms around the elderly butler; the only thing that stopped her was Gordon's clear embarrassment at her show of affection. He flushed and cleared his throat as if to remind her of her position in the household.

'What is the meaning of this?' Willa demanded.

'I have stolen Gordon from the Duke,' Leo stated proudly. He watched her face as Gordon held out his gloves for him.

Willa paused as a horrific thought occurred to her. 'Define *stolen*?'

'Don't worry so much, Willa.' Leo shrugged into the coat that the butler was holding out for him. 'I asked Matthew's *and* Luke's permission—and then bribed Gordon to the point where he would have had to have been insane to refuse.'

Willa looked to the butler for confirmation. 'You came willingly?' she asked and hurriedly followed the question with, 'It is a notable step down, from duke to viscount.' It didn't matter that Leo would be an earl one day soon—to be in service to a duke was an immense honour.

'I came willingly and with very little convincing, my lady.'

Leo snorted.

'God knows my husband makes a very compelling argument.'

Though he would never deign to confirm such a statement, Gordon bowed in reply. He walked to the door to open it for them.

Willa could not resist pausing one last time at the door to smile up at the looming butler. 'I am happy to have you,' she said sincerely. And, feeling the embarrassing burn of tears, hurriedly added, 'I shall try my best to refrain from calling you Gordy,' she promised, 'though it shall be a great test of my will.'

'I do not mind, my lady,' the butler replied.

'Please tell Wiggs and Peggy that there's no need to wait up for us, Gordon.' Leo took her hand and led her to the carriage.

It was only once they were safely inside, and the carriage was moving, that Willa lost herself. She hurtled herself across the small space separating her from Leo and flung her arms around him.

'Thank you,' she blubbered. 'This is the best gift I have ever received!' She pulled back slightly. 'Not that a person can be gifted, of course,' she corrected. 'But Gordon is a treasure! Do you know,' she carried on excitedly, 'that he physically prevented Gareth St Claire from entering Everett Place when Isabelle was ill?'

'Heavens,' Leo replied, laughing in surprise. But he did not let her pull back. Instead, he lifted her and settled her on his lap more fully. 'Who knew that all I had to do to get you back here was hire a butler?'

The casually intimate comment caught her off guard. Willa flushed with embarrassment, unable to meet his eyes even though she wore a mask. 'I have thought… That is to say, I have wanted…'

Golly, how did one proposition one's own husband?

'Me, too,' Leo said, saving her from having to explain.

'I do not know how to talk of such things, Leo,' she whispered, feeling more awkward, more *childish*, by the second.

'And I do not wish to rush you when you are not ready.' His hand found her face, his fingers brushing a stray lock of hair back from her mask. 'Willa… There is nothing you could ask from me that I do not already want to give you.' His voice came out thick. 'Do…do you understand what I am trying to say?'

'You want me,' she confirmed and, though she did not dare move or acknowledge him, she could feel his hard length beneath her thigh.

'Yes. But you are going to have to tell me how much of you I can have.'

She swallowed nervously because, while she appreciated that he placed the choice in her hands, it was also so much harder to have to open her mouth and actually ask. She had never been given so much power, the option to say yes or no. So, she took a deep breath and, before she could change her mind, blurted, 'I want you to kiss me again!'

The request sank between them. Leo froze, his muscles tensing. For one impossibly long, awkward moment, she thought he might not kiss her. But then his palm cupped her face and his lips lowered to hers. Unlike their first kiss, which had been a little stilted, this one was familiar, as if they both knew exactly how they would slot together now.

Leo changed the angle of the kiss, taking it deeper, but it was Willa who urged him on, her lips sighing open with need. Her hands rose to his head. Her fingers sank into his hair, drawing a groan from deep in his chest.

He moved away from her lips to trail kisses down her neck and Willa arched, pressing herself closer. Leo reached her collarbone and, instead of continuing his small kisses, ran the tip of his tongue along the long, slanting shape of the bone beneath her skin.

Her breasts ached, feeling too heavy, too tightly constrained in her corset. She trembled against the strange cool sensation of Leo's tongue and Leo, feeling her shiver, started to pull back. 'No,' Willa begged, holding him closer. 'Please. I…'

'Tell me, Willa,' he rasped. 'Tell me where you want me.'

Unable to speak the words, Willa did not reply. But needing relief from the tension coiling through her body, she reached for Leo's hand and raised it to her breast.

He growled his appreciation. His big palm moulded the shape of her over her bodice, cupping and pressing her through the restraining layers. 'Is this where you want me, love?'

'Yes,' Willa gasped.

'Do you want my hands or my mouth?'

She froze at the question, as unsure of herself as she was sure of him. 'I—I don't know,' she admitted, mortified by how truly inexperienced she was for a woman who had been married and widowed before the age of twenty-four.

'What if we try both and you can tell me which you prefer?'

Again, he waited for her to nod before dipping his hand into her low-cut bodice and gently lifting her breast from its confines, exposing her peaked nipple to his gaze. Willa tried not to flinch. She tried to stave off the flood of embarrassment that started eating away at her desire. When she wasn't quite successful, she buried her face in Leo's neck.

'Don't hide from me, Willa.' Leo cradled his wife on his lap and tried his best to calm his raging erection. It was no easy feat considering one of Willa's perfect breasts was peaked in front of him. He felt like a storm contained in a vessel that might explode from the pressure at any moment. Need practically vibrated through him.

'I… I'm not used to this,' she whispered quietly.

Leo wondered what she meant by that. Not used to being loved? Not used to being exposed? Not used to feeling lust? 'Am I scaring you?'

She shook her head. 'I am embarrassed.' Even as she said it, her hand rose to cover her breast. 'I know that I am not…*womanly*. Or well endowed. Or sensual.' She released a deep, shuddering exhale and whispered, 'I'm *frigid*.'

'Wilhemina,' Leo whispered, shocked by her perceived coldness. The woman he knew was all contained fire. The furthest thing from frigid. 'Where did you hear that?'

'That's what he used to call me,' she whispered. 'When I couldn't pretend to enjoy…*it*.' She turned those enormous eyes on him, and in them he saw doubt, self-consciousness and what looked eerily akin to shame. And though he did not know how it was possible that a woman as resplendent as Willa could be so insecure, it reminded him of what she had lived through.

'Willa—' he shook his head in frustration '—I am holding you in my arms and I can assure you that you are all woman. Your skin—' he kissed her neck once '—is as soft as rose petals. Your smell—' he buried his face against her hair and groaned '—is intoxicating. And your body—' he lowered his head to swirl his tongue around her peaked nipple once '—is perfect.'

Willa's chest heaved in response to his administrations, her chest rising, following his mouth even as he withdrew.

'Look at you,' he whispered and pointedly blew a breath over her straining nipple before tugging it into his mouth.

Her arms tightened around him. 'This is not the body,' he rasped, 'these are not the responses, of a frigid woman.'

When she did not reply, merely looked at him in confusion, he shook his head. 'I am undone by you—you have only to look at me to know that's true.' He nudged his hips, briefly pressing his iron-hard length into her thigh. '*Feel* me. My body aches for you. *You.* Exactly the way you are.'

He claimed her mouth in one fierce kiss that was as quick as it was intense. 'I will spend my entire life convincing you if that is what it takes.' As far as promises went, it was the easiest one he would ever make. While Leo knew that there was nothing he could do to guarantee her love, he was absolutely certain that he could give her this.

The carriage slowed. Leo, who had his wife on his lap with her breast out, barely refrained from calling for his driver to keep going. But it was Willa who groaned in frustration and plonked her head on his shoulder. 'I feel so *irritated*.'

Leo couldn't help but laugh at that.

He tugged her bodice back up and gave her one last look to make sure she wasn't too dishevelled. Willa was flushed with pleasure, her cheeks visibly pink even in moonlight. 'Willa…' How did he voice that he wanted to touch her without terrifying her? How did he ask her if she was ready for that, for *him*? 'I want to show you how it can be…'

And Willa did not demur as he'd expected. Though she could not quite meet his eye, she replied, 'Yes. I think it's time.'

'Tonight. After the ball,' he promised. But that was all Leo could manage through the intensity of his lust.

Chapter Eight

Any residual desire that had heated Willa's blood chilled the moment she entered the Earl of Heather's home. The guests behind her in the receiving line whispered as they recognised her, causing the guests in front of them to turn and see what all the fuss was about. The result was that Willa and Leo found themselves suddenly pressed by scathing looks and meant-to-be-heard whispers on both sides.

The Dowager Countess Rathbone fluttered her fan and deliberately averted her masked face, refusing to acknowledge them though they stood directly in front of her. Lady Georgianna and Lady Deborah Waller, twin sisters who had—or, at least, *thought* they had—vied for Leo's attention once, tittered and laughed, their matching white swan masks bobbing together. Georgianna's, 'How disgraceful, wearing red so soon after her late—or should I say *last*—husband's death', rang through the large hall, causing a round of ill-disguised laughter.

Willa fought to maintain her composure, but suddenly her dress felt too colourful, too red. Her lips, pressed into an austere expression, felt too stiff, too false. Still, she forcibly straightened her spine, trying desperately to appear unaffected though her stomach warred with sick dread.

Next to her, Leo did not seem bothered in the least. He

smiled like a fox in a henhouse, his mouth curving into a wicked grin that had his dimple popping, and though he did not reach out and take her hand, he leaned his upper arm ever so slightly against hers as if he wanted to remind her that he was there to protect her, to support her.

'Lord and Lady Pemberton!'

A hush settled in the hall as the Countess's greeting rang through the gathered crowd. Willa, unsure of what was happening, remained standing in place, waiting to be received. But Matthew's mother was not having it. The Countess skirted around the guests that she had been greeting—a deliberate affront—and glided towards where Leo and Willa stood, her hands outstretched. 'My dears, I am so glad you could attend!' she said, taking Willa's hands in hers.

'Lady Heather.' Willa bobbed into a curtsy. 'You have outdone yourself again. Everything looks beautiful.'

'Thank you, Wilhemina.' The Countess turned to Leo, her eyes twinkling with as much mischief as his. 'My dear boy,' she said at plain speaking volume, 'after all the years you have been received as a son in my house, you do not need to fall back on formalities. Go…' she waved a hand nonchalantly in the direction of her drawing room, which opened with the connecting room to serve as her ballroom each year '…find Matthew. He and the Isabelle are waiting for you.'

Leo bowed and kissed the Countess's hand. 'We will talk once you are done with your guests, my lady.'

The Countess tapped Leo's face twice as she would have done to one of her own children. The gesture was not lost on the assembled guests, most of whom looked genuinely insulted—undoubtedly as the Countess had intended. 'Yes. I shall find you later,' she said and, with that final word, resumed her place at the front of the line with an expression that almost appeared to be one of resigned boredom.

Leo escorted Willa away from the waiting guests. She appreciated the Countess's support—for there was no mistaking the woman's intention—but the kind gesture did not stop her from feeling every eye in the room as she walked away. The stares seemed to peel away her brave façade, leaving her anxious and full of nervous energy. She had half a mind to bolt.

'That went rather as expected,' she said to Leo, hoping to distract herself and counteract her strange urge to run.

'Chin up, love,' Leo replied, smiling gently. He raised her gloved hand to his lips, pressing a casual kiss to the back of her knuckles. 'We are only getting started.'

If Willa had not known what he'd meant, it did not take her long to figure it out. In minutes, Mary, Matthew, Isabelle and their entire extended family, which included the Earl Westmoor, who was married to Matthew's sister, Caroline, closed ranks around them, making it obvious to everyone in the room that the couple had retained some powerful allies through the scandal.

Willa's eyes burned behind her mask as her friends bracketed them from the censure of everyone else at the ball. But she did not have time to feel sorry for herself as they all started congratulating her and Leo on their wedding and talking over one another in their eagerness to appear to be having a grand time.

And if that had not been enough, soon Willa was being introduced to any number of people she had not met before. There was Lord Carmichael, a friend of Leo's from school, and his wife, Lady Carmichael. And the Viscount Cayden, a business associate of Leo's, and his sister, Lady Phillipa.

Even Cameron Sykes, who had never made an effort

with her before, came to greet them and wish them well. 'Lambert tells me that congratulations are in order,' he said and bowed in greeting.

Willa, who had never heard of her perfect, delicate friend Mary referred to by only her last name, risked a glance at the woman in question. Mary was a vision in a soft rose-coloured gown, her dark brown hair perfectly coiled and pinned. Instead of seeming offended or shocked, Mary just rolled her eyes behind her mask as if to say: Do you see what I have to put up with?

'Yes,' Willa replied, staring up at Cameron. 'Thank you, Mr Sykes.'

He grinned, his green eyes snapping with a humour that was certainly too brash to be considered gentlemanly. 'Though God knows you must have been in dire straits to accept a degenerate like Pemberton.'

'Sykes,' Mary warned.

But Leo just laughed and stroked one palm down Willa's tense back as if she was a displeased housecat in need of soothing. 'Fortunately for me,' he said, not denying the less than ideal circumstances. 'However, my wife knows the very worst things about me.'

Willa, becoming aware that Cameron Sykes had not been trying to cause offence, slowly relaxed. 'Yes,' she drawled, 'my husband has been known as a notorious rake in the past.' Leo tensed at her side, but Willa just leaned closer to Cameron Sykes and, lowering her voice, whispered, 'Fortunately for me.'

The innuendo was not lost on their company. Mary's eyes widened in shock at the brash statement. Sykes paused for only a moment before he threw his head back and laughed loudly. The deep sound echoed in the room, pulling several curious gazes in their direction.

'You're a dark horse, Lady Wilhemina.' He levelled a cheeky grin at Leo. 'If I'd known, I might have fought a round in the ring over you.'

'I am man enough to admit that once in the ring was enough with you, Sykes.'

'You...' She looked from Leo to Sykes, taking in their comparative sizes. While Leo was tall, he was long and lean. Sykes, in contrast, might have been the biggest man she'd ever seen, with height that rivalled even Matthew's and broad shoulders that undoubtedly caused his tailor endless grief. 'You *fought* each other?'

'Aye.' Sykes grinned. 'Your man probably came closer to beating me than anyone else ever has.' He raised a hand unconsciously to his jaw. 'The devil lurks in his right hook.'

'He's exaggerating,' Leo replied unselfconsciously. 'Sykes broke my nose and two of my ribs.'

'Heavens.' Willa tilted her head and studied her husband's face, trying to see any remnants of said broken nose beneath his half-mask, and, finding none, added, 'You didn't do a very good job of it, Mr Sykes.'

Sykes and Leo both laughed good-naturedly, their easy camaraderie telling Willa that they were closer friends than she'd initially thought. It was not every day that a viscount, a future *earl*, befriended and did business with a low-born merchant's son turned businessman. It showed her a side of her husband that she had not known before, one that she found herself curious to know more of.

Leo presented himself as a gentleman of leisure to society, but over the course of their short marriage, she had been surprised to learn that her long-held impression of him could not have been further from the truth. He worked harder than any other peer she knew, including Greyson, who had a rather famed reputation for being uptight and close-lipped in his business affairs. The revelation served as an important reminder to Willa that you could not truly know a person unless they deigned to show you their true self.

If she was very aware that he had promised to show her yet another side of himself later that night, she tried not to focus too much on it. She was too afraid that if she pondered it too long, she would become too anxious and say or do something wrong. Because even her brief interactions with Leo had told her that she did not quite know everything she should have as a woman who had been previously married.

The sound of the music starting up and the master of ceremonies announcing the waltz briefly redirected their attention. When it receded, Cameron Sykes held out his hand for Mary. 'Come on, Lambert. Have a whirl with me.'

Mary shook her head tiredly, but she surprised Willa by sliding her hand into her employer's, touching him with a familiarity that would have been scandalous if anyone had cared to notice. 'How could I refuse such a gallant offer?'

'You can't. I'd have to dock your pay for insubordination,' Sykes countered.

Mary sighed dramatically. 'When really one would think I deserved a raise for all my efforts.'

Cameron laughed and, with one final nod at Willa and Leo, led his assistant to where couples were preparing to dance.

Willa watched her friend walk away with the businessman, considering the two and their obvious familiarity. Cameron's head was bent attentively towards Mary as she said something. And it must have been something funny because he laughed loudly as he turned and gathered Mary possessively in his arms.

'You see it, too,' Leo observed, following the direction of Willa's gaze.

'They're...'

'Not yet. But knowing Sykes, it won't take him long to seduce her.'

Willa actually laughed at that. 'You only say that because you do not know Mary. She would not be seduced unless she absolutely wanted to be—and orchestrated the entire affair herself.'

'Would you like to wager on it?'

'A deal?'

Leo nodded and, taking her hand, led her towards the dance. 'I'm feeling lucky. After all, my last deal paid off immensely.'

Willa felt a tug of emotion at the words; they threaded through her, settling a deep peace in her heart, one that she had not known for a very long time. 'I would argue that it is *I* who gained the upper hand in that deal.'

Willa's soft admission caused a strange pang in his chest. It occurred to Leo as he led his wife into the waltz, that he had never had someone consider him important before. He had been sought for his title, of course, but he had always known that a woman wanting the title and wanting *him* were entirely different matters. Not even his own parents had wanted him—it had not mattered how hard he had tried to win their affections, or how well he had done in school, or how perfectly quiet and unobtrusive he had been when they were home. They not only had not cared, they had not even noticed.

But when Willa spoke of him of their marriage, he felt as if she were being honest, as if she valued him for who he was. She never even mentioned his title, though he supposed it mattered less considering she had already been a countess prior to their marriage.

Leo had known what he'd been doing when he'd proposed their *deal*. He'd had his eyes wide open. From the moment she had stormed his bedroom, telling him that Windhurst was dead, he had started planning.

He was not a good friend as Willa assumed, an honourable man who had stepped in to help her. He was selfish. Selfish enough to offer to help her because he knew, deep down in his soul, that she was the only woman he'd ever wanted to marry and that the only reason she would ever accept him was if she'd had no choice. He'd snatched her up when she'd been desperate and vulnerable, and he'd done it knowing he would never, even if she could not grow to love him, regret it.

And if his mind fell back through time, reminding him of when he'd originally approached Lord Russell to ask permission to court her, he stoically ignored the memory. It no longer mattered that he had been denied in favour of Windhurst, whose age and reputation had taken precedence. It no longer mattered that Willa's brother, Greyson, who had been a *friend* of Leo's, had, despite his obvious doubts, sided with his father. Because, even knowing that he *should* feel guilty, Leo did not. He finally had her. He had married Wilhemina Russell.

'What are you thinking about?'

Leo looked down into his wife's beautiful brown eyes, noting the flecks of gold that added warmth to their sad expression. 'I was thinking how selfish I was to trap you into marriage so soon,' he said honestly. 'But that I do not regret it in the slightest.'

'Trap me?' Willa's dark brows arched. 'Did you kill my husband, then?'

'No.' He laughed.

'Pity.'

'I took advantage of the situation knowing that it would

be easier to convince you when you were vulnerable,' he admitted quietly.

'Oh.' Willa's lips parted as if she wanted to say more, but her eyes snagged on someone over his shoulder and, instead of calming, she tensed immediately, her body going rigid in his arms.

Leo angled his head to see where she'd looked. Willa's older brothers—Greyson, Jameson and Gabriel—stood side by side like angry knights wanting to avenge her honour. 'Despite their ham-handedness, they love you very much,' Leo said, trying to calm her. 'Grey thought he was doing the right thing by you.'

'No. He and my father made the most important decision of my life without even *asking* me what I thought or how I felt. And in doing so, they not only deprived me of happiness, but subjected me to *years* of pain and suffering. And then, worst of all, even once Windhurst took to gallivanting around with Miss Pierce, they abandoned me. That is not *love*, Leo. That is possession.'

'It is not so different to our deal,' he said. 'I twisted your circumstances to suit my needs.'

'No. You did not coerce me or manipulate me or lie to me. You offered me a choice.'

He looked away as he struggled with the immensity of her faith in him. He did not deserve her, of that he was certain.

'Leo,' she whispered, 'look at me.' And when he did, she asked, 'If I had said no, if I had refused you, what would you have done?'

'I would have settled your debt and set you up somewhere safe,' he said without pausing. Though he had dreaded it, he had prepared for the possibility.

'On the night my husband died, you thought *I'd mur-*

dered him and, instead of panicking or denouncing me, you started making plans to run away with me, to *protect* me. If our deal had not already appealed to me, your infallible friendship would have. Which proves my initial point.'

'What point would that be?'

'That I rather got the better end of the deal.'

Leo couldn't help but smile. 'How about we agree to disagree?'

She nodded. 'On one condition.'

Leo tensed at her tone. 'Yes?'

'I would like for you to kiss me now.'

Leo stumbled. He caught himself almost immediately, just as the dance came to an end. Couples started to filter off, more started to join the floor for the next dance and Leo and Wilhemina stayed exactly where they'd stopped, their arms still in the waltz position.

'Are you sure?' he asked. Willa was becoming more relaxed with him every day, but a public kiss was far more than he knew her to be comfortable with. Even *he* felt anxious at the thought of public intimacy.

'Yes.' She tilted her head back to look at him. 'I would like to give everyone something to actually talk about behind their fans.'

'And make a point to your brothers?'

Instead of denying it, Willa grinned devilishly. 'You *do* know me well.'

Leo lowered his head, bringing her lips to her ear. 'Not as well as I intend to know you,' he whispered. And because he could not help himself, he added, '*All* of you.'

Willa blushed, but Leo did not give her embarrassment time to grow. He took her mouth in a fierce kiss, ignoring the gasps of horror and quiet chuckles that diffused through the Countess's ballroom at such a crude display.

He pulled back after only a few seconds, but it didn't matter. The damage had been done. People were staring. Matthew and Isabelle were grinning. Even Mary looked as though she might start applauding. Across the room, Willa's brothers were gaping, their faces set in strange looks of embarrassed confusion and, at least on Greyson's part, guilt.

Leo gathered his wife in his arms again, not giving anyone time to encroach before the next dance started.

'Two dances in a row with my husband,' Willa observed breathlessly. 'How shocking.'

Leo leaned down to nuzzle her neck, completely uncaring what anyone in the room thought of his puppyish behaviour. 'I wonder what they will say when we dance the whole night together then.'

Willa laughed loudly and it in Leo heard the echoes of Willa before Windhurst, of the spirited, happy girl he had first fallen in love with when she'd been just sixteen.

Chapter Nine

By the time Leo helped her out of the carriage it was nearing three o'clock in the morning. Per his instructions, none of the servants had waited up for them, though Gordon had left a single candle and matches in the hall.

Leo lit it and started up the stairs. 'Did you have an enjoyable evening?' He asked the question quietly, as if he were afraid of waking someone.

'I did.' Willa managed to smile sincerely despite her fatigue. 'Your above average dancing skills certainly made up for all the whispers.' She scrunched her nose. 'Though I don't suppose we'll be invited to any other balls in the near future.'

'Give it time. The worst of it will blow over.'

Willa did not have as much confidence as Leo, but she felt it necessary to reassure him. 'I don't mind, you know. I can be happy without them, Leo.'

They both fell quiet as they stopped outside her bedroom. 'I wish I could change the past,' he whispered sadly. 'I would have done everything differently.'

'Me, too.' Willa took the candle from him, deliberately ignoring the low stirring in her womb when their gloved hands touched. 'But seeing as we cannot…' She reached down and opened her door.

Leo did not move to follow her. 'Goodnight, Willa.'

She angled her face back to look at him, slightly panicked that he was planning on leaving. She remembered what he'd said. *'There is nothing you could ask of me that I do not already want to give you.'* Remembering gave her courage, just enough to ask, 'Do you think you could help me first?' She touched her mask with her free hand. 'I cannot take this off myself.'

It was a blatant lie; the mask was braided into her hair and Willa was a woman who was quite capable of unplaiting some braids. But Leo came to her immediately, his quiet 'Of course' skittering up her spine and filling her with anticipation.

She supposed if she'd been a seductress she would have just told him what she wanted as he'd asked her to. But Willa, for all her boldness, was not quite as scandalous as one would assume from her fallen position in society. She'd been raised properly, that is to say in ignorance of all the things she had come to realise a young woman ought to know prior to marriage.

She had been taught etiquette, dancing, drawing and French, and although it had always been assumed she would marry, and marry well, there had never been any talk of what happened after one had caught a husband—save to keep a good house and breed.

She placed the candle on her chest of drawers, lighting the room in a warm glow. Nerves danced through her stomach, but she managed to turn her back to Leo. 'The ribbons are woven through my hair.'

He removed his gloves and started loosening her coiffure without delay, his nimble fingers moving quickly as if he did not want to linger.

Willa, contrarily, wished he would slow down. She loved the feeling of his hands in her hair, each slight movement unspooling her by degrees. It was always like that with him; Leo had a way of slowly unravelling her, a way of loosening the tightness in her chest that nobody else had ever even known was there.

She sighed and closed her eyes as the tension left her scalp. Cool air brushed her flushed eyelids, adding a pleasant contrast, hot and then cold, when the mask started sliding down her face.

Leo's deep, even breaths whispered through the room, pulling the fine hairs on her arms upright. 'I think that was the last one,' he said and took a large step back.

Willa frowned and removed the mask completely. He was leaving?

Perhaps I was not obvious enough?

She turned to face him. Leo had both his hands behind his back like a child in a store who'd been told not to touch. His posture was relaxed. But his eyes... Willa's stomach tightened when she recognised the slightly wild look in his eyes, and when he spoke, asking, 'Is that all?', there was a tight pinch in his voice.

She cleared her throat. 'Actually, my dress and corset are laced up the back—if you could...' There was no need to *act* awkward; Willa felt genuinely mortified by her inability to seduce her own husband and her nervous dread was made obvious by her fluttering hands and stilted speech.

Leo made a strangled sound and blinked slowly. But after a long pause, he approached her again, his hands outstretched in front of him like some newly awakened Frankenstein. He gently turned her around so that he was at her back and started on her buttons, not touching her again, merely undoing the small obstacles expertly while she set about removing her gloves.

The dress opened by degrees, the heavy fabric loosening

enough that Willa could shrug her arms out of the sleeves. She raised her arms and Leo lifted the dress up and over her head, leaving her in nothing but her corset and white linen undergarments. And, *still*, he did not touch her. He draped her dress over one of the chairs by the fireplace and started loosening the laces of her corset, his fingers purposefully avoiding contact with her skin.

Wilhemina held her breath as the air in the room prickled her bare arms. She felt so odd—so anxious and frustrated and…flummoxed, really.

Her corset came away, leaving her in her chemise and stockings. Without a word, Leo threw it on top of the bed and started for his adjoining bedroom. Willa's heart sank. 'Leo…'

He paused at the door, his back stiffening as if he was preparing for an attack. He did not turn around. 'Yes?'

'Do you not want…?'

He turned around slowly, like a predator who'd just realised he'd passed some camouflaged prey animal hiding in the brush. He did not come towards her, but Willa could not help but take a step back when she saw the untamed looked in his eyes. 'Willa,' he said very slowly, 'what exactly are you asking me?' When she still did not reply, he added, 'You need to be very clear.'

'I…' Willa puffed out a frustrated breath, suddenly unsure of herself as she stood in her plain white chemise, trying to convince her own husband to bed her.

Leo did not move an inch. He just waited in silence, his blue eyes searing into her face as if he could burn back the layers of her to see her innermost thoughts.

She inhaled a deep breath and, without giving herself time to cower, said, 'I want you to stay. With me. I mean…' She slapped her hand over her eyes, mortified. 'How do people *routinely* do this?' she wondered aloud, becoming distracted in her embarrassment.

'Willa—' Leo did not relent '—in what capacity would you like me to stay?'

'What on earth do you mean?' she demanded, growing increasingly flustered. She waved a hand down her linen-clad body, noting that Leo's eyes tracked the movement, running from her chest to her ankles and back up again before settling on her face. 'To be quite frank, Leo, I thought I had made that quite obvious. And *you promised*.'

'I don't want to pressure you if you are not ready.'

Again, Willa looked down at her chemise and then back up at Leo. She raised one sardonic brow.

'Are you asking me to touch you?'

'Well, I *was*.' She wrapped her arms around herself, feeling dejected. 'Except now the feeling is gone.'

Leo came to her, his long legs eating up the space between them in a heartbeat. He gently took both her wrists, one in each large hand, and tugged her closer so that her body was plastered against his. 'What feeling is gone?' he asked, his voice hoarse.

'You *know*.'

He did not deny it. Instead, he lowered his mouth to her ear. 'I can bring it back, love,' he whispered. 'Is that what you want?'

His hands gripped her tighter as he waited for her to reply. His breath struck the side of her neck, making her shiver. And even though she nodded, she rather felt as if he, or his proximity, already had.

Her senses clashed, so that she became too aware of all of him—his smell, the sound of his deep breathing, the feel of his bare hands on her skin. Her heartbeat increased until it was frantically thumping against her ribs, stirring a new excitement through her that felt oddly like panic.

That same ache pulsed deep in her body and, although she would never actually do it, she had the strangest urge to rub herself against him like a needy cat seeking attention.

'Say it.'

'I want you.'

'To do what?' he demanded.

'To touch me,' Willa said, this time without hesitation. And in case her husband was still confused by her poor attempt at seduction, she added, 'Make me your wife.'

Leo groaned and crushed his mouth to hers. This kiss was not soft and gentle. He pried her lips open with his tongue, swooping inside her mouth even as his hands dropped her wrists and moved around her body to grip her bottom.

Willa returned the kiss eagerly, her tongue seeking, her hands fumbling. Her entire body felt overheated, as if there was a fire blazing out of control inside her, and when Leo nipped her bottom lip, she mewled in surprise as sensation flared between her legs, spreading slick heat down her upper thighs.

He pulled back immediately at the sound. 'I'm sorry,' he rasped and rested his forehead against hers. 'Just give me a moment...' But even as he took his moment, his hands kneaded her backside, his big palms alternately circling and cupping her as if he couldn't stop himself from touching. 'Willa...'

And Wilhemina, thinking she knew what he was asking her for, broke his hold on her and went to the bed. She did not remove her chemise or stockings, simply climbed on to the soft mattress and moved to the centre of the bed to wait for him.

* * *

Leo watched Willa as she lay prostrate on the bed, her legs straight, her hands lying nearly limp on the mattress beside her, her head angled to watch him approach. He did not have to ask her what she was doing; he knew in the depths of his soul that this was what she'd come to expect from the marriage bed.

And it destroyed him.

Again, he wished that he could bring Windhurst back so that he could kill him slowly. He did not understand how a man—*any* man—could look at Wilhemina lying on his bed and not want to worship her with his entire body. Leo himself felt as if he'd waited lifetimes for this exact moment.

But, conscious that she was easily embarrassed, he did not say anything. He removed his shoes, coat, cravat and waistcoat slowly, watching her the entire time, gauging her reaction and stopping, dressed still in his trousers and shirt, when she started tapping her fingers anxiously.

He went to her, his beautiful wife, and gently propped himself on his elbow next to her so that he could see her face. He wanted to make sure she wasn't afraid. Though Willa was good at masking her true emotions, Leo had spent every minute in her company for six years trying to decipher them.

Her long, blonde hair fell down either side of her face, the typically straight locks crimped from the tight plaits they had been in throughout the evening. Her big, brown eyes were wide with cautious need, as if she felt desire, but did not know what it was or what to do with it. 'What are you doing?' she whispered.

'I'm looking at my wife,' he replied honestly.

'Leo,' she chastised, rolling her eyes. 'Do not be obtuse.'

Leo chuckled, but he raised his hand and trailed the

tips of his fingers down the front of her chemise from the neckline to Willa's flat stomach, barely touching her skin beneath the flimsy garment. She trembled in response, her chest stuttering on a shocked little breath that he felt like a punch to the chest.

'I want to take my time,' he murmured. 'I want to touch you.' He shifted, hovering over her slightly so that he could trace his tongue over the shape of her peaked nipple beneath her chemise. 'I want to taste you.'

He lowered his hand, continuing on his lazy exploration of her slender body as he kissed her lips.

Willa opened her mouth, welcoming him, returning the kiss with her own eager strokes. Her hands rose to grip his hair and hold him in place as they lost themselves to one another.

Leo kept the kiss long and languid despite the base animal inside him that was desperate to finally take her. His body was aching, *throbbing* with the urge to bury himself in her, and still he was half afraid he would not last long enough to get there. She was his every fantasy come to life. She was his—and knowing it unravelled him in a way he had not come close to before.

His hand reached for the hem of her long chemise. 'May I look at you, love?'

Wilhemina swallowed, but after a small pause, she nodded and shifted her hips, allowing him to shimmy the garment up and off her.

She kicked off her drawers. And then she was naked but for her pink stockings and matching ribboned garters—which Leo rather thought he'd leave on. Her pale skin glowed in the candlelight. Her small, rose-tipped breasts heaved with her fluttering breaths and her hands instantly lowered to cover the small thatch of hair between her thighs.

Leo's mouth watered with temptation. He wanted to lap at her soft, wet core. He wanted to taste her salty heat, even as the scent of her lust drove him wild. Still, he did not touch her there yet. He rolled on top of her, levering himself on both elbows as he spread her thighs with his knees. 'Move your hands, love,' he commanded and, when she did, he slowly lowered himself, fully clothed, between her spread legs, covering her with his torso.

She relaxed immediately. Her thin body cradled his, her hip bones pressing gently into his upper ribs. The position did more than cover Willa, it put his mouth directly in the way of her breasts. 'These,' he murmured and blew a soft stream of air across her breasts. 'These were made for my mouth, Willa.' He paused to look at her, silently asking her permission.

She shivered beneath him and, instead of replying, buried her fingers in his hair and tugged his head down impatiently, making him smile.

He did not hesitate. He circled first one, then the other nipple with his tongue, gently lathering the small, straining peaks until Willa's chest was heaving, her pants of pleasure sawing through the room. Her hips pressed upwards in unconscious invitation and Leo, unable to resist, drew the soft flesh of her breast deep into his mouth.

She arched her back and moaned against the sensation, the loud, lusty sound filling his body with fire. 'Leo,' she urged.

He briefly released her to ask, 'Yes, love?'

'I… I don't know what's happening to me.' Her hands fluttered anxiously before finding a perch on his shoulders. 'I… I need…'

'What do you need?'

To his horror, her eyes filled with tears. 'I don't know.'

He didn't tell her not to cry—not now. Instead, he slid upwards and pressed himself firmly against her centre until she turned her sad eyes on him. 'Do you trust me?'

'Yes.'

Leo's heart bloomed when she replied immediately—still, he told her what he wanted to do so that she would be prepared. 'I want to kiss you,' he managed to rasp through his dry throat. He gently thrust upwards, pressing his hard shaft against her core, their intimate flesh separated only by his clothes. 'Here.'

Though he did not know exactly what her previous experience had entailed—and couldn't bear to think of it, of *her* with Windhurst, Leo knew that she had never been pleasured the moment the words were out his mouth. Willa's eyes went wide with horror. 'That sounds very uncivilised.' She crinkled her nose. 'And unsanitary.'

He couldn't help the raspy chuckle that climbed up his throat, nor could he help but bury his face against her chest as he tried to fight it.

'Leo?'

He kissed the deep, bony hollow between her small breasts and raised his head to meet her eyes again. 'It's not. It's…' How could he begin to explain that her smell and taste were designed to make him wild, and, yes, a little uncivilised? Or that, her pleasure aside, lapping at her wet heat was something that would drive *him* to his own completion if he let it. 'It's something I've dreamed of doing to you. For years.'

She did not say 'yes' or nod her head. She looked into his eyes for a long moment and replied, 'I trust you.'

The words sounded more like a reminder to herself than to him, so Leo promised himself that he would take his time, that he would show her what her trust in him meant.

He slowly shifted, moving down her body casually even as he felt her tense.

His mouth watered as she was slowly uncovered and her smell—sex and sin and Willa—wrapped around him. Her legs were tense and unmoving at his sides and Leo gently raised one and then the other, draping them over his shoulders so that she was open for him, glistening, her private curls damp with her lust.

Willa did not move, though her legs stayed tense over his shoulders. She did not speak or even breathe, but he saw the way her long, elegant fingers anxiously gripped the counterpane.

He blew a soft breath over her and then leaned down to trail small kisses on her inner thighs, slowly working his way closer and closer to her wet heart. He buried his hands beneath her bottom, lifting her hips slightly, and Willa released a ragged breath, one filled with equal parts fear and anticipation.

'Don't be scared, love,' he murmured. And then he bent his head to taste her. His tongue slid between her seam, his head moving back and forth slightly as he sank through the secret curls, deeper and deeper into her.

If he had cared less about her, he would have ravished her, eating at her until she was screaming his name. But Leo held back, knowing that this was new and frightening for her. Instead, he slowly lapped at her, fighting for calm as her salty taste flooded his blood with pagan greed. She started to respond, her heels pressing into his back, her breath changing and becoming laboured, and when she sighed, her long 'Ooh…' echoing in his head, Leo closed his eyes and fought for control.

Chapter Ten

In her wildest dreams, Willa had not imagined that something so sinful not only occurred, but that it would feel so incredible. As Leo gently licked at her most private part, her embarrassment slowly faded and was replaced by an impossibly pleasurable tightness that bordered on the verge of pain. She felt like an over-wound clock. Like the anchor of a too-fast ship dragging on the ocean floor, trying and failing to stop something much bigger and faster than itself.

Leo shifted upwards, placing his lips on the knot of nerves at the top of her sex, and suckled slowly. Willa moaned loudly as each pull of his mouth rippled sensation through her entire body, spreading from that point of contact outwards.

She squirmed erratically, her movements jagged, wanting to move away, but also begging him for more when words would not come. Her legs spasmed in time with the clever flicks from his tongue. She felt overheated and anxious, as if she was in desperate need of…*something*. Reaching down, she buried her hands in his hair, anchoring herself against the pleasure.

Leo gave a small groan and reared back slightly, making Willa pant in frustration as he momentarily left her. 'Shh, love,' he murmured. He freed his hands from beneath her and used both his thumbs to spread her open before his mouth found her again.

'Leo,' she begged, not quite sure what she was asking for. *'Please.'*

'My poor love,' he crooned and slid a single finger into her.

Willa braced against the intrusion immediately, but Leo did not let her panic grow. He withdrew almost all the way and then refreshed his advance, this time sliding his finger in and out of her in the tiniest of thrusts, only going as far as her tight body would allow. 'Relax, sweetheart.'

Willa didn't have a choice in the matter. Whatever he was doing felt glorious, completely different to anything she'd experienced before. Even her body seemed to take on a life of its own, pulling him in further each time that he thrust, as if it wanted more of him, more of whatever he was doing.

Her legs fell open, one dropping off his shoulder completely. Her chest tightened as she held her breath, her inexperience making her fight the cresting pleasure.

Leo licked her once, adding his tongue to that spot above where his finger tormented her. 'Wilhemina, the taste of you drives me wild,' he rasped. 'I could spend hours right here, feasting on you.'

Willa moaned her agreement and Leo rewarded her with another firm lick. 'Would you like that, wild girl?' he asked, his voice sinfully deep. 'Me, here, eating you until you are screaming my name?'

'Yes!' The single word punctuated the room loudly, but Willa didn't care. She heaved in great big gulps of air as her stomach tightened and her legs tensed.

'Good girl,' Leo murmured and bent his head to her again, burying his mouth in her as his finger wrung pleasure from her very soul.

'Leo,' she panted. 'Leo, please.'

He did not reply. And he did not stop. He doubled his efforts, increasing the speed at which his finger penetrated her while rhythmically suckling her damp flesh into his warm mouth.

And Willa, unable to contain her pleasure any longer, closed her eyes and simply exploded. She cried out his name loudly as unspeakable sensation roared through her body, each pulsing wave filling her with a rush of power that drained almost as soon as it crested, leaving her strangely loose-limbed and vulnerable.

Leo slowly gentled his movements as her body relaxed. It was obvious by his every touch that he had anticipated her, that he knew what he had been doing, and Willa, for all her experience in marriage, felt inexplicably sad, when really, she'd just had the most transformative experience of her life. She blinked rapidly, trying to stave her tears as her body drained of euphoria. She did not want him to see her like this, falling apart after he'd given her such a beautiful gift.

But he must have sensed the shift in her body because his head snapped up, his eyes finding hers. His expression fell. 'Willa.'

'No,' she hurriedly said and reached down to run a hand through his hair, comforting him even as the feel of his thick locks between her fingers comforted her in turn. 'I…' She shook her head. 'I didn't know,' she whispered.

He shifted, moving up her body to cover her again. 'I'm sorry,' he said quietly. 'I wish I could—'

'No. Don't,' Willa begged. 'I am so relieved that you are the only man who has ever shown me. It…it feels as if it is the first time…'

She paused, then looked down at him, her breath catching when she saw the glinting male pride in his eyes. He looked so much like a rake just then, eyes shining, hair dishevelled from her fingers, his lopsided smile conveying sinful pleasure. His broad shoulders and arms were taut with lean muscle beneath his shirt, his beautiful skin healthy and glowing.

'Could I…?' Willa trailed off, unsure of how to voice her question. It suddenly appeared as if there was an entire world she had yet to discover.

'What do you want to know?' Leo rested his chin on her flat stomach in a gesture that was overwhelmingly familiar and intimate, as if they'd done this thousands of times before. 'I will tell you anything.'

His ease calmed her. 'Well, I suppose I was wondering if… What I mean to say is: does it work both ways? Can I use my mouth…' Leo tensed against her. 'Was that a silly question?' she added immediately, flushing with shame.

'No. Not at all—there are no silly questions, my love. It's just…hard for me… No—' he fumbled '—that was the wrong word.' He took a deep breath. 'It is done. But we do not have to do anything you do not want to.' He relaxed by degrees. 'We have a lifetime to learn each other, Willa. There's no rush.'

'Do you like…*that*?'

'I love tasting you.'

'No.' She did not let him off. 'Do you like *receiving*?'

He cleared his throat. 'I do. But, as I said—'

'I want to try.'

'Willa, you don't have to—'

'I know,' she said, cutting off his protest. 'I *want* to.' And when he still didn't move, she placed her hand on his face. 'I want to know how to please you.'

Leo could not refuse her. And though he did not *want* to refuse her, there was also a part of him that was newly afraid that he would not be able to control himself. He was a good lover—he was confident enough to admit that. But this was not any woman; it was *Willa.*

Still, he pushed off her and moved off the bed to strip his clothes. He completed the task quickly and with no delay, not wanting to scare her, but the moment he attempted to climb back on to the bed, she held out her hand, stopping him.

Leo raised one eyebrow in question.

'I want to look,' she said, her embarrassment clear in the red blush riding high on her cheeks.

Leo took a large step back from the bed and let his arms drop to his sides.

Willa stared at him, drawing her bottom lip between her teeth in the way that had always knotted his stomach. Even if he'd wanted to control his erection, his naked wife would have made it impossible.

Her pale skin was flushed with a deep pleasure blush that painted her chest, throat and cheeks pink. Her brown eyes were wide with hesitant discovery, like a caged animal that was experiencing freedom for the first time and was still strangely unsure of leaving its familiar prison. She was everything he'd ever wanted, but thought he'd never have, and Leo still wasn't entirely sure how one man could be allowed so much.

'You know,' she said shyly, 'when I walked into your bedchamber on the night Windhurst died...'

'Tell me,' he begged, wanting her confession.

'I looked at you for a long time before waking you. I... I wanted to touch you in a way that I've never wanted before. You're so beautiful.'

Leo smiled. 'You mean handsome.'

She shook her head. 'You're not handsome. You are *far* more than handsome.'

Leo's throat constricted with her sweet praise. He went to her, climbing back on the bed and lying down beside her.

Willa did not move as she took in his manhood resting against his stomach. 'How do I…?'

He took her trembling hand in his, guiding her soft palm to wrap around him, showing her how to move in the way he liked before releasing her and lying flat on his back to give her room.

Willa did not hesitate. She leaned over him, intent on her task, her silky hair falling over his stomach, her soft hand moving firmly, if not confidently.

Leo closed his eyes as his body drew inwards towards release. He fought for control, wanting to last for her, wanting to give her the power. But every slide of her soft hand was the sweetest torture. Her silky hot palm wrapped around him and wrung the greatest pleasure he'd known even though her movements were shy and hesitant.

Her hand slowed by degrees. He felt her lips wrap around him. His eyes flew open just in time to see her open her mouth wider to take him deeper. Leo's entire body convulsed. His hand snaked out, gripping her hair, holding her still.

Willa froze, her eyes suddenly wide with panic.

Leo loosened his hold on her immediately, stroking her face to try to calm her. 'Sorry, love. You…you are going to make me spend too soon,' he explained. 'I can't control myself when you do that.'

'Oh.' She bit her bottom lip again, but this time her eyes were lit with mischief.

'You like that, do you?' he asked, only slightly teasing. Lord, the sight of her open lips had nearly finished him off.

'I do,' she said sincerely.

'Minx.'

Willa laughed at the easing teasing. 'I suppose I like to see that you really want me.'

Leo gently unwrapped her hand. 'When I touch myself, my little wildling,' he said, giving himself a firm stroke to demonstrate, 'I think of you. I close my eyes and imagine you, naked and quivering, your legs spread for me. It's been only you in my mind for a long time.'

Her lips rounded, a perfect 'oh' falling from her mouth.

'And your hands and your mouth.' He let his head fall back on a groan. 'Willa, I *love* your hands and mouth on me. But this first time,' he said, not wanting to hurt her feelings, 'I want to spend inside you.' He lowered his own hand to gently run his finger down her seam. 'I want to make you mine.'

Willa glanced at his engorged manhood, her throat bobbing with nerves. 'Will you be able to…? That is to say that you are…*quite* large.'

Leo couldn't help but smile, but he gently rolled over her, supporting himself on his elbows as she lay back and repositioned herself more comfortably. 'I'll go slowly,' he promised and gently spread her knees, opening her wider. 'But tell me if you are uncomfortable at any time. I'll stop.' He notched himself at her entrance, his own body tensing as she stiffened against even that slight protrusion. 'Relax, my love.'

'I'm trying.'

'Try less hard.' He nudged gently into her tight channel, stopping when he was only an inch inside her. 'Just feel me inside of you.' He leaned down to circle her nipple with his tongue as he started moving in small, rolling thrusts, making sure to keep his movements shallow as she started to relax beneath him. Willa's body was impossibly wet and tight around him, and Leo had to consciously keep himself from rutting like some unthinking beast. 'You're so perfect for me, Willa,' he whispered fervently.

She pressed her heels into the bed, raising her hips to take more of him, and Leo stilled so that she could control the depth. When she stopped moving, he flexed his hips. 'How are you?'

Willa reached up to brush his hair back from his forehead and, even though she smiled, tears fell from her eyes. She was quiet for a long moment as she considered, then her smile grew, as if she'd shocked even herself with her thoughts. 'Leo, *I'm happy*.'

The words caught in his chest and held for a long moment before he expelled what sounded strangely like a sigh and a sob rolled into one ragged breath. 'Me, too, love.'

Willa's hand moved to his face and she nodded. 'Now. Take me now.'

It was not how Leo had planned to claim her. He'd wanted to work her back to orgasm, slowly and thoroughly. But with her wet heat cinched around him, her body soft beneath his, her demand ringing through the room, he was helpless to do anything but push into her fully and let himself go.

Chapter Eleven

It took minutes for the blood to stop roaring in his ears. Exhausted, completely spent, Leo gently pulled out of Wilhemina and lowered his body down on top of her, careful to keep the bulk of his weight distributed throughout his bent arms, which he placed on either side of her head. He covered her body with his for both of them—so that he could be skin to skin with her and so she could hide from the embarrassment he already knew she would feel once her blood cooled.

Her thin frame cradled his, her hips bracketing his torso. Leo looked down at her, enraptured by her. He memorised the way her long, sandy lashes twitched restlessly even when her eyes were closed. Her pale face, still flushed with the faintest dusting of pink and framed by her long blonde hair, was a face that one of the old master painters would have begged for a chance to capture. But, as beautiful as she was, that wasn't why he loved her.

He loved her because she had never made her beauty the most interesting thing about her. In fact, she barely seemed aware of how gorgeous she was at all. Even the small vanities she did allow herself had more to do with her quick wit and skill in the saddle than her face or her clothes or any of the other number of things that noblewomen had been trained to value.

Wilhcmina was…uniquc. Shc was cntirely, well, Wilhemina and over the years she had somehow become his yardstick, the comparison he couldn't avoid making every time he met a woman—and found her to be…well, *not* Wilhemina.

Sensing his perusal, she slowly opened her eyes. She smiled softly when she met his gaze, the pink blush on her cheeks deepening noticeably. 'What are you looking at? Do I have something on my face?'

Leo gently lowered his forehead, resting it against hers. 'No. You are perfect. I'm just taking a minute to burn this moment into my memory so that I can look back and remind myself that I've already got everything I'll ever need.'

He looked up again, hoping that he hadn't scared her. Leo knew enough about Willa and what she had suffered to understand that one night in bed would not equate to winning her love. But Willa, to his absolute delight, didn't seem afraid at all. She raised her hands and ran them through his hair, brushing the thick mass off his forehead. 'I wish I'd married you the first time,' she said wistfully. 'Life would have been so different.'

Leo tensed against the emotion that gripped him, torn between wanting to tell her the truth and wanting to protect her from further pain.

'What's wrong?' she asked, feeling his body brace on top of hers.

Though he was terrified by the admission he would be making, Leo wanted to be as brave as her. Willa had just given herself to him despite her fear. The least he could do was tell her the secret he'd harboured all this time. 'I always wanted you, Willa—even before you married Windhurst.'

Willa tipped her head to look at him. Her hands in his hair stilled.

'You were—*are*—my favourite woman in the entire world.' It was a tepid truth and a complete lie at the same time.

Willa shook her head in denial. Her brown eyes filled with confusion and, worse, despair. 'Why didn't you ask? Why didn't you…?' She looked at him, her words trailing off, her eyes dimming when she read the truth there. 'You did.'

It was not a question. Leo nodded slowly. 'I did.'

'My father…'

'Thought that Windhurst was better suited. We were both set to be earls, both—on the surface in Windhurst's case—wealthy. But your father thought Windhurst was better suited. More mature.'

Willa's lips wobbled. She took a shuddering breath—he felt it enter her lungs, her chest expanding beneath his body with the force of it.

'Do not cry, love. It's over now.'

She shook her head, forcing the first tear to fall. 'I… I would have said yes. I would have… Leo, I would have been *so happy*,' she said, her voice thick. 'When I was younger, I used to dream of you asking for me. And maybe it was just a young girl's fantasy at the time, but I… I wanted you, too.' She frowned as if considering something. 'It's so strange,' she whispered, 'until this moment, I'd forgotten that. I was once a young girl with dreams and romantic notions, with hope…'

Leo's world stilled at her confession. Not for the first time, he thought he should have fought for her. He should have at the very least approached *her* and asked *her* to decide for herself. Because even if they had eloped and caused a scandal, he could have given her a title and wealth. He could have looked after her.

'I'm sorry I did not approach you,' he said now. 'At first, I thought you needed time to grow up—you were so much younger than me. I was going to wait another year, but then…'

'Then?'

'Jameson told me that Windhurst had spoken to your father, and all I could think was *I have to stop this—she's mine*. I went to your father and Grey that same day.' He braced, remembering the pain of rejection all this time later. 'Your father, I knew, would be wary. I was young and years away from inheriting. But I assumed your brother would side with me.'

'He did not?'

'He seemed unsure. But in the end, he did not want to oppose your father's wishes. And then when I considered fighting for you, I thought about the damage it would cause you and I couldn't do it. I couldn't subject you to the scandal an elopement would have caused.'

'Why didn't you tell me—that you'd approached my father?'

Leo tensed at the unexpected question.

'I would have eloped with you if it had been an option over marrying Windhurst. But…' she sighed '…I had no reason to think you were interested in me, no reason to suspect that you'd asked to court me.'

'I meant what I said earlier,' Leo said slowly. 'You were so young—barely eighteen to my twenty-eight. I wanted to give you time, let you live a little—go to balls and country parties, cause minor scandals and meet other men.'

She arched one brow. 'You *wanted* me to meet other men?'

Leo grinned at her tone. 'Not because I wanted you to

fall in love with any of them. I just wanted you to live, to gain some experience, so that when I finally approached you, you'd be sure that I was what you did or did not want.' He sobered, remembering back. 'It's never been easy for me, to imagine anybody wanting me for anything other than my title.'

'Why on earth not?' Willa demanded. 'Your title isn't who you are—it's just who you were born to become.'

'Not many people understand that there's a difference.'

Willa scoffed, but she raised her hands, sifting through his hair again. 'So, you thought I was too young.'

'Yes. But that didn't stop me once I found out about Windhurst. After I approached your father and Grey… I guess I was hurt. And surprised. That they would choose Windhurst over me… It was as if they'd affirmed everything I'd ever feared about myself—that I was not worthy.

'Every time I thought of speaking to you, of asking you what *you* wanted, I somehow managed to convince myself that they were right. I convinced myself that I was wrong for you and that I would ruin you. I convinced myself that they knew what was best for you and every time my mind rebelled at the idea, I told myself it was my own self-interest.'

'You were afraid.'

'Of course. Greyson *knew* me, better than almost anyone except the Blakes, Jameson and you, and he *still* felt that I wasn't good enough for you. It…it was crushing.'

'I'm sorry,' she murmured. 'I'm sorry my family hurt you.'

'Don't apologise for them, or for me. I knew, even back then, that we were right for one another. But I let others' opinions of me cloud my judgement and ultimately dishonoured both you and me.' Leo felt the bitter memories begin to rise. 'And worse, I put what could have been your entire future at risk and *that* is something I will not forgive myself for soon.'

It was terrifying to think that in some other world there was a Leo who was currently with the mistress he did not love while the only woman he ever *had* loved suffered under her husband's tyranny because of his insecurity. It chilled him when he realised just how lucky both he and Willa were that Windhurst's habits had ended his life prematurely.

'Before Matthew and Isabelle, I used to try to avoid you,' Willa said quietly.

'Really?'

Willa nodded and, although she did not cry, her eyes were glassy. 'Seeing you would make me *so sad*. You were a reminder of happier times.' She stilled. 'Do you remember when you and Matthew escorted me through the park that day?'

'Of course.' It had been the first time he'd seen her in almost six months and Willa had lost so much weight, she'd changed so much, that Leo had barely recognised her.

'I think that was a turning point for me. I… I heard you call me and when I turned and saw you… My heart sighed. And I remember being so afraid—'

'Afraid of me?'

'No. Afraid of how happy I was to see you. Afraid that Windhurst would see my happiness once I got home.' Her voice lowered to a whisper. 'Afraid that I'd never be happier than that brief flash again.'

'Is that why you stopped avoiding me after that?' he asked. He'd noticed, of course, but he'd always assumed it was because they didn't move in the same circles any longer and because she did not think of him the same way he had always thought of her.

'Yes. After that day, I… I stopped caring. And I started

trying to do things, small things, for myself again. I wanted to be happy, or at least try to find one or two things that would eradicate the sadness momentarily, and you… You were one of those things. You've always made me feel happy, Leo—even when I was at my most miserable.'

'Which is why you agreed to sneak away and play chess with me at your mother's ball?'

'Yes. But it also helped that Windhurst had just left for his whore.'

Leo heard the bitterness in her tone, but he did not try to cool it despite how much it scared him. She had a right to be angry. She should be furious—she *was* furious. His only hope was that one day she would not be, that one day the memory of her life as Lady Windhurst would be a far-off nightmare that she had lived through and moved on from.

'It did,' he agreed. 'And even though I could not touch you then, I loved having you all to myself.'

Willa frowned at him, her brow pinched. 'Why *didn't* you try to touch me? Was it because I was his? Because he had—'

'No, love,' Leo replied immediately. 'You were never his,' he said vehemently. 'I wanted to—touch you. I always have. But it wouldn't have been fair, to put you in a position like that.'

'I might have enjoyed an affair of my own,' she protested.

'No. You wouldn't have.' Leaning down, Leo kissed her gently, taking any sting out of the words. 'You are too loyal a person, even to people who don't deserve your faithfulness. You might have enjoyed me touching you in the moment, but the guilt of your infidelity would have hurt you every time I left and I couldn't have done that to you after everything else you'd suffered.'

* * *

Willa knew that he was right even as she hated that she could never have strayed from Windhurst. It would have served her husband right if she'd started an affair of her own with a man half his age and ten times his looks. But it wasn't only loyalty, as Leo assumed. It was fear. Her introduction to the sexual act had been by a man the same age as her father, a man who—she'd only tonight realised—had been more a blunt force instrument than a lover. And after Windhurst she'd been repulsed by even the thought of being touched.

Until tonight.

A raging blush consumed her when she remembered the things Leo had done to her, the things that *she* had done to *him*, and to her surprise, instead of wanting to defer or avoid talking of it, the reminder only served to rekindle that flickering weight low in her stomach.

She trailed her hands over Leo's shoulders, following the contours his muscles created. 'I don't want my past between us any more,' she said hesitantly. 'I want to pretend that it never happened so that I can experience all these firsts as your wife.'

Instead of agreeing as she'd assumed he would, Leo whispered, 'It's not going to go away just because you don't want to talk about it, love.'

'What would you have me do?' she asked, growing frustrated. Confused by his disapproval, she tried to wriggle free.

'No.' Leo released the arms he'd been holding his weight up with and let his full weight settle on top of her. 'Don't get mad.'

Willa stopped struggling immediately as his weight pinned her down. It was futile; he was too large. 'You don't look as though you have an extra ounce of fat on you,' she said pertly. 'But you, my lord, are ridiculously heavy.'

He grinned and, instead of getting off her, he shifted his body down slightly so that he could access her breasts. He trailed his tongue lazily across her chest, stopping briefly at each nipple to lathe it, slowly pulling both of them into tight buds.

To Willa's relief, he did not reopen the topic of her first marriage. Instead, he murmured, 'You're mine now, Willa. That's all that matters.'

And Willa exhaled the last of her tension as her hands found his hair again. 'Yes.'

'We've settled the last of your husband's debt and, as long as the Wolfe brothers don't come calling, the Windhurst name has no ties to you any more.'

That wasn't necessarily true. She would technically bear both her last and her new title until her death. But Willa didn't focus on that. 'What do you mean *we've* settled the last of my husband's debt? And don't call him *my husband*. He's not my husband any more.'

Leo didn't argue. 'I didn't want the gossips to know how much he owed because I didn't want you to suffer for it. Windhurst is dead. But you… Willa, you are the only one left to bear the burden of his sins—'

'So, you cleared the bastard's name,' she finished for him.

Shame like she had never felt before suffused her, spreading through her like some contagious disease transmitted by her late husband's corpse. How was it possible, she thought, that he could continue to humiliate her from the grave? The sting of self-pitying tears burned her eyes.

'Willa, I didn't do it for him. I did it for you. Because you do not deserve a moment's pain for how that bastard lived his life.'

'How much was it?' she asked, ignoring his justification.

'Why does it matt—?'

'How much, Leo?'

He rolled off her, but instead of leaving he gathered her close, holding her against him so that her back pressed into his chest and his big body sheltered her completely. 'After the sale of the Regent's Park house, it totalled six thousand pounds.'

Willa closed her eyes. If it had been anything less than three she might have eventually paid him back. She would receive a sum when her father died one day—*if* she reconciled with him. But *six thousand pounds* was a fortune that only her eldest brother, Grey, would ever receive and ever see, and only when he inherited the title and the annual profit it yielded. 'When my father—'

'Don't.' Leo did not wait for her to finish. 'Do not insult me or yourself by offering to pay me back.' His arms tightened around her. 'You are my wife, Wilhemina. I had no legal obligation to pay Windhurst's debt. I did it because I don't want his sins following you.' He used one big palm to brush her hair back from her face. 'I want you to be free and happy. I want you to start living again—with me.'

'If you are arguing that it was an entirely selfish act, I will not agree with you.'

'You don't always have to agree with me, my wild girl. But you have to let me love and protect you whenever I can.'

Willa's chest tightened with panic. *Love?* They'd never spoken of *love* before and, for some reason, it was an entirely overwhelming subject. Willa wasn't even sure she'd ever said the words to anyone before. Not her parents who, though attentive in their own way, had not openly brandished their affection. Not to her brothers, who, as boys, had never been very emotionally astute.

Perhaps sensing her panic, Leo levered on to one elbow and rolled her on to her back so that he could look at her face. 'If I can't do that, I'll be demoted to a mere instrument of pleasure,' he said, looking mock-devastated by the notion.

Willa felt her lips curl and fought the smile. But she grabbed hold of the new topic of conversation. 'If you are trying to make me laugh, it's not working.'

'Hmmm.' He seemed to consider his options for a moment. 'I suppose I'll just have to accept my role then.' A wicked gleam entered his eyes.

Willa's stomach gave a little kick of recognition. 'I suppose so,' she said pertly, but her lips wobbled.

'If you say so.' And with that, he lay down on his side and pulled her closer, so close that she felt his hard length slide between the gap in her upper thighs.

Willa did not pull back. She kissed him, pouring everything—all guilt and frustration and fears—into the kiss. And if Leo did manage to distract her from everything he had done for her, Willa let him.

But the thing with distraction, she realised later, as he drifted off to sleep and she stared at the heavy ceiling beams above the bed, was that it was only fleeting, lasting for as long as you had something else to occupy your mind.

Chapter Twelve

Were Leo not so besotted, he would have been embarrassed by his own infatuation with his wife. But even when his friends, who he'd been neglecting in favour of spending time with Wilhemina, laughed at his behaviour, Leo could only shrug. There was no point in trying to deny it and no sense in pretending that he wanted to change anything.

If Willa was in the study reading, Leo took himself there to work, trying his best not to disturb her—though he usually succumbed to his need to touch her after only a few minutes. If she retired early, he followed her like a dog on a leash. If she did not want to go out, he stayed in with her, knowing that he would be happiest wherever she was.

Willa, too, seemed to be slowly shedding her life with Windhurst. She laughed often and she laughed loudly, making him smile each time he heard it ringing through his previously quiet house. She'd gained back some of the weight that she'd lost under her late husband's neglect and the result was that his already beautiful wife slowly morphed into a healthy young woman who was so devastatingly gorgeous that she turned heads wherever she went—and none more so than her own husband's.

There were still times when she did not know that he was watching her, moments when he saw flickers of sadness play across her features, but Leo tried not to let it dampen his own resolve. He was determined to slowly eradicate her previous fears and doubts and return her to the carefree young woman she had once been.

Though she still sometimes became shy and uncertain during their lovemaking, it never lasted long. Leo was able to slowly coax out her long-dormant playful personality, encouraging her to take what she wanted until they were both wild with need and rushing towards completion. And as if that wasn't satisfying enough, she had abandoned her rooms and taken to sleeping in his bed every night, her slender body curled up against his as if she wanted to be close to him even in her dreams.

I should go and find her.

It was that thought in Leo's mind when the door suddenly opened and Willa herself came into the room. Her dark blue day dress contrasted against her pale skin and blonde hair. Leo's body immediately tightened with the need to touch her. 'I was just coming to find you,' he said, meeting her gaze.

His smile died when he saw that she held a letter in her trembling hands and that her eyes were glazed with shock. 'Willa?' He stood and went to her immediately, taking her upper arms in his hands to steady her. 'What has happened?'

'Oh...' She seemed to briefly battle with some internal decision before collecting herself and replying, 'It is nothing. Only another invitation from my mother.'

Leo knew that she was lying to him immediately. Although invitations from her family did still get sent to the house, Wilhemina did not open them. And she did not become pale and drawn as she was now—she became furious. Still, he steeled himself against the stab of disappointment that her lie wrought. 'Is there anything I can do?' he asked, leaving the question deliberately non-specific in the hope that she would confide in him.

He wanted to rip the letter from her hands and read it. Who could possibly have written her something that would distress her this much? Something that she couldn't tell him about?

She shook her head vigorously and turned away from him, pulling out of his loose grasp and starting for the door without further explanation. 'I think I'll just go lie down for a moment.' She exited the room as abruptly as she had entered, her feeble 'I have a headache' barely reaching him.

Leo was torn between wanting to go after his wife and demand answers and wanting to give her the freedom to make her own choices. Willa had already come so far in a relatively short period of time and Leo didn't want to jeopardise the relationship they had started to build. Still, he knew that whatever news she had received had scared her.

He swore roundly and began pacing the study, his anxious footsteps taking him from the large, mahogany desk to the floor-to-ceiling bookcase on the opposite side of the room and back again. But no amount of restless activity could remove the image of Willa, pale and trembling, with that letter in her hands. So, finally, Leo did the only thing he could think of: he went to find her.

Willa had been so alarmed by the letter that she hadn't even stopped to consider where she was going or that Leo might have been in the study. So, when she had barged into the room and realised he was present, it had taken her a moment to think of some adequate excuse to explain her rattled nerves and strange behaviour. Her only consolation was that he had seemed to believe that the missive had been from her mother, when in fact it was from none other than Camilla Pierce, her late husband's lover.

The letter had come in the morning post on a crisp, clean piece of paper that had been folded and sealed with wax.

The letter read:

My Lady,

Please, I beg of you, forgive my impertinence. There is nobody else I can appeal to. My parents have been dead these past six years and though I have an older brother, I have advertised these past months but still cannot find him. I fear that he is lost to me for ever.

There is a matter which I must discuss urgently with you. It pertains to your late husband and, while I am sure it will not sway your decision in any way, my life depends upon your reply. If you would visit me at Number Four High Street, Shadwell, at your earliest convenience, I shall explain everything.

Camilla Pierce

Willa was no simpleton. She knew in the depths of her soul that Camilla Pierce would not have contacted her unless she'd had no other choice. She also knew that the mistress would have found another protector easily—unless she was with child. *Windhurst's* child.

The possibility had left her shaken, ill with dread and also, surprisingly, pity. How much worse would her life have been if she had caught Windhurst's eye as a young, defenceless girl with no family to offer the appearance of protection? How much more would she have suffered?

Wilhemina opened her bedroom door and went inside. She kicked off her shoes and collapsed on the big bed without removing her dress, too exhausted by the strange missive to care if she crumpled her clothes.

I lied to Leo, she realised and that, even more so than the letter, settled a heavy weight in her chest. She hadn't wanted to, but she had also known Leo for a long time and he would not like her associating with Camilla Pierce in any way. He wouldn't understand, if only because he had never been a woman trapped by a man.

And, though she tried to deny it even to herself, Willa wanted to spare him one more humiliation. She wanted to handle the situation herself so that Leo, who had only ever been kind and protective of her, didn't have to. She cared about him too much to subject him to another blow. He had done too much for her already and she was the one who had to draw the line—because Leo never would. Not when it came to her.

Moreover, Willa wanted to finally close the chapter of her life that included Windhurst. She wanted to finally put it all behind her so that she could move on—with Leo.

Her only option was to see the other woman in secret and pray that Leo never found out. She could take the few pieces of jewellery that remained from Windhurst and give them to Camilla Pierce to support herself with.

Leo would never have to know.

Her plan might have actually worked if Leo hadn't knocked on her bedroom door and entered at that very moment.

Willa rolled on to her back so that she could watch her husband approach. He looked like some predatory lion, his golden hair catching the daylight that filtered in through the open window, his blue eyes focused on her face, reading her distress easily.

He reached for her, lifting her into his arms without a

word, and carried her to one of the big chairs by the cold hearth.

'Leo, what are you doing?' Willa asked, though she did not resist. It felt so good to be close to him, to be held by him. As if nothing, no sadness or harm could befall her as long as she was sheltered in his arms.

'I'm comforting my wife,' he murmured, and sat down. He gently rearranged her on his lap so that her skirt-clad legs draped over the arm of the chair and her head came to naturally rest against his neck. He exhaled a deep breath, one filled with dread, and added, 'And hoping she tells me what was really in that letter.'

Willa tensed immediately, her body becoming brittle in defence. 'Leo—'

'Don't lie to me.' He didn't snap or snarl. He said the words quietly, calmly. 'Tell me to mind my own business or leave it be, but don't ever lie to me, Willa. I can live with you being afraid to trust me with everything so soon into our marriage, but not with deceit.' When her eyes filled with tears of shame, he gently swiped them away with his thumb and kissed the side of her head. 'But I can't make it better if you don't tell me what it is, love.'

'She...she wrote me.' Willa didn't know why she told him the truth, only that she couldn't stand to feel the distance her lie had created between them.

'*Who*, love?'

She pulled the folded letter out from inside her dress sleeve and tried to pass it to him. 'Camilla Pierce.'

Leo shook his head, as if he was sure that he had misheard. 'Pardon?'

'Camilla Pierce—his m-mistress. She...' Unable to go on, she flattened the letter against his chest. 'Read it.'

Leo took the letter and unfolded it awkwardly, his movements hindered by Willa on his lap.

Willa relaxed into him, burying her face against his neck, their newly acquired familiarity eradicating any hint of shyness or reserve.

Leo's entire body went taut beneath her as he read and reread the letter. His typically friendly eyes turned ice blue with anger. His usually easy demeanour became brittle with impatience.

'She can only be pregnant.' The comment came from Willa, issued gravely but with dry eyes. 'It is the only reason that she would be desperate enough to seek my help.'

'Perhaps.' Leo turned the letter over several times, as if searching for a clue that she had missed.

Willa did not give him a chance to dwell on the letter. She levered herself up so that she could face him, readjusting her slight weight on his thighs. 'I want to see her.'

'Willa—'

'There is no use trying to dissuade me,' she countered immediately. 'My mind is made up.'

'What benefit could such a meeting accomplish?' he argued quietly. 'Must you be *plagued* by this woman after everything else he put you through?'

'It's not that simple.'

'What could she possibly tell you that would help you and not hurt you?' he demanded. His voice rose in his anger. 'Name *one thing* she could say to you that would balm your wounds instead of inflame them.' When she did not reply, he raised his hand and turned her face back to his. 'My love, you have no obligation to respond to her plea. Let it go. Please.'

'I want to close this chapter,' she said, her frustration

leaking into her tone. 'I want to rid myself of any reminder of my past.'

Leo closed his eyes, clearly trying to quell his frustration. 'If you do not go, it *would be over*.'

'No.' Willa pushed to her feet and moved a little away, adding space between them. 'I have thought of her,' she whispered, her back to him, her spine rigid. She roped her arms around her waist. 'I have thought of her and I have wondered if she suffered as I did. I…' Her breath hitched as she bit back tears. 'Leo, I *need* to face her.'

Leo came to where she stood. He ran his hand down her back, stopping immediately when she flinched against his touch. 'Willa,' he rasped. 'Look at me, love.'

She turned slowly, squaring her shoulders as she did so.

'We agreed that you would let me handle Windhurst's affairs as I saw fit,' he reminded her.

'That's not fair—that was before Camilla Pierce was involved!' She advanced, her fists clenched at her side, her jaw stubbornly set. 'This is *my* responsibility, *my* problem to solve.'

'Wilhemina.' Leo's voice was so cold that she stopped moving closer immediately. 'You are *my wife*. Therefore, it is, unfortunately, now *my* problem to solve. I will not have you traipsing to the bloody East End to visit that woman, *especially* given her involvement with your husband's murder!'

Willa, who had spent years defending herself against verbal and physical abuse, straightened her spine reflexively. It didn't matter that her heart was not cold as it had been when she'd fought Windhurst—instead, it beat frantically, her blood hot and fast with fury. 'You promised that you would never tell me no.'

Leo cursed—loudly. 'This is not wearing breeches or

fencing or refusing invitations. This is dangerous! Traipsing to Shadwell to meet with Windhurst's whore!'

'And yet you are allowed to go in my stead?'

'Yes!' Leo bellowed, losing his temper completely.

If Willa had stopped to think, she would have realised that, though they were shouting at one another, she felt no fear when arguing with Leo. She was absolutely secure in the knowledge that he would never harm her. All she felt was stubborn fury at his insistence on handling everything when, really, it had nothing to do with him save for his association with *her*.

Over the past four weeks of their marriage, Leo had been kind and attentive and passionate—perfect to the point where every one of Willa's flaws and problems, including her marriage to Windhurst, reflected tenfold. And it smothered her. Instead of enjoying the way he assumed all of her burdens, she felt ashamed.

Still, having grown up with three older brothers, Willa knew when arguing was futile. She calmly walked to the door, opened it and stepped to the side. 'Then we have nothing more to say to one another, *my lord*.'

'Willa—'

'Get out.'

Leo cursed. He did not move for a long moment, only averted his eyes like some injured predatory cat who had taken a moment's rest to contemplate his next move.

As she watched him struggle, Willa was overcome by the urge to reach out and touch him, to comfort him. The terrified woman that had first come to him longed to make peace.

She wanted to run her fingers through his thick hair and feel the heavy locks sliding beneath her hand. She wanted to wrap her arms around his waist and rest her head over his heart until he calmed down enough to wrap his own arms around her. But she didn't. She couldn't. She was too aware of the new distance between them, too conscious of the divide that suddenly seemed unbridgeable. And Willa, who had never had the desire or the chance to reconcile after a lovers' quarrel, did not know how to.

Then Leo left without a word, his heavy footfall sounding down the hallway, down the stairs and straight out the front door.

Willa closed her bedroom door gently.

He had left.

She straightened her spine mechanically, letting her pride consume her pain. She would not be cowed by a man—ever again. Especially by Leo, who had always treated her as an equal. She would solve her own problems and those left behind by Windhurst. She would face Camilla Pierce now, tonight, before Leo returned and had a chance to intervene. She would show him that she was capable of solving her own problems without his help.

And she would, finally, be free.

Chapter Thirteen

Willa hurriedly removed her dress and replaced it with her black trousers, white shirt, black vest and tall boots. Instead of one of her shawls, she asked Peggy to bring her one of Leo's long, black coats and a hat. She might be a lady, but she'd be damned if she'd travel to the East End looking like one.

'Pardon, milady,' Peggy said as she watched Willa hide her mass of hair with the black hat, 'but may I ask where you intend on going?' The question was asked nonchalantly by a maid who had accompanied Willa on any number of inadvisable ventures.

'Shadwell.'

'Shadwell?' Peggy parroted.

'Yes.'

'But, milady,' the maid gasped, her eyes rounding with horror, 'that's no place for a lady! It's dangerous. And it's nigh dark out.'

Wilhemina tried not to let her maid's observation hinder her, but she felt the resounding pulls of hesitation all through her body. Maybe she was making a mistake? Maybe she had been too hasty?

But then she remembered Leo's anger. She remembered his words: *'I will not have you traipsing to the bloody East*

End...' And her fury returned, spurring her into action. 'I am not a simpleton, Peggy. I will be careful.'

Peggy seemed to want to argue. She opened her mouth and closed it several times as if she were testing arguments in her head and discarding them. After several iterations of this same process, she nodded and whispered, 'Yes, milady,' and fled the room.

Several minutes later, when she was sufficiently attired and had packed the last of her jewellery from Windhurst into a black drawstring bag, Willa made her way down the stairs, only to find Peggy and Gordon waiting for her by the front door.

Peggy wrung her hands anxiously. But it was Gordon who Willa's gaze focused on. He was not uniformed, but dressed in brown breeches and a white shirt beneath a coat similar to hers, except his was brown where hers was black. 'Good heavens, Gordy. I don't think I've ever seen you so casual. It feels positively scandalous.'

The butler did not smile. 'My lady, I beg of you, please wait until Lord Pemberton returns.'

Willa's heart raced in her chest, but she stepped past the butler, his plea falling on deaf ears. She had to do this—for herself. For Leo, who had already taken the burden of so much of her shame. Willa was frantic with energy, with the desperate need to right her wrongs and defend her heart from further grief.

Gordon did not reach out to stop her. He followed her out into the dusky air. 'Gordy,' she said, fully prepared to demand that he return home.

But the old butler kept walking, down the front steps to the street. 'My options are to physically detain you until Lord Pemberton returns, or accompany you,' he replied gravely.

Willa felt another ripple of that same hesitation, urging her not to go. 'I don't need a bodyguard.'

'Forgive my impertinence, my lady, but have you ever walked the East End?'

'No, but—'

Gordon tipped at the waist, smartly cutting her off, and moved into the street to stop an approaching hansom. He did not speak again, but Willa did not miss the pointed look he shared with Peggy, who stood at the top of the stairs wringing her hands.

It riled her that even the servants took Leo's side. She could see the disapproval clearly on his face. 'You could ask a footman to accompany me if you think I need protection, Gordon,' she said flatly.

'I'll not entrust your safety to anybody else,' came the terse reply.

Seeing that he would not be swayed, Willa stepped into the cab and took a seat. Given that the hansom cabs had been specifically designed for economy of movement on the busy London streets, the interior fit only two people, forcing Gordon to sit down beside her. It was clear that the butler was immensely uncomfortable with the situation, but he sat down stiffly, keeping his back upright and his eyes forward.

The driver sat on a raised seat outside, behind the cab. 'Where to?'

'High Street, Shadwell,' Willa replied, leaning closer to the trapdoor to ensure that she was heard.

Willa sat back in her seat as the light cab started to move, the wheels rolling roughly over the cobbled streets of the West End. Her heart thrummed with excitement and anxious dread, equally eager to finally lay her life with Windhurst to rest and dreading Leo's reaction when he found out that she'd gone to do just that. 'I don't suppose there's a way I can convince you not to tell my husband about this?'

Gordon turned his head to look at her, his bushy eyebrows gathered in a frown. 'My lady, when Lord Pemberton finds out I accompanied you, I won't have much of a say in anything.'

A new, dreadful thought occurred to Willa. 'Leo wouldn't dare sack you. Not when he finds out that you had no choice.'

'There is always a choice, my lady,' the butler replied ominously.

Willa felt the words skitter down her spine. 'This is not his problem to solve. It's *mine*,' she said desperately, trying to make the butler understand. 'And Leo… He has done everything for me.' Growing increasingly panicked, Willa tapped her fingers impatiently on the seat on either side of her. 'He agreed to marry me, knowing that he would lose friends and business associates in the ensuing scandal. He settled Windhurst's debt, even though he had no legal obligation to, because he didn't want me to be humiliated by it.'

The shame of it all swelled in her chest, suffocating her. But still Willa's words spewed from her. 'And he stood by me when my own family did not. If I don't do this, our marriage will be perpetually one-sided. And then he will realise that he made a mistake.'

Her words, barely whispered, escaped from her lips with a fervour that she could not tame. 'And he will regret me and, worse, he will find somebody else.' Her heart chilled at the thought and then she breathed her worst fear into the cab. 'And what will people think when they find out that not one, but *two* husbands did not want me?'

'That is bloody bollocks.' The statement was issued by Gordon, loudly and with complete austerity despite his foul language.

Willa reared sideways, shocked that she had admitted her darkest fear to her elderly butler and horrified that he'd been paying close enough attention to argue with her.

Gordon focused on Wilhemina's face, his gaze stern and unflinching. His tone was severe. 'For years, you were married to a man who was afraid of your spirit; he saw it as something to be tamed and tried to tear you down because of it. And you defended against his bullying the only way you knew how—you became brave and resilient.' His eyes gleamed with anger. 'Stubborn, too.'

Willa's eyes burned with unshed tears.

'But now, my lady, you have married a man who does not want to tame you and you're still chafing at the bit even though it's not there, grinding your own teeth to powder.' The butler trailed off with a shake of his head, perhaps realising he had spoken to her quite roughly.

And Willa, not wanting him to regret his honesty, replied, 'You are not the first man to compare me to an animal, you know.'

Gordon's mouth twitched. 'I dare say I won't be the last either, my lady.' They were both quiet for a long moment, each thinking over Willa's situation. 'There's no shame in trusting people to help you when you need it.'

'There is if that is the entire nature of your relationship,' Willa insisted. 'I don't want Leo to always have to rescue me. He's done enough.'

Gordon fell silent after that, as if he finally realised that there was no point in arguing with her. But his words had had an odd effect on Willa, who was woman enough to admit that she still carried the fear and associated defences that she'd had to learn during her marriage to Windhurst. And, instead of that fear dying and those defences slowly eroding as one would have expected, they seemed to grow stronger with each day that she grew closer to Leo.

With each piece of her heart that Leo stole, she had to make a defensive countermove to try to ensure that he kept it, that he *wanted* to keep it. Because at the centremost of her soul, that foundational core that made her everything that she was, she understood that Leo had the power to do far more damage than Windhurst ever could have. And that terrified her in a way that nothing ever had before. If Leo grew bored of her or realised that she wasn't worth all the trouble and abandoned her, she wasn't sure how she would survive it.

She thought about this over the long journey, which even in the quicker hansom took them over an hour, and by the time the cab slowed, she felt cold, tousled and surly.

She passed the driver his fare through the trapdoor and hobbled to the ground when he unlatched the door. While Gordon descended, she looked up at the driver. He was an elderly man, wizened and hunched over with age. 'If you wait thirty minutes for us to return, I'll pay double your fare to take us back to Mayfair.'

'I'll need three shillin' in advance t'wait and after thirty minutes I'll need t'move on if I'm to return to the yard in time.'

Willa passed him the three shillings and beckoned Gordon to follow as she started down High Street, counting the house numbers as she went.

Although it was already seven o'clock at night, it was not yet dark. The dusky street was bustling with people, some on their way home, others on their way out. Drunken laughter and shouts echoed in the evening air.

Willa watched her step, skirting piles of refuse and puddles of indeterminate liquid. The stench was ripe and she crinkled her nose, letting her mouth fall open as she tried to avoid using her sense of smell at all.

When she saw a group of four men approaching, she hunched into her coat and hid her face, keeping her gaze downcast to avoid attracting any attention. Gordon's large frame at her side made her feel infinitely safer and she issued a brief prayer of thanks for the butler's stubborn insistence that he accompany her.

'Oy! Evening!' an unidentified man shouted to her as he passed, clearly falling for her gentlemanly attire.

'Keep walking,' Gordon instructed.

She hastened her steps, barely faltering when the same man laughed loudly and shouted, 'He's running now, boys.'

The sound of heavy footsteps fell in behind them and Willa instinctively tucked the drawstring bag into her shirt. Her heart screamed with fear, its fretful tapping knocking her ribs and forcing quick pants of air from between her lips.

'Quickly,' Gordon urged. 'Number Four is right up here.' He gripped her elbow and dragged her into a slight run, not pausing when loud laughter greeted their hasty escape.

'This was not my most inspired idea,' Willa panted.

Gordon grunted his agreement and tugged her up a short flight of stairs to the front door of a rough brick row house. Before she could compose herself or think what it was she wanted to say, Gordon reached out his hand and slammed the knocker down repeatedly.

It was only when he let his hand drop that she saw the knocker. It was similar to the brass lion's head door knockers that had gained popularity over the years, except instead of a lion's head with the ring in its mouth, this one was a big, brass wolf. Its ears were pricked, the knocking ring ensnared by snarling jaws.

If the Wolfes' obvious insignia had not scared her already, then the fact that the street had fallen eerily quiet behind her, their pursuers swiftly disappearing when they'd seen her destination, most assuredly did. So much so that Willa instinctively took a step back as she weighed the known dangers of the street versus the unknown dangers of the dark house.

'Gordon,' she started to say, her voice dying in her fear as the door swung open to reveal a giant man with the looks of a pirate and the devil's own smile.

'Lady Windhurst,' he drawled in a surprisingly refined accent, his eyes glinting wickedly. 'I must say, I didn't think you were stupid enough to actually come.'

Wilhemina was silent for a single second before her rage erupted. It came upon her like a house fire, burning through her body and heating her blood with reckless intent. 'I am not *Lady Windhurst* any more. And I am not *stupid*,' she snapped, her fear dying in the heat of her fury.

She took a brave step forward, going head to head with the oversized stranger. 'I am *tired*. And I am *cold*. And I am, quite frankly, sick and tired of being taken advantage of by silly men who think I will be manipulated and cowed!' Her voice rose with each word until she was practically shouting at the stranger on his own doorstep. 'Either show me to Miss Pierce or leave me damn well enough alone!'

The stranger didn't seem cowed by her. In fact, he seemed to find her—or perhaps the situation?—humorous. He leaned his massive shoulder against the doorframe, blocking her entry, and raked his blue eyes suggestively down her body. 'You're not what I was expecting.'

Neither are you, Willa thought. The man standing in

front of her was beautiful, big and broad with muscle. His hair was black as midnight. His blue eyes gleamed with wicked humour that reflected in the subtle twitching of his lips. 'I don't give a damn if you were expecting the Queen herself,' Willa stated. 'I would like to conclude my business with you for good. And if you keep delaying me, I will leave and you will not see a penny of what my dead husband owed you.'

The stranger's eyes darkened, not with anger, but with something that looked strangely like appreciation. And curiosity.

'For Christ's sake, Rafe,' another voice sounded from inside the house, 'stop playing with the woman and show her in.'

'I can't help it,' the man—Rafe—replied. 'She's a stunner, Bruv.' He winked cheekily at her.

Willa frowned, suddenly unsure of the game he was playing. 'Is Miss Pierce here or not?' she demanded.

'Aye.'

She raised one eyebrow haughtily. *'Well?'*

The man chuckled as if he were enjoying her lack of manners immensely. 'What I would do with that pretty mouth if it wasn't already spoken for,' he said wistfully.

Willa opened said pretty mouth to spew some rather ugly words, but another familiar voice, cold with fury, so cold that it stopped Willa's heart, interceded. 'Do not speak to my wife in that manner.'

Leo.

Leo could not even look at Wilhemina as Rafe Wolfe stepped aside and allowed his wife entry into the room. He was afraid that if he did, he would throttle her until she regained some of the common sense that she seemed to have completely disregarded. She had come, despite his express instructions not to, she had lied him and, worse, *unforgivably*, she had put herself in direct danger in the process.

He had tried so hard to be the husband she deserved. He had helped her with her list and fanned her scandal, even though it had hurt his business, his friendships and his relationship with his father—though, admittedly, that hadn't been stalwart to begin with. He had wanted to give her everything—money, safety, love. He had tried so hard. And for what?

Though he tried to separate his past from the current situation, it proved almost impossible. How many times had he done this? How many times had he put himself on the line only to be found an inconvenience to be ignored and walked around? And if, in the back of his mind, he was aware that Willa was not his parents and the situation was entirely different, the fear of seeing her there, the pain he felt over her clear inability to trust him blurred the line.

Leo did not spare his wife a glance as she came to stand in the room, wisely keeping to the other side of the small space. It was only when he heard Gordon say, 'I'll wait outside', that he chanced a glance at the door, a fraction of his fury dying when he saw that she had brought the butler with her—not that Gordon would be able to do anything should the Wolfes decide to hurt her.

'There seems to have been a misunderstanding between you,' Rogan Wolfe, commonly called Rogue, commented from where he lounged on a red velvet sofa.

The Shadwell house that the brothers used for business had been rearranged, the entire bottom floor opened to form one large receiving room and counting house. The room was furnished expensively with sturdy furniture. Bookcases holding account books, manuals and large unmarked tomes lined the back wall behind a set of three desks that faced the door, as if their occupants were prepared for an attack even as they worked.

An enormous safe that must have been six cubic feet sat in the far corner of the room, its conspicuousness boasting the brothers' dangerous reputations. Leo assumed that the upstairs rooms functioned as the house, though he did not dare ask.

He wanted to be done with this entire day. He wanted to take his wife home and lock her in safety for the rest of her life. He met Rogan's blue eyes. 'That's none of your concern. I want to conclude this business.'

Willa, thankfully, did not argue.

Rogue nodded. 'Lord Windhurst borrowed five hundred pounds over a year ago,' he said calmly. 'Given his dire circumstances, we refused to lend him more than that.'

'What was his interest rate?'

'Ten percent.'

'A month,' Rafe added.

Leo did not even flinch. It was a thankfully small sum, less than a tenth of what he had been expecting—and willing—to pay. 'Where can I have the money sent?'

Rogan considered him for a long time. 'You would pay another man's debts for this woman?' he asked, his eyes flickering to Wilhemina.

'Yes.' Leo did not add that he would do it a thousand times over. He knew that any show of affection for Willa might sway the brothers to use it to their advantage and push for more. At his wit's end, and unable to handle another threat against her, he added, 'I want to be done with my wife's dead husband so that I can move on with my own damned life.' He heard Willa's small inhale and tried his best not to let it affect him.

'I will write you instructions.'

'You do not doubt that I will pay?' Leo asked.

Rogan shrugged his massive shoulders. 'I doubt you would have come here if you didn't intend to pay. Whatever you want to believe of us, we are not in the habit of knocking off men—particularly ones who owe us money.'

'He owes you nothing,' Willa snapped.

Rogue's gaze turned to her and Leo grit his jaw against the urge to haul his wife over his shoulder and start running. Before the other man could speak, Leo said, 'We both know that I am the only one with the means to settle it. She has nothing.'

Rogan raised his eyebrows, but he must have sensed that it would do him no good to address Wilhemina again. He reached forward, extending one hand for Leo's. 'We are agreed. And given that it was not your debt to settle, we will only require the original five hundred he borrowed.'

Leo dipped his head in thanks and returned Rogan Wolfe's handshake. 'My thanks.' He stood and only then did he dare to look at Willa. His coat hung on her thin frame, making her look so much smaller than she was. The hat had fallen askew, allowing several heavy locks to escape down her face and neck. She was drawn and pale, her shoulders rounded, he knew, by his callous words.

She ignored him completely. She stepped past him, facing Rogan Wolfe bravely. But Leo couldn't help but clench his fists; to him, she was a lamb confronting a wolf. She reached into her shirt and removed a black drawstring bag. The obvious clink of jewellery reached his ears. Willa did not open the bag. She held it out for Rogan Wolfe. 'For Miss Pierce.'

'She has no need of your finery, my lady. We will take good care of her.'

Willa dropped the bag at his feet. It made a beautiful tinkling sound as it hit the floor. 'Throw it to the cutpurses, then.'

'Why?' Rogan's question was weighted with a curiosity that scared Leo. Rafe was already looking at his wife as if she was a prime joint of Christmas ham. The last thing he needed was for Rogan to take an interest in her, too.

'If she put up with half of what I did, then she deserves it.'

'She was your husband's whore,' Rafe pointed out, clearly not understanding why Willa would try to help Camilla.

'One man's whore is another man's daughter,' Willa whispered. 'I am lucky in that *although I have nothing*.'

Her choked words tore through Leo's chest.

'I w-want for nothing either. Take it or throw it in the Thames—I don't give a damn. I don't want it.'

She turned and strode past Leo, not bothering to say goodbye to the Wolfe brothers, both of whom watched her predatorily as she left.

'You're going to have a right time of it with that one,' Rafe observed, grinning. 'Lucky bastard.'

Leo couldn't smile. He knew that whatever progress he'd made with Willa over the past weeks had been unravelled, all in the space of a few minutes. He looked from Rafe to Rogan. 'I'll wait for those instructions,' he said and left.

It was only once he was out on the street that he realised Wilhemina had not waited for him. She had left, forcing Gordon to follow her. He caught sight of them walking into the shadows in the distance and followed, making sure that they reached the waiting hansom cab safely before walking into the darkening night to find his own.

He couldn't go home. He couldn't face her in his current mood. He was too angry, no, *furious*. His very blood had frozen in his veins when he'd heard her voice outside and now Leo determined that the only thing that would get his terrified heart pumping again was a bottle of spirits.

He waited for a passing hansom and the moment one pulled over, he gave the driver the address for his club and sank back into the seat, exhausted.

But as the cab rattled and bounced through the dark streets of London, Leo thought of Willa. He had loved her for so long and longed for her love so intensely that he'd done everything he could to win her. He had coerced her into marriage when she'd been vulnerable, he'd paid her late husband's debts and flamed her scandal as he'd thought she'd wanted to, all the while lying to her, telling her it was his responsibility as her friend and her husband. Because he had been too afraid to tell her that he loved her—had only *ever* loved her.

But perhaps it was time to reassess? Ignoring that familiar empty ache of inadequacy that settled in his chest, Leo began to plan.

Though the thought of adding distance between them pained him, he could not deny the facts any longer. While he had been frantically trying to win her love, Willa had not even been conscious of it. She had been trying to survive. And, for the first time, he realised that perhaps he had not given her the space to do that. Perhaps his own need for her affection and approval had clouded his judgement and resultantly hurt them—hurt *her*? Well, not any more. It was time he took a step back and gave his wife the freedom she'd craved for so long.

Chapter Fourteen

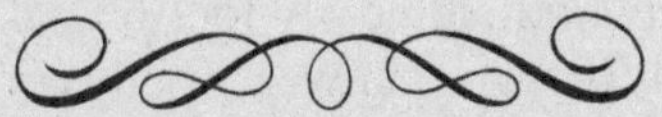

Leo did not come home. Wilhemina knew this because she had bathed, changed into her nightgown, then slipped beneath her sheets and waited, listening for any sound of his arrival. None came. No footsteps or the familiar sound of his bedroom door, which was right next to hers, opening and closing.

And, perhaps worse, Willa had become so accustomed to curling up next to him in his big bed that her own felt foreign, cold and uncomfortable despite the thick blankets and plush pillows. She tossed and turned all night, long after she realised that he would not be coming back.

She lay awake and wondered where he was and who he was with, and even though her heart rebelled at the idea, she couldn't help but convince herself that he had gone back to his mistress. Why else would he have stayed away the entire night?

The thought left her drained with exhaustion. There wasn't even any panic, only deep vindication. And resentment. She had been right. Just as she'd started to get comfortable, to believe the things Leo had said, to believe that things could be different, he'd gone and betrayed her.

How shall I live with it a second time? she wondered.

Even then, she knew it was not quite the same. It had not

mattered what Windhurst had done, he never could have hurt her like this. Simply because she had not cared about him one way or another. But Leo… When Leo abandoned her, he would be depriving her of far more than her pride.

Willa was so distressed by the idea that sleep evaded her completely until, at nearly four o'clock in the morning, she finally dragged her weary body out of bed, put on her shawl and slippers and went in search of a cup of tea.

The kitchen, scullery, pantry and storeroom took up a large portion of the basement floor, one level below the street entrance of the terraced town house. Willa carried a single candle down the narrow, wooden staircase, keeping her hand cupped in front of the wick to protect the small flame.

The fire in the range had already been lit to heat the boiler and the room was filled with warmth. Though the kitchen and adjoining scullery were glistening and clean, the faint smell of stale smoke hung perpetually in the air, reminding Willa that this was a place that rarely saw rest. If the servants weren't cooking and cleaning, they were preparing the weekly wash or scrubbing the floors, and almost every household chore originated and ended here, downstairs.

Since her marriage to Leo, Willa hadn't had any reason to interfere with Mrs Smith's impeccable housekeeping. Although she still spent a small portion of her Monday and Friday mornings meeting with the matronly housekeeper and making sure that the woman had everything she needed to run the household smoothly, Willa had been delighted by the fact that she wasn't particularly needed.

While she was sure most husbands would have wanted a wife who adored her domestic role, Leo hadn't seemed to care that Willa was more than happy to give the reins almost entirely to Mrs Smith. And why not? The woman was trustworthy, dependable and far better at managing a large house than Willa ever would be—or would ever want to be.

She carefully placed her candle on the large kitchen table and went in search of a serviceable tea kettle. She was rummaging around in the pantry when a throat cleared behind her and she turned to find the cook, Ada, standing in the doorway.

Ada was still a young woman, maybe thirty years old. She had a round, homely figure and a healthful, ruddy complexion made more wholesome by her wild brown hair and twinkling green eyes. 'Good morning, milady.' She dropped into a quick curtsy. 'May I help you with something?'

'Oh, good morning, Ada. I was hoping for a cup of tea and didn't want to wake anyone so early.'

'That's no problem, milady,' the cook hurried to reply. 'I'll bring it up to the drawing room.'

Understanding that she was not being given a choice in the matter, Willa smiled. 'Thank you. If you could send it up to the study instead.'

'Yes, milady.'

Wilhemina picked up her candle and retraced her steps to the ground floor. Although the cook had not intended to be brusque, Willa felt the sting of loneliness as she walked down the short hallway to the study. The first weeks of her marriage had passed so quickly that she had not made much of an effort to see her friends. She had been trying to find her footing in her new house and with her new husband, but now the loneliness was starting to creep in.

Before Leo, Isabelle and Mary had been the only constant, dependable people in her life. They had cared for her and quietly made sure that she knew that she had a place to go when things with Windhurst were bad.

And she needed them now.

Although Isabelle, Matthew, and the children had returned to the country after the masqueade ball, Mary lived close by. Willa made a mental note to pay a call on her as she opened the study door and stepped inside.

She pulled up short when the first thing she saw upon entering was Leo. He was fast asleep on the sofa, his arms crossed over his chest, his long legs dangling off the end. His mouth was slightly open, the soft sound of his deep, even breathing barely reaching her where she stood. He was dressed in the same clothes from the night before, sans coat, cravat and shoes.

Willa's heart constricted in her chest as she looked at him. Even though the cynical part of her whispered that he could have returned only an hour earlier, she felt in her heart that he had slept most of the night on that very sofa.

She hovered for a moment, unsure of herself, unsure of what to do.

She had never felt this fretful, anxious need for a person before, had never wanted to go to someone so much—and she had certainly never felt this awful urge to punish someone as she did Leo for the hurtful things he had said the night before.

She was aware that she had nothing—that was, after all, why she'd married him so soon after Windhurst's death. But to hear *Leo* say it, and to other people, too, to *strangers*, had reminded her briefly of what it felt like to be married to Windhurst: as if she were something broken and useless, a woman unworthy of him. The only difference was that with Leo, she actually believed that might all be true.

A yawning chasm seemed to open within her, one that

being married to Leo had temporarily sealed shut, but that reopened with a vengeance now, spewing all her insecurities and fears back into her until her chest was tight with panic.

She took a hurried step out of the study and closed the door quietly behind her just as Ada was coming up with a tea tray. 'I'll take it in my bedroom, please, Ada,' she said breathlessly.

She followed the cook up the stairs and waited patiently as she placed the tray down on a nearby table. Without being asked, Ada knelt on the floor to rekindle the fire, her efficient movements belying years of experience doing just that. 'May I send up some breakfast, milady?' she asked once she was done.

'No. Thank you, Ada. I'm not particularly hungry. But could you have George fetch Atalanta for me when he wakes up?' she asked. Remembering Leo's fury from the night before had her hastily adding, 'And ask him to saddle a horse for himself, too—I'll need him to accompany me. Oh, and, Ada,' she added right as the cook turned to leave, 'a regular saddle, please. Not a side-saddle.'

Ada bobbed a quick curtsy and left the room, leaving Willa alone with her tea. She sat in front of the crackling fire, cold and aching despite the rapidly heating room.

With Windhurst, the expectations had been clear. She was to be quiet and obedient and elegant. As long as she adhered to that framework she could largely escape his notice—and punishment. But with Windhurst gone and Leo now here, she wasn't quite sure who she was any more. And, perhaps worse, she wasn't sure who she was *supposed* to be either. Somewhere between her father's house and her two husbands', she had become lost, uncertain of where her place in the world was.

* * *

Willa contemplated this loss for nearly two hours, growing more and more unsettled with each minute that she mulled. So, when Peggy knocked on the door at only six-thirty and entered the room to tell her that the horses were saddled and ready, she did not hesitate to quickly swipe at her eyes and say, 'Could you tell him I'll be down momentarily, Peggy.'

She hastily scrawled a note to Leo, telling him that she would be back later, and then, before she could overthink it, she went outside to her horse. She mounted the mare quickly and without help, her trousers, coupled with the regular saddle, making it unusually easy.

George followed her lead as she turned Atalanta in the direction of Mary's home, a set of tidy rooms that she rented from Cameron Sykes above her place of work on Maiden Lane, only a short two-minute walk south of the Covent Garden Market.

The neighbourhood was one that was relatively safe during the day as the popular market flooded with people from all walks of life and the surrounding establishments drew men of business. But once the sunlight faded, the area became notably dangerous, so much so that both Willa and Isabelle had vehemently objected to Mary's decision to live above Sykes Trading. But no matter how much they tried to argue, barter and bribe her, Mary had been resolute to start her new independent life with no assistance from either of them.

Given the early hour of day, the ride took them only twenty minutes on horseback, but Willa couldn't help but bask in the city at dawn. The air was cool and crisp, the faint smell of woodsmoke rising up through the morning fog. As they drew closer to Covent Garden Market, costermongers sold their wares, some from carts laden with produce, others from simple woven baskets holding small tokens like single roses and ribbons. Willa even noted a young girl, not even twelve, with a basket of fat, wriggling terrier pups. Men hawked their articles, their cries rising, merging and echoing all around her like some strangely harmonic choir.

Willa relaxed by degrees, the novelty of London in the early morning distracting her and soothing over some of her distress. By the time they arrived at the austere building with Sykes Trading over the front, she was almost herself again.

She dismounted and gave her reins to George. 'You may go home, George. I'm sure Mr Sykes will lend me his carriage when I am ready to return.'

George nodded uncertainly, but he did not move and, at Willa's frown, he explained, 'Beg your pardon, milady, but Gordon said I'm to see you into the building before leaving.'

'Oh. I see.' Willa supposed that, after last night's adventure, the elderly butler deserved that much at least. 'Thank you, George,' she said and started for the door. 'You may tell Gordon that I made it to my destination unscathed.' Still, the footman waited patiently outside until she had rung the bell and been admitted by a maid before he remounted his horse and turned both animals towards home.

Despite the early time of morning, inside the Sykes Trading building, business was already underway. Young clerks sat at their desks, their heads bent over their work as a pair of maids hurried to stoke fires, refresh the fare at a nearby laden sideboard and clean around the studious young men.

'This way, milady.' The same maid who had admitted her led her to a flight of stairs and up to the first storey where three large, glass-windowed offices formed a U shape around the stairs. The doors were all closed, their occupants undoubtedly not in yet, but Willa was fascinated to read the names stamped above each door. The central, largest office had *SYKES* above the door—as if anyone could mistake the monstrous room for anyone else's. The office to the left read: *MOORE*. And the one on the right, in the same big letters, read: *LAMBERT*.

It was strange for Willa to see the obvious marker of her friend's success and independence, and the fact that Mary was a woman was the least of it. Mary was smart and good with numbers. She was rational and relatively unemotional. Her personal qualities made her an excellent candidate for her position.

No, Willa found Mary's situation strange only in that her quiet, austere friend had always seemed like the last person who'd *want* to work in such an environment—and work for a man like Cameron Sykes, none the less. Mary was conventional down to her marrow. Or, at least, Willa could acknowledge, Mary *used* to be conventional down to her marrow.

Willa's lips quirked at the irony of their situations. Willa, who had not wanted to remarry, had been forced to by her dire circumstances. And Mary, who would have made an exemplary wife and mother—and probably wanted to be both—had not.

Willa pondered that as the maid led her silently up to the second floor, where they were met by a short, dark hallway that ended in a single door. She knocked on the door and when Mary's voice replied, enquiring who it was, it was Willa who responded, 'Are you decent?'

The door opened a moment later to reveal Mary. She was awake and alert, though still dressed in her demure nightgown, her long hair falling in a long braid over one shoulder. 'Willa!' she exclaimed, but her happy expression faltered when she saw Willa's face. 'Is anything the matter?'

'No, of course not,' Willa replied quickly. 'Can't I visit my friends any more?'

Mary opened the door to admit her, only briefly pausing to ask the maid to bring some tea and toast, before closing it again.

Willa took in her friend's rooms, noting how they'd changed since Mary had settled in. They were simple yet well furnished. The main living area contained a sofa, two chairs and side tables set atop a plush red rug and centred around a large fireplace. A small dining room table and four chairs occupied one corner of the room, while a large writing desk and bookcase occupied the other. A separate bedroom with an *en suite* bathroom and lavatory sat off the main room.

'You don't mind if I change while we talk, do you?' Mary asked, not waiting for a reply before walking to her bedroom. She left her door open so that she could be heard. 'I received your letter about visiting Isabelle next week,' she said, her voice momentarily becoming muffled as she pulled her dress over her head.

'I was thinking it would be nice to visit her and the children before travelling to the Vickery estate for the summer.' Willa had originally hoped that Leo would accompany her, but now she wasn't so sure he'd even want to. They'd have to pretend that was everything was fine between them, which might have worked for strangers, but not for their two best friends. Matthew and Isabelle would know that something had happened.

'And Leo?' Mary asked, perhaps sensing Willa's deliberate avoidance.

'I'm not sure yet,' she managed to say hoarsely, banking her emotion. 'I know he is eager to get back to his estate. Apparently, there is much to do given that he has been gone for the entire Season. And his father's health means he cannot manage much without Leo any more, so it's been left almost entirely to his estate manager in the interim.'

Mary came back through after only a few minutes, clad in a simple, brown day dress that only accentuated her creamy pale complexion, green eyes, and rosy cheeks. 'Why do I have the feeling that you're not telling me everything?'

'Because you have a naturally suspicious nature?' Wilhemina suggested.

Mary's brows rose. 'Willa...'

She shook her head as emotion clogged her throat. 'Leo and I had a...'

What had they had?

It wasn't a fight. It hadn't become heated enough to be a fight—had it?

Mary came to her immediately, her eyes filled with concern. 'Tell me,' she said quietly and led Willa to one of the chairs in front of the fire.

And Willa did. She poured out her soul, not even stopping when the maid brought in a tray of tea and toast. The words came fast in her panic, one falling over the next until she was breathless and on the verge of tears, her entire body trembling with the effort to contain her emotion.

Mary listened in silence until she finished with, 'And all I could think last night when I thought he hadn't come home was that he had gone back to his mistress.' She blinked rapidly, avoiding her friend's kind gaze when she added, 'I can't live through it again, Mary. I didn't really care about Camilla—she kept Windhurst away from me. It was only the public humiliation that was hard to live with. But if Leo...'

'I thought they parted ways before your wedding?'

'They *did*,' Willa replied. 'But that doesn't mean that he's incapable of seeking her out again.'

'Willa... Have you told him how you feel?' Mary asked, skipping straight to the heart of the matter.

'No.' Willa shook her head, rejecting even the thought of telling Leo the depth of her feelings for him.

Mary took a delicate sip of her tea, her face completely neutral. 'Why not?'

Wilhemina struggled with the truth for a long moment. Tears fell freely down her face now. 'I don't want him to have any more of me, Mary. I can't, because...'

'Because?'

'He already has too much. And I didn't even know it had happened until it was too late.' And then, to her mortification, she burst into big, racking sobs that seemed to steal all the air from the room.

'All right,' Mary crooned. She put her teacup down on the nearby table and came to Willa, gently brushing her hair back from her face in a maternal gesture. 'It's normal to feel this way, Willa.'

'H-how can you s-say that? I think I might actually be going crazy,' she added with a small sniffle. Her chest felt tight, each breath pinching her lungs until the air barely filled them. Her eyes were red and swollen and itched like the devil. And worse, her heart seemed too broken to ever mend and Willa felt hysterical with fear that she would always be this way. Just barely held together, barely sane and always the subject of pitying glances and vindictive gossip.

'You're not going crazy.' Mary dragged one of the small

tables closer to Willa's chair and sat on it before taking Willa's hands in hers again. 'You're grieving.'

'No.' Willa shook her head vehemently. 'I felt nothing for the bastard.'

'Not for Windhurst,' Mary clarified. 'You're grieving for yourself. For the years you could not mourn the parts of you that he took away without your permission. You're grieving for the girl you were.'

To Willa's immense mortification, a keening cry slipped from between her lips. She doubled over in the chair and buried her face in her hands as she tried to choke it back.

But Mary kept talking. 'That girl is gone, Willa. And no matter how much you try, you will never bring her back to life. However,' she added after a long pause, 'you can build yourself into someone completely new, a woman who is stronger and better than before.' Mary's hand rubbed gentle circles on Willa's back. 'But you have to give yourself time. One day, you'll wake up and you won't feel like a stranger in your own skin. And that woman will know she's worthy of her husband's love.'

And it was that last statement, delivered with nothing but simple confidence, that broke Wilhemina. It tore down the small pieces of her that remained, like some wild winter storm sweeping away the ruins of an ancient castle with no thought to what it had once been or how proudly it had once stood, and with no consideration for the scar it would leave behind, even once it was gone.

Chapter Fifteen

Leo awoke to a firm knock on the door just after nine with a splitting headache and an aching back, both of which pushed his already sour mood to the brink. His feet hit the floor with an ominous thud. He sat up on the sofa and ran one hand through his hair, trying to smooth it down as much as possible before hoarsely calling, 'Come!'

The door opened and Gordon stepped inside, his bushy eyebrows gathered together in concern. 'Forgive me, my lord, but Mrs Lambert is here to see you.'

Leo frowned in confusion. 'Show her to my wife,' he said as he began to put his boots back on.

'Er… Lady Wilhemina is not here, my lord.'

Leo paused what he was doing, one boot on, one boot off. Before he even asked, he knew that something terrible had happened. 'And where, pray, is she?' he asked coldly.

'George escorted her to Mrs Lambert this morning,' the butler explained, 'and now… Well… Mrs Lambert is here.'

'And my wife is not,' Leo concluded grimly. He took a deep, steadying breath and tried to rein in the desperation that clawed through him. 'Bring me some coffee, please, Gordon. And show Mrs Lambert in.'

'Yes, my lord.' The butler hesitated slightly. 'Should I bring some tea for Mrs Lambert?'

'No.' Leo did not know why, but he knew that Mary would not be staying.

The butler bowed and hastily left the room. He must have sensed that whatever was happening was grave indeed because he did not re-enter to re-introduce Mary, merely opened the door, ushered her in and quickly shut them in together.

'Mary.'

'Hello, Leo.' Mary sighed tiredly, as if she were exhausted at just the thought of the conversation they were about to have.

'Is Willa with you?'

'She is.' She sat down in the chair opposite his and folded her hands in her lap, so calm and demure when really all Leo wanted was for her to shame and chastise him so that he could fight back. 'She came this morning, and I didn't know what to do. She was—' she shook her head lightly '—distraught. I thought it would be best if she rested before returning, except the moment her head hit the pillow, she fell into an exhausted sleep. I didn't want to wake her.'

Leo's heart ached in his chest. He didn't curse or pound his fist, suddenly too goddamn fatigued to do anything except ask, 'Does she need anything?'

Mary considered him, her green eyes missing nothing. She was quiet for a long moment before replying. 'No.'

'She told you what happened? Last night?'

'She did. She said she'd never seen you so angry before.'

'Angry?' Leo rasped with emotion. 'I was goddamn furious! I *am* furious! She did not listen to me and, instead, put herself in danger!' He swore ripely, enraged all over again at the memory of Willa standing between the Wolfe brothers. His entire body vibrated with fury. In over thirty years, he had not come close to the panic or the desperation

that had surged through him when he'd first heard Willa's voice and Leo, who had never loved anyone so intensely, could not make sense of the violent helplessness consuming him even now, with Willa safe and sound.

'Yes, I can see that.' To his utter frustration, Mary only smiled gently.

'She could have been hurt, Mary!'

'She knows that.'

'She *has* to be able to trust me.'

'Why?' Mary demanded, a laugh in her voice. 'Because you are a man?'

Leo groaned in frustration. 'Yes. Because *I am her husband*.' Unable to contain himself any more, he added, 'Because I love her and want her to be safe and happy. And because if anything ever happened to her, *I* would not survive it.'

'You forget, Leo, that every single man that Willa has ever loved or been entrusted to has betrayed her in one way or another.'

'I'm not like them! I would never—' He took a deep breath. 'Last night was different. What was I supposed to do? Let her traipse through Shadwell alone, visiting with whores and paying off illegal debts to a notoriously dangerous gang?'

'No.' Mary remained completely calm, her soft voice making Leo sound unreasonably angry, almost petulant by comparison. 'Of course not. Willa knows that you're different, Leo. In fact, I think that's the crux of the issue. If she opens her heart to you, she'd be giving you the power to destroy her completely.'

Leo's heart stopped beating for one perfect moment. 'I would never hurt her.'

Mary's green eyes sparkled with a cat-like, superior

amusement. 'I know that. And I think Willa does, too. Last night… She was acting on impulse born of all that fear she's been carrying. And then when you didn't come home afterwards, she…'

'She what?'

Mary's blush reached her hairline and, although she held his gaze, Leo sensed that it cost her. 'She convinced herself that you had gone to Elaine.'

'What?'

His first response was surprise, swiftly followed by anger. How could Willa not see that he was *obsessed* with her? Blinded by her?

'Windhurst damaged her, Leo. Truly and deeply.'

'I am not Windhurst. I would never… I was home by ten, Mary,' he said, as if he had to convince her. 'I didn't go upstairs because I know Willa prefers my bed and I didn't want to disturb her sleep after the night we'd had.'

'You don't have to convince me, my lord.' She stood and tugged on her gloves as if preparing to leave. 'I only wanted to help you understand: Willa is recovering from a long period of suffering and doubt. She might not feel secure with herself for years. And she certainly won't feel secure with you until then.' She smiled kindly and with no hint of malice. 'Trust me on this.'

'I am trying,' he said, closing his eyes momentarily. 'I am trying to show her that she can depend on me, but… What else can I do?' he asked desperately.

'I know it may not feel like it now, but I truly believe that you're doing everything that you can already. Be patient with her. And continue to love her. The rest is up to her and it will come. But it will take time. Leo, it may take *years*.' Mary's smile was soft. 'It did for me.'

Leo exhaled a deep breath, trying—and failing—to rid

himself of the morose sense of inadequacy that stamped down upon his soul. If his own wife could not trust him, could not feel safe and secure with him… 'I only want her to be happy.'

'I know. *Willa* knows. But at the end of the day, *she* must choose her own happiness. It is not your responsibility, Leo—it is hers. It has to be hers, irrespective of how much it pains you, pains *us all*, to watch her suffer.'

Mary started for the door. 'I have to get to work. I just wanted you to know that Willa is safe. I'll make sure she has the carriage to get home once she is up and able.'

'Mary…'

'Yes?'

'Can you tell her I'm sorry—for scaring her? For hurting her?'

'No.'

Leo laughed tiredly at the abrupt answer.

'That is for you two to sort out.' Mary opened the door, only pausing to add, 'But you should tell her the truth, Leo—that you love her. Don't leave things unsaid in your marriage—you never know when it will be too late to say anything at all.'

Leo went up to his rooms and washed and changed, feeling a little the worse for wear. More than the hangover or cricked back from his sofa slumber, he felt weighted down by the circumstances. He was tired, his energy drained from equal parts worry and helplessness. He would rather die than hurt Wilhemina, yet it was exceptionally humbling to think that he was the one person in the world with the ability to hurt her still. He'd rather saw off his own arm than cause his wife a moment's misery.

Perhaps, he thought, Mary had been right and he had been going about wooing her all wrong, trying to bring back the girl he'd known instead of giving Willa the time and space to discover the woman she wanted to become. Again, he remembered that, though he had lived with his desperate love for her for a long time, Willa had not. And he had not paused in his own happiness to think that she might be terrified instead of overjoyed, that instead of their love freeing her as it had him, it might make her feel trapped and insecure instead.

When he returned to his study, he wrote a quick note to Matthew and rang for Gordon. The butler entered almost immediately, his typically stoic expression undermined with fatigue. 'My lord?'

'Gordon, I wanted to thank you for accompanying my wife last night. God knows it was not expected of you; however, I appreciate that you did not let her go alone.'

The typically stoic butler visibly sagged with relief, his face relaxing with the first genuine emotion Leo had ever seen the man show. 'Of course, my lord.' He clasped and unclasped his hands in front of him, as if he wanted to say more.

'Speak, man.'

'I considered trying to detain her, my lord. But… She wasn't herself. I was afraid that if I tried, I might harm her. She was feverish and anxious, almost hysterical.' The butler dropped his eyes. 'She was nervous and rambling, talking on about how your marriage is one-sided and that you would feel the effects of it eventually and…'

'And?' Leo urged.

'And that you'll eventually leave…'

Leo buried his head in his hands, unable to face the elderly butler. Gordon, who was the epitome of discretion, would never have mentioned Willa's confession if he had not been exceptionally worried about her—Leo knew that.

And somehow it made everything worse. As much as he couldn't regret going to the Wolfe brothers in her stead, he could have handled the entire situation better. Somehow…

He just had no bloody idea what he could have done differently. And, now, instead of lying in bed or breakfasting with his wife, he was miserable and alone and she was seeking safety somewhere that was not in his arms. The entire situation seemed irredeemable.

'Sometimes, my lord,' the butler added hesitantly, 'hope can be the most terrifying possibility. If hope is all we have left within, then the fear that it will not materialise or be substantiated is *terrifying*.'

Leo exhaled a long breath. 'I think you're right, Gordon.' His wife had gone from a sheltered existence to the worst kind of hell with no time in between to adjust to hardship.

Gordon resumed his silent and austere position and a strange calm came over Leo as he handed the butler the letter to Matthew. 'Please see that this is posted right away.'

'Yes, my lord.'

'I'm expecting his reply tomorrow or the next day, by which time I want my wife's things packed and ready to visit Lord and Lady Ashworth at the Heather estate. I want you and Peggy to go with her, Gordon. Mary has already said that she will see if she can take time off, but I need someone who can write me an objective account of my wife's health.'

The butler frowned. 'You are not going too, my lord?'

'I have business to conclude here. It shouldn't take me more than two weeks, at which point, I'll join you all there and we'll carry on to the Vickery estate afterwards.'

Although sending Willa away was not what Mary had recommended or what he wanted, Leo knew that he could not be in proximity to his wife without falling into the same patterns. He loved her too much. Willa needed time away from him to heal. And though it pained him to admit it, perhaps he needed time away from her, too?

He had been so caught up in the fact that he finally had her, had become so obsessed with giving her everything she wanted in the hope that she might grow to love him that he had completely undermined the strength of the bond they'd had before their marriage. Because they had been friends—equals—once, not so long ago. Before he'd put Willa on a pedestal in the centre of *his* world and, perhaps worse, not given her the space to get off it should she wish to.

Chapter Sixteen

By the time Wilhemina got back home it was nearing noon. Despite the fact that she had slept deeply for nearly five hours at Mary's, she did not feel refreshed at all.

'Is my husband home, Gordon?' she asked as she entered the hall and began to remove her coat and gloves.

The butler took her gloves in hand and draped the coat over his arm as he replied. 'Yes, my lady. He is in his study.'

'Thank you.' Willa steeled herself and made to move past the butler, stopping abruptly when thoughts of the night before threatened to erode her resolve. 'Gordon…'

'Yes, my lady.'

'I wanted to apologise to you, for my behaviour last night.'

'Please, my lady,' Gordon hurriedly said as he flushed. 'An apology is not necessary. I am *in service*.' He said the last part in a whisper that belied his embarrassment.

Wilhemina tried to remind herself that the man in front of her had been employed by the Duke of Everett for many, many years and that prior to working for Isabelle he had most likely been treated like a piece of furniture rather than a human being.

Still, her own shame would not let her leave the subject alone. 'Yes, you are. However, that does not mean that you should be put in an uncomfortable or dangerous situation—especially one that you clearly wanted no part in. For that I am sorry.'

'It is done now, my lady. Perhaps it is best if we both forgot that it occurred.'

'If you'd prefer.'

'I would, my lady.'

'Very well then.' Willa stepped past him and started for the study.

She bypassed the drawing room and the dining room. With each door she passed, she had to actively resist the urge to fling it open, lock herself inside and avoid the task before her.

So much so that when she came to the study, she stood outside contemplating the particular shade of the wooden door for a full five minutes.

'Come now. Enough of this,' she murmured to herself, knowing that her nerves were getting the best of her. She raised her hand and knocked, quickly and firmly, so as to leave her no chance of escape. When Leo called for her to enter, Willa did not hesitate, though her feet practically itched to move in the opposite direction.

The study had always been her favourite room in the house, not only because it smelled faintly like whatever shaving soap Leo used that had the softest notes of citrus in, but because the room was an almost perfect replica of the man: handsome, with heavy, expensive furniture that could only have been inherited down the long line of Vickerys, clean, with no dust or grime, and still impossibly cosy, with hundreds of books packed on to the shelves with no thought to order, plush rugs that were heaven beneath bare feet and a fireplace that always emitted a warm, welcoming glow.

'Willa.' Leo's voice, the strangely cool tone of it, seemed

to contradict Willa's rambling thoughts immediately upon entry. 'Is something the matter?'

Unsure of what to say to the question, unable to begin her apology on such strange footing, she floundered. 'No. I'm assuming you received my note—about going to visit Mary?'

Leo sat back in his chair and regarded her from across his desk, his eyes running from her feet to her face and pausing there, waiting for her to say more. After an exceptionally awkward silence, he replied, 'Yes. I knew where you were.'

Another long silence ensued, this one so heavy and insurmountable that Wilhemina couldn't have voiced her original apology through it even if she'd wanted to.

'I should leave you to it,' she said softly, feeling strangely out of sorts.

He was acting as if nothing had happened even though his entire demeanour towards her had changed. Where was the man who had held her while she'd cried, the man who'd told her she could always go to him when she couldn't sleep at night? Where was the man who'd taken her riding in Hyde Park and bought her fencing lessons?

Have I really ruined everything so neatly?

Confused, distraught and not knowing how to begin to repair their relationship, Willa turned to leave without as much as a farewell or—as she might have done only yesterday—a promise to come find him later.

'Wilhemina.'

She turned at the door. Leo stood now and, though he was still behind his desk, he was angled as if he wanted to move around it— but couldn't.

She waited in silence.

'I have written to Matthew in advance of your visit to the Heather estate. He and Isabelle will be expecting you in as few as three days.'

So, this is what it had come to? He was sending her away as another man might an unwanted inconvenience. 'I see.'

'I think it might be best for you to spend some time with your friends,' he carried on, gentler now.

But Wilhemina couldn't stay a moment longer. She bowed her head demurely, when really she itched to throw a few of her brothers' choicest curse words at him. She did not argue. She did not say anything. She merely left the room and closed the door behind her.

She walked up the stairs calmly, her steps measured and even.

She opened her bedroom door, entered and locked herself inside before walking to the door that adjoined her and Leo's rooms and did the same to that.

And only then, once she was sure that she was alone and could not be disturbed, did she lie down on the big bed with its cold counterpane and let the agony come. The pain, the *torment*, bracketed her from all sides, mummifying her in a familiar place within herself where she had spent many a day married to Windhurst.

There were no tears.

Even her rage, which she had always brandished against Windhurst once she'd needed to pull herself back together, was not there. Instead, and to her relief, she felt…empty, as if nothing, *nobody*, in the world could reach her any more.

And maybe that was better, Willa thought, and promptly fell into a dreamless sleep.

'Sodding idiot.' Leo paced his study ten minutes later, still berating himself. He'd had a plan. He'd thought it through extensively. He was supposed to remain calm, listen to what she'd had to say, then apologise and explain why he'd reacted so poorly to her appearance at the Wolfes' the night before.

Instead, he'd been consumed with nerves and Willa hadn't seemed wanting or willing to say anything, her hurt still so fresh and clear. And he, in his flustered confusion, had acted like a semi-mute incompetent.

'Christ.' He gripped his hair with both hands as he tried to find some excuse to go to her, some reason for seeking her out when he was clearly the last person she wanted to be near to.

'Don't be a coward, man!' he urged himself aloud. 'You simply have to walk up the stairs, knock on her door and apologise. Beg if you have to!' He would, too. He could survive without her returning his love—hadn't he done just that for years? But if Willa cut him out of her life completely, if this new distance between them persisted and he couldn't see her or talk to her or touch her… He closed his eyes, bracing against the familiar inadequacy and the suffocating panic that accompanied it.

His palms *itched* to touch his wife, to run down the gentle slope of her spine as he soothed her and promised he would try to be more understanding, try to be better. God, just having her in proximity and not being able to reach for her was its own kind of torture. How the hell was he supposed to live without her for *two weeks*?

Overwhelmed by the torrent of emotions consuming him, Leo yanked his study door open and, after apologising to a passing maid he'd startled, hurried for the stairs.

He didn't give himself time to think, knowing that he would lose courage if he did. He took the stairs two at a time, too eager, too desperate to act calm, so that by the time he came to Willa's door he was sweating beneath his waistcoat and panting for breath.

Aware of his own appearance, he took a long minute to level his racing heart and regulate his breathing. Then he knocked gently.

His heart seemed to stop beating entirely as he waited for a reply, as if even that organ was aware of the silence needed to hear Willa's voice through the closed door.

But no reply came…

Frowning, Leo knocked again, louder this time, and when Willa still didn't answer, he reached out and turned the knob—only to be met with cold resistance.

The reality of the situation dawned on him suddenly and with some alarm; he felt much like a prisoner who, after awaiting the gallows, finally had the hangman's rope in sight and was only then beginning to see that there was no redemption forthcoming. Willa had locked him out and, perhaps worse, she would not even respond to him.

In a daze, thinking that perhaps she had locked the door to take a bath—people bathed at midday all the time!—or use the commode, he entered his own bedroom and walked, like a battle-dazed soldier, to the door that joined their two bedchambers. He raised his hand slowly and placed it on the doorknob, deliberately ignoring the memories of all the times he'd hurried home and come through this very door to find her waiting for him. After one deep breath, he gripped the cold brass knob and turned it, his hand cinching helplessly around the hardware when he met the same resistance.

Wilhemina had locked him out.

For one heartbeat, he considered kicking the door in and confronting her anyway. He even took a step back to give himself the leverage to do just that. But then he thought of Willa, thought of how hurt and afraid and confused she must have been to brave the Wolfes, and the fight drained from him, leaving him unsure of…well, *everything.*

And his energy simply left him. Leo rested his forehead against the door for a long moment. Much like Willa, Leo, despite his confident appearance, had not come far enough from the neglected boy he had been to understand that he did not have to be perfect—the perfect friend, perfect Viscount, perfect husband—and that real love transcended such things as lover's spats all the time.

So, unsure of himself, but knowing that he would give anything for his wife to feel safe, even if that was a locked door between them, he turned around.

And he left.

Chapter Seventeen

Willa watched numbly as her trunk was carried down the stairs by two young footmen. Although she and Leo had spoken and politely dined in each other's company since the Shadwell incident, it had been so different, so foreign to both of them that neither of them had lingered long. Leo had not visited her room. He had not even touched her and Willa was too unsure of herself—and him—to know what to do or how to move past the impasse her husband seemed intent on enforcing.

She wished she could go back in time, just to the point where she'd panicked and decided to visit Camilla Pierce. Because while Leo seemed to have moved past her ill-advised foray to Shadwell, mentioning it only once to inform her that the last of Windhurst's debt had been paid off to the Wolfe brothers, Willa understood that it was her decision to go to them in the first place that had ruined everything.

Leo stood beside her in complete silence now, his handsome face calm and devoid of all emotion.

'Do you promise you will come in two weeks?' she asked suddenly, overcome with panic. Where was the man she had married? There was no glint of humour in his expression, no smile tugging at his lips.

'Willa...' Leo paused. He seemed to take a long moment,

perhaps to think over how to let her down gently. He cleared his throat and straightened his spine. 'I promise,' he said eventually, but the words lacked conviction.

He sounded so unfeeling that Willa couldn't help but nod and feign a smile. But the truth was that she didn't particularly want to go to Hampshire. Or, rather, she *did*, but not without Leo. She didn't want to leave him alone in London and, although the thought left her reeling with guilt, she knew it was partially because she didn't trust him. And *that* seemed to be where their problems began and ended.

'That's the last of it, my lord,' Gordon informed them. 'At your leisure, my lady.'

'Thank you, Gordy.' Willa stepped forward to leave, but Leo gently grasped her elbow. Even that small touch sent fissures of awareness travelling up her spine. Willa froze, blinking back self-pitying tears as she turned to look up into her husband's face.

'I'm going to miss you, Willa.' His colour heightened perceptibly. He opened his mouth again as if he wanted to say more, but then seemed to think better of it. 'Write to me?' he asked. 'Let me know how you are.'

'I will.' Willa steeled her nerves and, quickly, before she could second-guess the impulse, plastered herself against him in a spontaneous hug. 'I'll miss you, too,' she whispered and took a deep inhale of his familiar scent to try to calm herself.

Leo paused for only the briefest moment before his arms wrapped around her tightly, as if he could not bear to let her go. He kissed her forehead gently and the small gesture seemed to crack through some of the tension that had separated them for the last few days.

They both sighed deeply and relaxed into the embrace. 'Willa…'

Hearing the new desperation in his voice, she pried herself away for long enough to meet his eyes. 'Yes?'

He opened his mouth, to say what she had no idea. And then just as quickly snapped it shut.

'Leo?'

He gently stepped back, out of her arms, leaving her cold and alone. Bereft. 'I'll see you soon.'

Disappointment swamped her. Though tears burned her eyes, she refused to let them fall. 'Yes.'

Before she walked out the door, he passed her a small jewellery box and a letter. 'Open these when you get to the Heather estate.'

'Not now?'

'No.'

She frowned quizzically, confused by his odd behaviour, but tucked the box and the letter into her small, crocheted wrist bag for later. 'Goodbye, my lord,' she managed hoarsely.

'See you soon.'

Willa forced her feet to move in the direction of the carriage and, even though each step felt weighted and strangely off balance, she did not stop until she was seated next to Mary. Peggy sat opposite them. Gordon sat out on the box seat with the driver.

Then they were off.

There were several ways to travel the seventy-odd miles from London to the Heather estate in Hampshire. Although the London and Southwestern Railway would have been the fastest, Willa had been too anxious to brave the chaos of trying to get everyone and their belongings to the Nine Elms Railway Station in Battersea and had promptly declined Leo's offer to book first-class tickets.

The journey would have taken between eight and nine

hours by a public coach, but, with Leo's own carriage and horses, a pair of beautiful Cleveland Bays, they planned to go slow and steady over two days instead, stopping at a coaching inn at approximately halfway to let the horses rest overnight.

Almost four hours into the drive, Mary and Peggy both rested, their eyes closed as they dozed away. Though Willa had feigned sleep initially, not wanting to talk to the other women when her mood was so foul, she found that her mind was too distraught for rest, her entire body too anxious, too fidgety to relax.

She constantly repositioned herself on the cushioned seat, first putting her ankles together beneath her knees, then stretching her legs out in an unladylike manner. But it didn't matter how she sat, she could not get comfortable. Her stomach ached. Her legs felt numb. And, perhaps worst of all, she had a splitting headache that soured her mood further.

The streets of London had long faded to be replaced by ever-increasing greenery, but Willa couldn't bear to look out, too aware that the further into the beautiful country they travelled, the further from Leo she went. And not just geographically; it felt as if, with each mile travelled, she lost her connection with him just a little more. Angry with him for insisting she visit Isabelle, irritated with herself for agreeing to go and terrified of the repercussions of their separation in general, Willa could do nothing except restlessly shuffle in her seat and mull.

By the time they pulled up to the small coaching inn, aptly named Halfway House, she was too afraid to even talk to either of her companions in case she snapped and said something terrible that she would later regret. Instead, she organised rooms and asked for a meal to be sent up to her, then promptly excused herself, begging the need for sleep though it was only six o'clock in the evening.

Her room was small and comfortable, and although it lacked any fuss or frills, Willa did not care as long as the bed was clean. She placed her wrist bag down on a nearby table, the small clunk it made when it hit the surface reminding her of the jewellery box and letter from Leo.

She hesitated for only a moment, conscious that he had asked her to wait until she reached Hampshire to open it—then pointedly did what she wanted anyway. Willa, who had never understood the need for patience—or virtue—couldn't wait an entire day now that her curiosity had been excited.

She tugged open the drawstring bag and removed the box first. It was a typical black, velvet box with a gold Muller & Son jeweller's stamp on the front. She took a deep, steadying breath and opened it to reveal a glinting golden brooch in the shape of a swan.

The bird's neck was elegantly curled, its engraved wings tucked neatly over its back as if it were swimming calmly on a lake. The gold had been shaped and moulded so that each feather seemed displayed in detail. The swan's eye, a single, sparkling diamond, glinted up at her as if with genuine life.

The swan was undoubtedly beautiful, but Willa was still perplexed as to why Leo had given it to her. Unable to resist, she unfolded his letter, her pulse pattering excitedly in her throat the moment she saw his familiar handwriting.

She read it slowly, her heart caught between breaking and healing with each word that he wrote.

Dearest Willa,

By the time you read this you will be tucked safely away in Hampshire with Isabelle and Matthew, far from the innumerable dangers of London—or at least the innumerable dangers of Willa in London.

My wild girl, if you only knew how my heart stopped the moment I heard your voice outside that Shadwell house. If I loved you less, Wilhemina, I might have reacted better. But to see you there, as it were, to know that you were in danger and that there was nothing I could do to extricate you from the situation...

Sweetheart, I could live my entire life without ever being that afraid again. If something were to happen to you, my love, what would be the point of anything? My every heartbeat is for you. I feel as if I have some terrible affliction, for which you are both the reason and the cure.

Even knowing that you need distance from me, I hate every second that we are apart, and thirteen days is an eternity when you are counting in seconds. And still I want you to use this time, Willa.

Think about what you want your future to look like. Think about what you want to do and who you want to be, and as soon as you know we can work on making them real. Life is long, my love. We have thousands of days to discover whatever will make you happy—as happy as I am just knowing that you are my wife.

I won't carry on like a milksop, babbling on about the many ways I am going to miss you. Instead, I will leave you with a symbol of my love.

Knowing you—and I rather think I do—you opened the box first and have already seen the swan and wondered what in God's name I am gifting you a gold avian for...

The swan is not, as you may imagine, in deference to our monarch or country—though if anyone asks, and you are embarrassed by the truth, I would be amenable to you using that excuse. The real reason I asked the jeweller to make a swan is because a naturalist friend of mine once told me that swans are famed for their lifelong mating habits, often forming partnerships before they even reach maturity.

This conversation happened soon after you married Windhurst and all I remember thinking was that if a blasted bird could know its true mate, then so could I.

The next part you may not think so romantic... On the night that we went to see Windhurst's body, I took his wedding ring from his finger once you had left the room. Forgive me, but I had the jeweller melt it into this brooch. Before you hurl it into a Hampshire lake—and, believe me, I understand the sentiment—hear my reasoning: your marriage to Windhurst happened and, though I hate myself for it still, there is nothing either of us can do to change the past. It is a part of you, my love. And it is a part of me, although less so.

But in the scope of our long life together, your marriage to Windhurst will be but a drop in the pond, an experience that will slowly, over time, become diluted by the many happy memories we will make, until one day, when you look back, all you will see is the beautiful whole.

I didn't want a necklace to chain you with, my love, but a brooch that you could pin or remove on your own whenever you need to be reminded that I always knew we were destined.

I am counting the seconds to seeing you, Wilhemina, Lady Pemberton.

For ever your mate,

Leo

Willa placed the letter back on the table with a trembling hand as soon as the first tear fell, smudging Leo's signature. That he would tell her he loved her after sending her away! She had half a mind to order a horse and return to London immediately.

And, still, for some reason that she could not fully explain even to herself, Willa understood that she must heed his advice. She needed to take the time apart, two short weeks out of a lifetime, to think about the things that she had not had a chance to ponder since Windhurst had died and she had married Leo. Things such as who she was and who she wanted to become, things such as how she felt about her husband and what she wanted their marriage to look like, though, she supposed, at some point she would just have to tell him the truth: that she was hopelessly in love with him, too—and terrified of it.

Exhausted from the events of the past three days, the journey, and, yes, the letter, Willa picked up the brooch and collapsed on the bed without bothering to remove her dress. She curled up, trying not to miss the feel of Leo's big, warm body at her back, and gently unclasped the brooch pin. She fastened it on to her dress and fell asleep in minutes, her tears drying on her cheeks, her hand still pressed against the brooch, and no thoughts of Windhurst or his ring even entering her mind.

Chapter Eighteen

On her second day in Hampshire, Wilhemina finally managed to sneak away from her well-meaning friends and the entire Blake family to reply to Leo's letter. Although Matthew's family were well intentioned, plying her with love and attention, their kindness was all rather overwhelming to Wilhemina. She had mostly been left to her own devices for years, only interspersed by brief visits with Isabelle and Mary at her own convenience. So, the Blakes, with their unhindered comings and goings and chatty way of communicating with each other, were a rather overwhelming novelty.

She sat down at Matthew's large desk in the study for a full five minutes as she thought about what to say. Whereas Leo seemed to have no problem with words of love and affection, Willa felt as if she might choke on them every time they started crawling up her throat.

Despite being quite madly in love with her husband, she had no idea how to tell him, let alone broach the subject, whereas Leo had *showed* his love with his every word.

'You look as though you are contemplating something unpleasant.'

She looked up and, seeing Matthew standing in the doorway, smiled. 'I apologise for invading your space, my lord.

I was trying to write a letter to Leo.' Overcome with helplessness, she whispered, 'Only I have no idea what to say.'

To her complete mortification, Matthew heard her. He hovered for a second before stepping fully into the room. 'I find that it's easier to write the truth than to speak it.' He came into the study and pointed his hat at a nearby chair. 'May I?'

'Of course. It is your house, after all.'

He sat down on the edge of the seat as if he did not plan on staying long. 'Do you know,' he said after a moment, 'when I first started writing to Isabelle, every time I would sit down, I was overcome by this urgency…this madness. I wanted to know everything—everything about her, everything about the daughter I had not known I'd left her with. But we were strangers still and half of what I wrote turned out to be entirely inappropriate.'

'It seemed to work out well for you,' she observed, thinking about all the ways in which Matthew and Isabelle were compatible.

Matthew shook his head. 'I didn't send most of the letters.' He turned his hat in his hands and looked down at the carpet, smiling at his own memories. 'I would write them and then leave them for several hours before going back to reread them.' He leaned forward conspiratorially. 'At which point I would rewrite them—*heavily.* Keeping only what I knew wouldn't scare her.

'It became a journaling exercise, of sorts. Because even though I never sent most of what I wanted to say to her, I knew in my heart and committed to paper my true feelings.' His dark eyes settled on her face, his gaze intense, as if he could see her innermost thoughts. 'And now, when I'm struggling with an important decision, whether it's concerning business or family, I still write every thought down, leave it for a period, then go back to it once I've had time to compose myself.'

'Are you advising me to do the same?'

'What harm could it do?' he asked gently. 'Nobody has to see it except you.'

'Leo is so good with words,' she countered. 'Anything I say will sound like drivel in comparison.'

'Leo is not better with words than us. He's better with emotions than us. But, Willa…' Matthew hesitated as if unsure of the confidence he was imparting. But one look at Willa's face seemed to strengthen his resolve.

'Leo… He has his fears, too. He is terrified of failing—at anything. And once he has made a friend—or, as it were, found a wife—he would do anything to protect them, even if it involved hurting himself. He is terrified of being abandoned, so he thinks he must do everything within his power to become invaluable to a person.'

'I had not thought of that,' Willa admitted and it was rather humbling to realise that there were still things that she did not know about the man she loved. Matthew's words also made her think that perhaps all the things Leo had done for her—riding in Hyde Park, fencing in breeches, and dancing every dance with her—he had done to please her despite how difficult they must have been for him. Before their marriage, Leo had been society's golden boy, the most-favoured bachelor. Yet, he had willingly cast all of that away to make her happy, to complete her scandalous list and to let her live without the typical bounds of marriage.

Matthew was quiet for a long moment. 'You know, most people raised in his circumstances would be exceptionally lonely and selfish. But by some stroke of luck, his parents' abandonment made him very good at recognising true attachments and holding on to them—if a little too tightly.

To my knowledge, he had never lost a friendship until he married you and severed ties with your brothers—and even then, and despite how difficult it was for him, he did it because it was what you needed.'

Willa raised her fingertips to trace the gold swan pinned to her dress. Matthew was right, of course.

'Whatever you do say, Willa, Leo will be glad to have heard from you.' He smiled kindly. 'I've known Leo twenty-odd years and I've never seen him so happy. To be completely honest, I can't believe I didn't see how he felt about you before…'

'Nobody did,' Willa affirmed. 'He wanted to protect me, to avoid putting me in a situation that might make my life with Windhurst more difficult.'

He started for the door, only stopping when Willa asked, 'Do you think it lasts?'

'Do I think what lasts?'

'This—' she placed her hand over her rapidly ticking heart '—panicked love.'

'No.'

Willa's heart sank.

'The fever calms,' Matthew said with a soft smile. 'Thank God—otherwise we'd all be quite useless. But the love grows deeper and takes on new meaning. Like a tree sapling,' he observed. 'With each year, it grows bigger and stronger, the roots sink deeper, and the tree becomes more equipped to withstand hardships and shade other people.' Matthew's smile grew into a devilish grin. 'Try not to overthink it so much, Willa. Men never do, you know, and as far as I can tell we have a much easier time because of it.'

Willa laughed as he left the study, closing the door behind him. She contemplated the blank sheet of paper in front of her. If she took Matthew's advice, what would her letter say? How would it differ from any other letter she might have sent her husband?

Deciding that she had absolutely nothing to lose, she began writing, committing her darkest fears and deepest fantasies to paper, knowing that she would be the only person to ever read them.

Chapter Nineteen

Wilhemina never did send the letter to Leo. Though she had admitted things in text that she had not realised before, or, perhaps, simply been too afraid to admit to herself, she knew that she wanted to wait to speak to her husband in person when she told him everything.

Because Matthew was right. Although she had not seen it before, and although she had loved that Leo tried so hard, with distance, she was able to see how desperate he had been to please her. And it did not comfort her. It made her feel ashamed. Because while he had been fighting for her love and approval, subjecting himself to ridicule and scandal over and over again, she had been too steeped in his attention to notice that, perhaps, he needed more from her, too. More reassurance and communication. Perhaps, even some boundaries—for both of them.

Willa, who had been out alone, walking the Heather estate, raised one hand in a small wave as she approached her friends. Isabelle and Mary were sitting together on the bench in the rose garden.

'How was your walk?' Mary enquired as she drew near.

'Invigorating.' Willa lowered down to the bench with a sigh, relieved to be off her feet. She had been feeling lethargic and irritable for days, and though she was too afraid to hope, she had been plagued with a sore, swollen stomach, a feeling that she remembered well as a precursor to her monthly courses.

Mary's eyes narrowed on Willa's face. Her nose crinkled. 'Are you all right, Willa? You look quite pale.'

'I think…' She trailed off, embarrassed to be discussing such an inappropriate subject. Her feminine problems were something she had only ever talked about in any detail to her doctor and even that had been humiliating.

'What is it?' Isabelle asked, looking worried. She took Willa's hand in her own. Her eyes rounded suddenly, filling with hesitant joy. 'Are you…with child?'

Mary gasped and turned to stare at Willa, waiting for her to answer the question.

'No. Definitely not. I… I can't. What I mean is… My courses stopped during my marriage to Windhurst.'

To her horror, Isabelle's eyes instantly filled with tears and the words, 'Oh, I'm so sorry I asked', slipped from between her friend's lips.

'It's all right,' Willa hurriedly assured her, knowing that any prolonged sadness from her friends would start to crumble her own defences. Children of her own were something she had trained herself not to think about. 'Leo knew before the wedding,' she said instead. 'He said he would rather me without an heir than any other woman with one.'

'Oh.' Isabelle sighed. 'That's so romantic.'

'Like something out of a novel,' Mary agreed, blinking rapidly.

'Only…' Willa wondered if she was going to sound crazy, but one look at her friends' intrigued faces told her she couldn't back out of her confession now. 'I've felt… *aware* the past few days. Do you know what I mean? How even when you aren't counting the days, you know in the back of your mind that your courses are coming and make sure to prepare?'

'Yes,' Mary replied with no hesitation. 'I often find myself tucking extra rags in my pockets even before I've checked my calendar.'

Isabelle's big, dark eyes turned back to Willa. 'You think they're returning?'

'I hope so. Either that or there is something terribly wrong with me.' Lowering her voice, she added, 'My stomach is as hard as a melon. And everything aches.'

Her two friends nodded knowingly and Willa, needing to focus on something other than her own meagre hope, said, 'Izzy, I'm surprised you are not pregnant yet.'

Isabelle's blushed. 'I told Matthew I wanted to wait a year or so, until Seraphina is a little older. The thought of being pregnant again is overwhelming—and this time I'd have a small child in tow, too.'

Willa and Mary both grinned, remembering how short-tempered and anxious Isabelle had been throughout her confinement with Seraphina. Isabelle, who was small and agile and loved to ride and go for long walks, had felt constantly constrained by her 'waddling' as she'd called it. She'd been uncomfortable and unhappy throughout her pregnancy as a result. 'I think it'll be different this time,' Willa commented. 'Now that you have Matthew.'

'One can only hope,' Isabelle replied, sounding unconvinced. 'But this time, Mary, I'll have Matthew attend my labour.'

Mary laughed aloud. 'Poor Dr Taylor was torn between helping Isabelle deliver Seraphina and making sure that I didn't faint and fall off my chair.'

Isabelle reached out and took Mary's hand, linking all

three of them. 'But you were there. And you insisted on staying even when Dr Taylor told you to leave.'

'And I was the first person to hold Seraphina,' Mary added. 'Which *almost* made it worthwhile.'

Isabelle squeezed their hands. 'None of us has had a particularly easy time of it, have we?'

'No.' Willa thought back to Isabelle's offer to support her if she ran away from Windhurst. She thought of Mary's honest, unflagging friendship. 'But we've always had each other, which counts for something.'

'Everything,' Mary corrected. 'Having true friends counts for everything.'

And Willa and Isabelle nodded their agreement.

Chapter Twenty

By the time supper rolled around that evening, Willa was in too much pain to go down. She sent her excuses, knowing that there was no chance she could sit through one of the Blakes' long meals in her current condition. Her stomach was swollen, sensitive and filled with a constant, deep throbbing. Her back ached. Her breasts hurt. And to make matters worse, no amount of tossing or turning improved her situation, so she had taken to lying with a pillow wedged beneath her stomach in the hope that the pressure would relieve some of the pain.

'Is there anything I can do, milady?' Peggy asked. The maid hovered by the foot of the bed, her eyes filled with concern.

'No. Thank you, Peggy. I'm afraid it's just a waiting game.' She sighed deeply and closed her eyes against the sting of tears, too overwhelmed to talk, too afraid to hope.

'I'll ask the housekeeper if there's any laudanum.'

Wilhemina nodded, but did not reply as the maid left the room. She wished that Leo was there. Even though it would probably be humiliating to be coddled by him in her current condition, she would have preferred it to anything else. He had a way of holding her that made her feel sheltered from the world. And just then, while she was in pain and suffering from equal parts anxiety and hope, she wished she had fought him, she wished she had told him she would stay in London with him until they removed to the Vickery estate together.

She mulled over this until a gentle knock on the door admitted Isabelle, who poked her head in. 'Willa? Peggy said you're in need of some laudanum?'

Willa was helpless against the tears that spilled down her cheeks. 'I don't know what's wrong. It's never been like this before…'

'Have your courses come?'

Willa shook her head and then blotted her damp brow on a pillow. She wasn't typically a dramatic woman, but for some reason she felt completely overwhelmed—and not only with pain. It was too much—all of it. She couldn't think about what was happening or what it might mean for the future.

She couldn't face it at all. She wanted to go home. She wanted to tell Leo she was sorry for not listening to him. She wanted to tell him that she had only done it because she loved him and couldn't stand the thought of being a burden to him any more. She wanted him. She *needed* him.

Isabelle came to the side of the bed and placed one cool palm on Willa's face. 'You're quite feverish,' she observed, her brow pinched in concern. 'I'm going to send for the doctor.'

'No.' Willa managed to lever on to her elbows for long enough to glare at Isabelle. 'I don't need a *doctor*, Izzy. I…' To her absolute horror, her voice wavered. 'I need Leo,' she whispered. She braced against a wave of pain, lowering her head down for a moment as she fought it. 'Please write to him.' Swallowing her pride, she managed to say, 'Just tell him I need him…'

'All right. I'll send for him right away.'

The promise immediately spread relief through Willa and a strange sob sigh left her lips.

'But I'm sending for the doctor anyway,' Isabelle stated in a tone that broached no argument. 'This is not normal, Wilhemina.'

Even if she thought she could have changed Isabelle's mind, Willa didn't argue. She didn't have the energy. She propped herself up for long enough to swallow the laudanum Isabelle insisted she take, then collapsed back on to her stomach to wait for it to take effect.

She felt the opium spreading slowly through her like a heavy blanket of morning fog. It soothed her raw nerves, a balm over the worst of the pain and confusion, until only twenty minutes later she fell into a deep, troubled sleep.

Leo's heart stopped beating for one perfect moment when he opened a letter from Matthew that read:

Leo,
Willa is not well. Do not panic. The doctor says she will be fine; however, she has asked for you.
Matthew

Leo, who had not heard from Willa in the week she had been gone, did not pause to ponder what on earth could have befallen his wife in Hampshire, or why Matthew would be so deliberately vague when writing about something as serious as Willa's ill health. He pushed back from his desk and hurried to the door, calling for Wiggs as he started up the stairs to his bedroom.

'My lord?' Wiggs entered Leo's bedroom moments after

him, his face mapped with confusion as he watched Leo's harried movements.

Leo rapidly changed into a pair of riding breeches and secured them with braces, refusing his valet's assistance in his haste. He didn't bother with a waistcoat or cravat, knowing that both would only prove meddlesome in the fast-paced ride. He threw on a linen shirt, a loosely tailored riding jacket and boots. 'Lady Pemberton has taken ill,' he hurriedly explained. 'Have George saddle two horses—one for me and one for him.'

Wiggs's face fell at the news and Leo did not doubt that the man was genuinely concerned for his wife. 'Yes, my lord.'

'I'm leaving you to pack my things and follow, Wiggs. I can't delay.' Even the thought of the mad race ahead and the hours in the saddle were almost too much for Leo, who suddenly felt as if the world had come to a jarring halt. Willa was sick…

'Will you return?'

'No. I'll write to Mrs Smith from Hampshire with instructions to close up the house as soon as I've assessed the situation.'

The valet nodded and, seeming to understand that Leo had no further instructions, hurried from the room, his footsteps echoing as he bounded down the stairs.

Leo took a moment to compose himself, knowing that if he rushed, he would unnecessarily endanger himself and George. While they were both confident horsemen, hours riding at pace were no laughing matter. His mind raced as he calculated where he would have to stop to change horses and how soon he could be with Willa. Six hours at the soonest, seven at the latest.

It didn't seem soon enough—not even close. And, still,

Leo didn't pause to pack a single item. He ran down the stairs ten minutes later to find the horses already saddled and waiting, George holding both by the reins. 'Have Wiggs pack anything you need with my things, George,' he instructed as he mounted his leggy thoroughbred mare, Gypsy.

George patted a small bundle secured to the back of his horse's saddle. 'I have what I need, milord,' he replied and climbed into the saddle.

They were off in minutes, neither one of them feeling the need to try to talk over the sound of ponding hooves and the occasional shout to slow down as they fought their way through the London streets, heading south towards Hampshire, towards Willa.

His wife was fierce and courageous and stubbornly independent, and he didn't dare think about what had scared her enough to need him, especially after how they'd left things between them. So, he tried not to think of it at all. He focused on the stretching road ahead and keeping to his saddle as they raced the horses at a bruising pace.

They came to the first stop only three hours later, both horses lathered in sweat and breathing fast with exertion. Leo left George with some money to stay overnight and care for the horses. The footman would follow with their horses to the Heather estate the next day, while Leo travelled ahead on a rented horse that would have to be returned within the week.

Leo rode the second stretch without stopping once, maintaining a pace that the leggy mixed breed handled well. By the time he rode down the long, shaded lane to the Earl of Heather's country home, he was shaking with fatigue, his entire body covered in so much sweat and dust that he knew he must look a fright.

Any other time, Leo would have dawdled and admired the familiar Queen Anne–style home with its tree-lined lane, impressive stone façade, verdant grounds and man-made ponds. But today, he didn't care. He didn't even see his surroundings. His only thought was getting to Willa, his vision narrowed on the rapidly approaching door.

He dismounted by the front stairs and took two stumbling steps forward as his legs resisted his efforts after six and a half hours in the saddle.

The young groom who ran out to take the horse stared at Leo with alarm, his eyes widening as he took in Leo's dishevelled state and bent-over form. 'You all right, milord?' the boy asked hesitantly.

Leo forcibly straightened and took a moment to stretch out his cramping legs before replying, 'Yes, thank you.'

The boy looked sceptical. He hovered as if he wasn't quite sure if Leo was going to keel over and die. It was only when Matthew himself opened the door that the boy relaxed enough to lead the horse away, only pausing once to look back at the mad Lord.

'Good God, man,' Matthew exclaimed, his eyes raking over Leo in obvious surprise. 'I didn't expect you for at least two more days. I thought I might be imagining it when I saw you galloping down the drive…'

Leo winced as he climbed the two short stairs to the front door. 'You wrote a letter telling me that my wife was ill, Ashworth. And you did not say what is wrong with her or how serious it is. What was I supposed to do?' he demanded. 'What would *you* have done?'

Matthew's dark eyes softened considerably. 'I'm sorry. I should have made it clearer that there was no need for such haste.' He shook his head, his lips curving into a knowing grin. 'Why don't you go inside and bathe? You look a little worse for wear, my friend.'

'Not until I see my wife,' Leo argued, his heart pounding with fresh panic. 'What is wrong with her?'

Matthew dipped his head. 'It's best you talk to Willa. Come. I'll show you where she's staying.'

He climbed the steps at Matthew's side, his throat thick with emotion. With each inch closer to Willa, he felt oddly more centred but also more anxious, as if he knew his place in the world, but worried that she might not. He wasn't sure what he'd do if he couldn't touch her, couldn't hold her after a week apart.

'Relax. She'll be happy to see you.'

Leo smiled mockingly. 'It's been the longest damn eight days of my life, Ashworth.'

Matthew laughed quietly. 'It is strange, is it not? How quickly the scope of a man's existence can be condensed.'

He raked both hands through his hair, sending a cloud of dust dancing through the air. 'I feel mad.' He rubbed his sore chest. 'Like I should be committed to an asylum without delay.'

Matthew placed his hand on Leo's shoulder as they reached a closed bedroom door. 'You are both going to be just fine, you know.'

'How can you be so sure of that?' Leo demanded, feeling sick with panic and relief and fatigue.

'Because you both love the other enough to keep trying. Leo, you rode to Hampshire in—what?—*seven hours*? And Willa… She's doing fine. She didn't need you here—she *wanted* you here. That's not the behaviour of two people who aren't aware of what they have and wouldn't fight for it.' As if he could sense how close to the edge Leo was,

Matthew gave Leo's shoulder a quick squeeze. 'Just take it one day at a time.'

Matthew stepped forward and opened the door himself. He didn't follow Leo inside, but closed the door behind him. The soft click pulled Isabelle, Mary and Willa's attention to him. But while his wife's friends gawked at his appearance, Leo only had eyes for Willa.

She was sitting up in bed, propped against a mountain of pillows. She was deathly pale, her eyes eerily large, dark and unfocused, and when she spoke his name, 'Leo', it rasped from between her lips.

'Don't panic,' Isabelle said quickly and pushed to a stand. 'She's had some laudanum, so she's slightly…well, foxed.'

As if to prove Isabelle's point, Willa collapsed into a fit of giggles, which almost made Leo smile—until her giggles turned to deep, heaving sobs.

While Leo stopped advancing, filled with horror at the sight of Willa breaking down, Isabelle only smiled and patted his arm as she and Mary moved to exit the room. 'She's had a difficult time,' she whispered. 'I think the opium has made her a little more vulnerable.'

Mary's eyes were lit with mischief. 'We'll have some water sent up for a bath.'

'And some food and wine,' Isabelle added. 'Don't worry about seeing the family tonight. We'll visit with you both in the morning.' And with that, she closed the door, leaving him alone with his wife after eight days—or, as it were, approximately seven hundred and nine thousand seconds.

Chapter Twenty-One

Willa swiped at her eyes, embarrassed by her inability to control her emotions. She was not, or at least not typically, so prone to feminine hysterics. 'It's the laudanum,' she said, trying to explain though her tongue felt thick and clumsy. 'It's making me emotional.' Even as she spoke, she was aware of the numbness spreading through her, masking the worst of the pain. Everything except her heart—which beat furiously—seemed slightly out of reach, as if she was aware that she had arms and legs and toes, but that it had become suddenly exhausting to try find them, let alone *use* them.

She watched Leo as he approached the bed cautiously. He was dressed casually, wearing no waistcoat and cravat, the hem of his long coat falling to his calves. He was covered in dust from head to foot, so she knew that he had come straight to her upon his arrival.

He didn't seem to notice or care that he looked as though he'd survived a minor skirmish. 'Willa,' he murmured hoarsely and reached for her. Whether he saw the state of his own hands or simply thought better of it, he drew back without touching her at the last moment. Instead, he stood at the side of her bed, his blue eyes running over her repeatedly as if he needed to confirm that she was all in one piece. 'What's the matter, love?'

'I'm fine,' she replied hurriedly. 'It's...' She closed her eyes, humiliated that he'd obviously left London the moment he received her letter from Matthew. 'It's a...feminine complaint.'

He nodded once, very slowly, but his eyes darkened with confusion and he still did not touch her.

Willa's own medicated exhaustion made it difficult to focus. She closed her eyes and relaxed against the pillows at her back, relieved to finally have him back. Still, she was aware that she didn't want him to go. She wanted him to stay—and she would need to be the one to say it. 'Please don't leave,' she said, forcing her eyes back to his. 'Stay.'

Leo ran one large palm through his hair. 'I'm not going anywhere, my love. I'm here.'

'You must think I'm awfully silly,' she observed drowsily. 'I don't have an excuse, I just...' She swallowed down a self-pitying sob. 'I wanted you to hold me.'

He cursed under his breath and, although he stepped closer, he still didn't touch her. 'I need to bathe first, Willa. I'm covered in dirt.' But he hovered, his thighs pressed firmly against the bed as if he wanted to be as close as possible while actively preventing himself from reaching for her.

'No, you don't,' she insisted. She forced her eyes open to look at him, and, noting that he had not moved, chose to go to him instead. She fumbled with the bed linens, pushing them back with clumsy, heavy hands.

'Willa—'

She didn't listen. She freed herself from the cosy confines and crawled awkwardly across the bed to get to him, only pausing when her knee got stuck in her chemise and it threatened to choke her. When she reached him, she plastered herself against him, wrapped her arms around his waist, laid her head on his dirt-covered chest and used his stoic strength to steady herself against the roll of light-headedness that passed through her.

'You're going to get yourself dirty,' he said quietly, but his arms wrapped around her anyway.

'I don't care,' Willa replied on a tired exhale, one that she immediately followed with a deep breath that filled her lungs with the scent of him. His familiar smell entered her blood stream like the opium had, heavy and calming, centring her world once again. 'I don't care,' she repeated.

He held her tightly, as if he could not bear for there to be even an inch of space between them, and buried his face in her hair, inhaling deeply.

Willa absorbed the feel of him, the smell of him, after too long apart. In some dark corner of her mind, she understood that she should stop talking, that the laudanum had made her weepy and sentimental, but she couldn't hold back now that he was there with her. 'I don't like being away from you,' she whispered, her tears starting again. 'I don't feel as though I can be myself when you're not with me.' She shook her head against his chest, knowing that she wasn't making much sense even as an adequate explanation eluded her.

Leo's heavy hand started painting small circles on her back. 'I'm not going anywhere, Willa. The only way I could let you go was if you wanted to leave me.' A tremor rolled through his body and into hers as he spoke. 'And even then, it would take every power I had to stop myself from going after you.

'My love…' he pulled back slightly and used one hand to gently grip her long braid and tilt her head back '…I want to be where you are—always. I want to fall asleep beside you and wake up next to you in the morning. I want to hold you when you're sad and laugh with you when you're happy. I want to be the only person who's allowed to fight with you. I want everything you're prepared to give me.'

His thumb brushed her cheekbone, sending a languid shiver through her. 'I love you, Willa. I don't know how to make you believe me, but I'm committed to spend my entire life trying.'

A deep sob worked its way free from her. The painful sound sawed through the room, surprising them both. Willa wanted to give the words back to him. She wanted him to know how much she loved him too. Only, they wouldn't come. Humiliated, frustrated, and exhausted, she tried to explain, 'I'm s-sorry,' she managed to stammer. 'I— It—'

'It's the laudanum,' he concluded softly for her, his arms tightening around her. 'It's all right, love. Relax.'

Willa did not argue when he picked her up off the bed and carried her to the nearby chair. Although she was vaguely aware of the sound of servants coming and going, she did not open her eyes to confirm it. She lay in Leo's arms as he brushed her hair back from her face and whispered words of love in her ear, only for her to hear.

'Leo...' she croaked after a long moment. Though she was losing the battle against the laudanum, which pulled her under even as she spoke, she wanted to explain why she was so sad and confused and—terrifyingly—hopeful.

'What is it?'

'When they stopped...my courses...' Willa released a hiccupping sob. Leo's arms tightened around her in silent support, giving her the ability to continue. 'He was so angry. He...'

How did she even begin to describe how Windhurst had

made her feel? How did she tell Leo the things he'd said to her—that she was useless to him, that her father must have known and used her sizeable dowry to coerce him—without falling apart? Leo wouldn't understand… Because he loved her. But for most other men, especially men of Windhurst's age, marriage to a woman thirty years younger was supposed to guarantee one thing: healthy children, at least one of whom would be a boy, an heir.

'He hurt you,' Leo encouraged quietly.

'He did. But I…' She trailed off as her emotions warred, unsure, through the laudanum, if she was going to laugh wildly or sob hysterically when she told him.

'Tell me, sweetheart.'

'I burned my baby things—the little blanket and clothes that I brought with me.' In her clouded state, she didn't feel the tears falling down her face or realise that she cupped one hand in front of her when she said, 'Tiny knitted shoes.' She released a hiccupping sob. 'Things that had been mine as a child… And… My mother…'

'Things your mother had given to you for your own children,' he put into words for her.

Willa could only nod.

Leo released a deep exhale, as if he needed to calm himself. 'I'm so sorry, sweetheart,' he said eventually.

Through the laudanum, she managed what she hoped was a wicked grin. 'I wish you could have seen his face… For just one moment as we stood and looked at each other as the fire blazed out of control, Windhurst… He was *terrified* of me, Leo.'

'I always knew he was, love,' Leo said simply. 'He married a young girl thinking he'd get an ignorant, malleable bride. And he got a wildling instead. A woman he was too cowed by to meet as an equal.' He rocked her slightly, lulling her as he might one day a child—*their* child. Though the thought struck Willa, she found that she still could not open her mouth and tell him. Because what if her courses *didn't* come back? She'd rather not say anything and suffer the disappointment alone.

Ignorant of her internal battle, Leo continued, 'While it's small consolation, I'm sure my nursemaids would have stored all my childhood things. Perhaps we can go through them when we get home?'

Willa sighed. 'Yes. I only… I wanted you to know,' she whispered drowsily, 'why I'm *s-so...confused.* I… I feel like my life is finally restarting and I suppose I had not realised how terrifying that could be…'

If Willa could smell him—sweat, dirt, and horse—or feel the grime covering him—and now her—she did not show it. She slept deeply in his arms, completely oblivious to the servants who'd brought hot water for the tub and food and wine and then promptly left, leaving only Peggy behind.

Willa's maid hurried about the room, making small adjustments to the food trays and laying out a clean nightgown for Willa, given that he had dirtied hers, streaking the white cotton with brown dust when she'd hugged him.

Leo looked up, surveying the bedroom for the first time since entering. It was large and comfortably furnished with a rococo mahogany bed that had gold gilt edging along the top of the headboard and base. A thick gold and red carpet, on top of which sat a small writing desk and chair, an armoire and a chest of drawers occupied the rest of the room. The plumbed bathroom adjoined.

'Peggy,' he called the maid's attention quietly, 'how much laudanum did they give my wife?' Although the drug was common enough, Willa was so slight and he worried that they might have accidentally overdosed her. Even as he spoke, Willa didn't stir, merely slept deeply.

Peggy approached, her eyes gleaming with tears when she no longer had anything to distract herself with. 'Not very much t'all, milord. Lady Wilhemina doesn't sleep well.' Peggy frowned. 'Or she never used to before—' she cleared her throat '—your marriage, milord. So, she's been up at all hours this week.' Once she got started, Peggy didn't seem able to stop. She vented her fears and frustrations to Leo with barely a breath. 'Then with the pain from her courses starting again, I think she just became overwhelmed.'

The last pieces clicked together in Leo's mind. His heart shuddered in his chest—and not from joy. It was too soon to hope. But at least now he understood why Willa had needed him, why she was so confused and afraid.

He touched her face, gently tracing over her cheek and nose with a single finger, memorising the bone structure underneath. 'She's going to be fine,' he said, trying to convince Peggy as much as himself. 'She just needs time.'

'Yes, milord.' Peggy sent him a shaky smile. 'She's already doing much better, although…' The maid caught herself. She flushed scarlet.

'You may be honest with me, Peggy. Especially when it concerns my wife.'

'You shouldn't leave her alone, milord. She doesn't like it.' Peggy wrung her hands anxiously. 'She needs to know that you'll stay even when she's feeling angry or maudlin.'

'Yes, I think I'm beginning to see that,' he said quietly.

Peggy dipped into a small curtsy and sent him a wobbly smile. 'May I wake her and help her wash and change, milord?'

'No. You may go, Peggy. I'll see to my wife.'

The maid didn't argue and the moment she left the room, Leo gently placed Willa back on the bed. He hurriedly bathed, making sure to clean all of the travel grime from his body and hair, then changed into the clean trousers and shirt Isabelle had had the foresight to send up with the food and wine.

Once he was finally clean again, he took a small porcelain bowl and the pitcher of clean water from the nearby table and gently cleaned the smudges of dirt off Willa's hands and face. He helped her change into the clean nightdress, all the while murmuring soothing nothings every time she asked him a confused question.

'Leo?' she mumbled. 'You came?'

'I'll always come for you, my love.'

And a minute later, 'What are you doing?'

'Helping you change for bed.'

And finally, 'Did they tell you?' She drew in a hiccupping sob.

Overcome by the uncertainty in her voice, all he could reply was, 'Yes.'

Willa opened her eyes and struggled to focus on his face. When she finally managed to hold his gaze, she whispered, 'What if my courses don't come back?'

Leo shook his head. 'Whatever happens, we have each other, Willa. We'll get through it.'

She seemed unsure for a moment, as if it took her a minute to make sense of his words. But then she smiled and closed her eyes, and when Leo forwent food and wine, choosing to cuddle up against his wife instead despite his hunger, she burrowed back into him, sighed deeply and mumbled, 'You know I love you, don't you?'

His heart slammed into his ribs. But, Leo, who knew that his wife was barely cognisant, merely tucked her hair behind her ear and whispered, 'I do now, my love.' He kissed beneath her ear, murmured, 'Go to sleep', and the moment that she did, her breathing deepening, he followed her into the darkness, exhausted. But smiling.

Chapter Twenty-Two

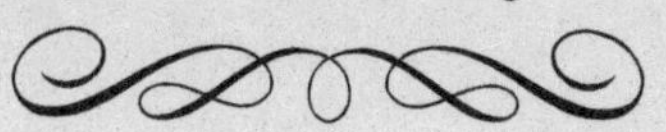

Willa awoke at dawn the next day with an unpleasantly dry mouth and the bitter taste of laudanum on her tongue. Her head throbbed, her tongue felt heavy and her stomach still ached—all of which she immediately forgot when she felt the solid warmth of her husband in her bed behind her.

After almost two months of marriage, she could not mistake his hard chest against her back or his smell enveloping her senses, nor could she resist cuddling back into his warmth and laying her own arm over his, which was roped around her midriff as if he were afraid that she would leave in the night.

As her mind cleared, she felt a deep calm come over her, one so heavy and peaceful that she could have wept from the relief of it. Leo had come for her the moment she'd asked, his prompt arrival telling her that he had not even delayed by replying with a letter or finished sorting his affairs in London.

That he had come for her when she'd needed him, no questions asked, was more proof of his love than any words he could have spoken or any physical affection he could have shown her. The immensity of it overwhelmed her. It filled her with an unfurling warmth that spread through her chest, her heart, and her mind.

She gently lifted his arm and prepared to roll over. She wanted to face him as he woke up. She wanted to watch awareness come into his eyes, wanted to see his love for her on his face when he was drowsy and unguarded. Only, the moment she tried to turn, she became aware of the wet, sticky moisture coating her upper thighs.

Her mind blanked. For a long moment she didn't move, then slowly, in shock, she reached a hand between her thighs—and touched blood. Still, she raised her fingers back into her line of sight, almost too afraid to believe it when they came back smeared red.

She exhaled a shaky breath. Tears burned her eyes. And, as if he had somehow sensed her distress even in his sleep, Leo snapped awake, his eyes popping open so suddenly that Willa startled.

His gaze settled on her face, his eyes softening when he realised where he was and who he was with. He reached out one hand to touch her face, pausing mid-air when Willa skirted back out of his reach. 'Don't,' she gasped, mortified by the situation.

Leo dropped his hand immediately and, although he tried to smile, she saw the hurt that lanced his expression before he could hide it. 'Good morning,' he whispered.

'Leo,' she managed to speak through tears of embarrassment, 'it's not what you think. I'm…' She floundered for the right words. This was hardly something she spoke about with other women, how was she supposed to broach the topic with a man? It didn't matter that Leo was her husband—some things were not done.

'What's wrong, love?' he asked quietly.

'I'm afraid I'm…rather…'

'Willa?' Leo was frowning now. He shifted, as if to move closer.

Willa shot out one hand, stopping him. 'Don't.' She groaned aloud, humiliated beyond reason. She closed her eyes so that she didn't have to look at his reaction when she said, 'I'm afraid I seem to have…bled…well, *everywhere*.'

There was a horrifically awkward silence in which Willa couldn't open her eyes, only buried her face in the pillow like a child, not a grown woman. A hot blush of embarrassment flamed through her, heating her throat and cheeks. It would be her, she lamented, that would be caught in such a situation and by Leo, the image of perfection himself.

Leo didn't say anything, but she felt him climb from the bed and breathed a sigh of relief when she realised he was leaving her in privacy. She didn't move as he walked around the room, she presumed to change. She barely breathed when he spoke to a servant at the door. And minutes later, when the room was silent, she peered out from her pillows to see if he was gone.

He was not.

Her husband stood at the door, dressed in a black, velvet robe, his blond hair glistening in beautiful contrast. His broad back was to her, his hand on the doorknob as if he was waiting for someone. 'Leo?'

He turned to look at her over his shoulder. His serious blue eyes softened. 'One minute, love.'

And, sure enough, soon after, a trio of maids, each carrying two large buckets of steaming water, entered the room and, without pausing, carried their burdens to the adjoining water closet.

Willa exhaled in relief when she realised that he had ordered her up a bath. Even though she still felt the sting of embarrassment over the situation, the knowledge that she would soon be clean was enough to balm over it.

The maids left, exiting the room as quietly and efficiently as they had arrived.

Willa levered herself up on to her elbows and waited for Leo to close the door. 'Thank you.' She couldn't meet his eyes. 'I'm sorry; I didn't know my… I mean, I didn't know they would return. The doctor seemed unsure and then—'

'Willa,' Leo cut her off gently, 'why are you apologising?'

She sat up in the bed, twisting the sheets in her hands. 'I… I'm not usually this…uncouth, I suppose. I mean, in regard to…' Unable to even speak the words, she mumbled, 'It's humiliating.'

'No, it's not.' Leo came to the bed and, before she could stop him, he threw back the white bed linens, leaving her horrifically exposed.

Her hands hurriedly lowered, trying—and failing—to cover the stark evidence of her unladylike situation against the white nightgown and bed linens. 'Leo,' she hissed, consumed with humiliation and outrage, each of which vied for the lion's share of her.

'Yes?' he replied nonchalantly and, reaching down, gripped her by one ankle and dragged her across the bed until she was closer. He lifted her easily into his arms, completely disregarding her mortifying condition.

Willa sputtered as her panic spread. 'You don't have to—' She pushed at him with both hands. 'Please, put me down—'

He silenced her with a kiss, one that was deep and long and drugging, one that Willa was helpless to protect against. His lips pressed firmly against hers. His tongue coaxed hers open and then slipped inside her mouth, the gentle pressure encouraging her to relax.

She sighed and, instead of pushing him away, roped her

arms around his neck and nestled against him, finally content after being deprived of contact with him.

Leo's arms tightened around her, lifting her higher, bringing her closer. He broke the kiss and rested his forehead against hers, his eyes closed. 'Please don't ask me to leave,' he said quietly. 'I don't want to go.' He opened his eyes to look at her, the blue depths filled with sincere longing.

She wanted him to stay, yet still Willa couldn't help but remind him, 'But... I'm...'

'Perfect.'

'No.' She rolled her eyes.

'Beautiful.'

'Leo,' she pleaded.

He smiled and, leaning close, whispered, 'Mine.'

Defeated, Willa dropped her head to his shoulder and sighed. 'Yes.' She would allow him that; there was no point in trying to deny it.

'Let me help you, Willa. Let me be the only person in the world allowed to see you like this.' He kissed her head. 'There is nothing about your body that isn't beautiful to me.' And when she still couldn't reply, he whispered, 'Please, my love. I... I don't know if I can leave you just yet.'

And it was that admission that finally swayed her. Because instead of sounding irritated or resigned, Leo sounded as if he genuinely couldn't bear to be apart from her now that they were together again. She remembered his letter, remembered the beautiful things he had said and, wanting to be as brave as he had been, as vulnerable, she nodded once.

'Yes?' Leo asked hoarsely.

'Yes,' she said, firmly this time, and he carried her into the adjoining bathroom.

It was a small room, just big enough to house a pine

chamber pot commode, a bathtub and a small table that held washcloths, soap, various oils and linen towelling. The steam from the hot water filled the room, filling it with warmth and chasing away the chill.

Leo gently released her, placing her feet on the floor. Without a word, he unbuttoned her nightdress and lifted the soiled garment over her head. He dropped it on the floor without commenting. Slowly, his easy, unembarrassed manner started to relax her.

Willa held his hand and climbed into the bath, only releasing him so that she could grip the folded lip of the tub as she lowered herself down into the scalding water. She closed her eyes and leaned back, a long moan of relief escaping her as the hot water soothed her tight, swollen stomach and washed away the blood.

She wallowed in the hot water, opening her eyes again when Leo started to gently wash her with one of the nearby rags, his movements slow and gentle as if he was enjoying her bath as much as she was. He knelt on the floor, the sleeves of his dressing gown rolled back to his elbows, his large, strong hands impossibly tender. His eyes were dark with an intensity that reached for her, flooding her with self-conscious awareness.

'Did you think I would want you less because you are bleeding?' Leo asked quietly, seeing her abashed look.

'Yes,' she replied frankly.

He laughed quietly. 'I'm sorry to disappoint you, love.'

'Is it...*done*?'

'It probably varies by couple,' he replied. 'But with you...' He shrugged. 'I want you always and irrespective of how you come to me.'

'Oh.' The word seemed inadequate to describe the heat

that sank through her bones, eradicating her embarrassment. That deep, pulsing ache started between her legs.

And with each minute that passed, each stroke of his hands over her body, the ache grew until she had to consciously fight the urge to grab his hand and lower it between her legs.

When her skin was clean and glistening pink from the heat, Leo poured some of the rose oil from the nearby table into his hands and instructed her to lie back. The moment she did, he leaned over the tub, angling his body over her so that both his hands could rub her stomach, his thumbs working in long, repeated strokes down her lower abdomen, slowly unknotting some of the tension there.

Unable to help herself, unable to brace against the pleasure his touch wrought, Willa closed her eyes on a long moan. 'Leo…'

'Do you want me to show you, Wilhemina?' He sounded pained. Desperate. As if he were undone by only the thought of touching her.

Willa opened her eyes. Leo was still bent over the tub, but his big hands on her had stilled and he was watching her face, she knew, for any sign of fear or discomfort. 'Yes,' she said firmly, leaving no room for him to doubt that she wanted him, too.

Leo released a ragged exhale. But he did not stand or remove his clothes. He did not move to help her out of the bath either. He bent back to his task, his oiled hands working over her with firm, rounding strokes, his thumbs fanning over her swollen stomach, moving lower.

Willa held her breath as those clever thumbs moved lower still, parting her, exposing her inner flesh to the warm water. 'I can't look,' she murmured, even as her body responded to his touch, that place between her thighs coating with a slickness she could feel through the water.

'Close your eyes, Willa,' Leo said, and when she did, he gently gripped her ankles and pushed her knees up so that her feet could brace against the bottom of the bath-tub. He used both hands in long soothing strokes down her inner thighs, slowly pushing her legs wider. 'Relax,' he murmured. 'Feel me.'

'It's not very easy to relax in this position—' The words died on a shocked little gasp as Leo slid one finger through her seam, parting her for the warm water even as his finger ran whisper-light over her sensitised flesh.

Willa let her head fall back even as she pressed herself more firmly into Leo's hand, asking, *begging* for more.

Leo groaned. 'Your body is so beautiful, my love.' His other hand rose to her breast, cupping her as his fingers rolled her nipple. 'Seeing you like this—ready, wet for *me*—is my every fantasy come to life.'

Unable to hold back against the sensations pummelling her, Willa began to move her hips in small thrusts. 'Please, Leo.' She was mortified to hear the plea in her tone.

Leo circled her entrance with that same finger. 'Here, love?'

'Yes.'

With a growl of pleasure, he sank into her. He stilled for a moment and, when she dared to open her eyes, she saw him with his hand between her legs, his blond head bent, jaw wired shut, eyes closed as he tried to control himself—for her.

Her heart swelled with emotion. Her body sighed, re-laxing fully.

Leo, sensing the moment she relinquished herself to him,

began to move, thrusting into her with long, languid movements that pulled her to the brink in seconds.

'Leo,' she panted.

'Be patient, wild girl.' And, so saying, he added a second finger, stretching her body, adding tension to the sensations bracketing her from all sides. Leo's own breathing sawed through the small bathroom with hers. 'The way your body tightens around me drives me wild, Willa. It makes me feel wanted.'

Tears rose to Willa's eyes even as her body took over, riding his hand as she strove for release. 'You are wanted, Leo,' she managed to gasp. 'Mine.'

And then she exploded.

The single word *mine* hurtled through him as he gentled his movements and helped Willa ride through her release.

Leo was overcome. His body ached. His mind, though clouded with lust, understood with clarity what she meant. And his heart, filled to bursting with equal parts love and relief, simply broke.

He supposed he had not realised how long he had yearned to belong. His entire life had been spent striving to be someone important—son or friend or lover—to people who could not give him the only thing he craved: to be *the* one to someone. Then he had married Willa and had been so terrified of being found lacking, of her not feeling the same way, that he had very nearly bungled everything completely.

'Leo.'

He raised his hands out of the water and looked at her, his *wife*.

His blood drained to his feet when he the tears streaming down her face. 'What's wrong?'

'Nothing,' she replied. 'I just wanted to say out loud that I love you.' She said the words quickly, as if she needed to get them out before she lost courage.

He moved to embrace her immediately, but Willa held up one hand, stopping him so that she could say the rest. 'I know I'm not perfect and that I still have to work on trusting you completely. But I don't want to withhold my love from you just because I'm afraid.' She placed her palm on his cheek, drawing his lips to hers. 'I want your love,' she murmured against his mouth. 'I want you.'

'You have me, Willa,' he replied, his eyes burning. 'You always have.'

'You're the only person who's ever made me feel completely safe to be myself. I don't know why—'

'Because I love you exactly the way you are, wild girl,' he replied for her and silenced her with his lips.

Chapter Twenty-Three

Although he would have loved nothing more than to take his wife back to bed after eight days without her, Leo knew that Willa had been through enough, given her situation. So, instead, he refrained from touching her anywhere else as she climbed out of the tub. He helped her change, lamenting the tightness in his crotch with each button he fastened and with each inch of her skin he covered up.

At her insistence, he took her downstairs to breakfast once she'd organised her rags, where everyone else was already sitting down at the table, enjoying the full English fare laid out on the sideboard. The Blakes talked loudly among themselves, laughing, teasing and arguing over every subject imaginable. Even Isabelle, who had once been shy and reserved, joined in, teasing the Countess, her mother-in-law, about the town butcher's fascination with her when the subject turned to the remarkable quality of the bacon and the fact that the man always sent the Countess his choicest cuts.

When Willa didn't eat, merely poured herself a cup of strong tea and went to sit next to Mary, Leo piled a plate with bacon, eggs, sausage and toast and placed it in front of her without a word before going back to get himself some food. He'd been half expecting an argument, so he couldn't help but smile when he turned around and saw her pointedly take a vicious bite of toast with a small mock-glare in his direction.

He merely raised his eyebrows and shrugged innocently, as if to say 'Yes?'

'Come sit by me, my boy,' the Countess demanded when he had his breakfast in hand.

Leo, understanding that it was not a suggestion, went to her immediately though it pained him to not go straight back to Willa. He pulled out his chair and sat down next to the woman who had been more than a mother to him than his own. 'Forgive my unannounced arrival, Lady Heather,' he said quietly.

'Leo, you are welcome at our home any time and without an invitation.' She frowned, her grey eyes clouding. 'I don't know why I always assumed you knew that.' Leaning forward, she lowered her voice. 'You know that the Earl and I consider you ours, don't you?'

Leo managed to smile through the lump in his throat. 'Thank you, my lady.'

'Lord, don't thank me!' she protested. 'It's rather selfish, you see.'

At Leo's perplexed expression, the Countess started counting the reasons off her fingers. 'Well, four successful children are so much better than three. I'll have more grandchildren, more people to stay with when I'm old and the Earl has—' she raised her voice for her husband to hear '—died from his penchant for bacon.'

She lifted both her eyebrows when the Earl, who was still superbly fit, just grinned and took a deliberate bite from another rasher of bacon, but Leo could see that she was fighting a smile. 'And, besides all that, your own parents never deserved you.' As Leo struggled for an appropriate response amid the emotions that tightened his chest, the Countess put her hand over his. 'Despite their neglect, you are remarkable, Leo. And we're very proud of you.'

'Thank you.' Leo barely managed to meet her eyes. 'I love your family very much and I've always considered myself honoured to be included in it.'

She gave his hand one last maternal pat. 'I used to hope you'd marry Nora, you know. Make it official and legally binding.'

Leo blinked once, genuinely surprised. 'No. I didn't know that.' He thought of Nora, who was the same age as Willa and yet more like a little sister to him than any other woman he knew. In fact, Leo didn't think he had ever even *looked* at Nora in the way a man looked at a woman, which was strange because she was beautiful with the same black hair and Blake-grey eyes as her mother. 'Perhaps, if I had not been in love with Wilhemina for so long, the idea would not seem so strange to me,' he said finally.

'Perhaps. Irrespective, I knew it would never happen once I saw you with Wilhemina last year—the first time she attended my ball with Isabelle.' The Countess laughed at the memory. 'The way you smiled, as if the sun and moon rose and set by her power alone. And even when you forced yourself to walk away from her, I saw you sneaking glances every few seconds. It was as if you thought she would disappear at any moment and you needed to hoard as much time with her as possible before she did.'

Leo grinned, remembering well what it had felt like to be in the same room with the only woman he'd ever loved, knowing he could never have her and that her husband was in attendance, too. 'And here I thought nobody knew how I felt about her,' he said quietly.

And the Countess laughed. She wagged her finger at

him and, leaning closer, whispered, 'Mothers always know these things, my boy.'

Leo nodded. Though he would have loved to be able to verbally return the sentiment, which he felt most keenly, he could not manage it. He supposed he had spent so long focusing on being unwanted, *unloved*, by his own parents that he had forgotten that he had two families who had taken him in as a boy with no expectations of gaining any advantage to themselves.

After considering this for some time, he quietly asked the Countess, 'Do you think that I will be a good father one day?'

The Countess looked at him with genuine alarm.

'My parents…' How did he even begin to describe the emptiness their neglect had hollowed within him? And the fears it had bred in all that space? 'They couldn't love me.' He said the words quickly, too afraid that he would baulk if he hesitated. 'And I worry that I might have the same… *inadequacies…*' He supposed when he'd known Willa couldn't have children, he'd been able to protect himself from the possibility. But now…

'My dear child, you have already surpassed them in every way imaginable!' Her eyes narrowed on his face. 'Do not tell me that you have harboured that ridiculous notion this entire time?'

'They did not—*could not*—love me, their own child, even though they adored each other.'

'Leo… How to put this nicely?' Seeming to think better of it, the Countess said, 'You never knew your parents and certainly not well enough to know that they loved each other. *I* knew them, Leo. And they were both selfish, vapid people.' She paused in her rant to look at him again. 'Did you ever think that their neglect was better than their attention? And that, in their absence, you became a far better boy, then man, than they ever could have raised had they paid the slightest attention to you?'

'No,' he replied honestly. But her words sank through him, filling him with relief and *peace*. All through his childhood, he had thought that if he could just be *better*, be *more successful*, then maybe his parents would feel more for him. And, in his desperation to be loved by Willa, he had approached their marriage the same way. But, perhaps, he had simply needed to find someone who could show him that being perfect would not solve all of his—their—problems.

'May I ask you a personal question?' the Countess asked.

'Of course.'

'How do you feel about the idea of Willa having your children?'

Leo looked across the table at his wife as she laughed about something Isabelle was teasing her about. When she saw him watching her, she winked cheekily at him. His heart gave one pathetic kick in his chest as he grinned back.

For the first time, he allowed himself to imagine her pregnant, then, as a mother—to *his* children. He imagined what their children would look like and—with Willa as a mother—the mischief they would find. And the emotions that hurtled through him—awe, joy, anticipation—settled a new peace through his heart.

He turned back to the Countess, and he replied, rather hoarsely, 'There are no words.'

She smiled. 'Well then.'

And for the first time ever, Leo supposed it really could be that simple.

Chapter Twenty-Four

They stayed a week at the Heather Estate, each of them content to delay the journey to Leo's country home a little longer. While the Blakes carried on with their typical pursuits and Mary travelled back to London for work, Wilhemina and Leo spent every minute together.

Following the Blakes' long, leisurely breakfasts, they would either walk or ride side by side. They explored the hundred-acre estate slowly, navigating the verdantly green pasture, heathland and small thickets of beech forest with no destination in mind and no need or desire to rush home.

During these outings they talked of nothing in particular—and essentially started to discover everything they didn't already know about one another. With each discovery, whether big or small, they not only grew closer, but became more and more comfortable with one another. Their defences fell. Their attachment blossomed.

During the day.

Night was another problem altogether.

Leo, who knew that Willa was overwhelmed by her courses restarting and who wanted to give his wife the time and distance he'd promised her, insisted upon sleeping separately.

So, when everyone retired for the night, he would watch

his wife leave, yearning—*aching*—to go after her. He wanted to hold her. He wanted to make love with her. And after almost six days in her company with no respite from his wanting, he'd taken to dreaming of her naked skin rubbing over his, her nipples pebbling against his tongue. He dreamed of tasting her again, her slick warmth filling his mouth, and, instead, woke up with a raging erection and a desert-dry throat. But, still, he did not go to her because Willa would need to be the one to take that first step again.

Now, on their last night at the Heather Estate, he lay awake in his bed. He stared up at the heavy ceiling beams above him, counting the visible grain lines in the wood in an attempt to distract himself from the thought of Wilhemina. And when that didn't work after ten minutes, he rolled over and tried to imagine meeting the Queen—an image that quite effectively stole what remained of his passion.

But as he quietened, the faintest scuffling sound reached his ears, pulling his attention to the closed door. He didn't move or even breathe as he strained to listen. Outside, it rained heavily, but even the sound of the rain did not muffle what he heard as distinct conversation.

His entire body settled into an alert state.

The moonglow coming in through the window illuminated a diagonal strip of the wooden door, beneath which Leo caught the faintest shadow.

Someone was outside.

Wasting no time, he silently climbed from his bed and slipped into his black nightgown, barely pausing to ensure that the sash was tied. Although there were several reasons why people would be traipsing around the house at midnight, none of them was a good one and he was resolved to out the miscreants before their crime was committed.

With his heart racing in his chest and his body flooding with vigour, he approached the door, his footsteps completely silent. He stopped, took a deep breath to steel himself for a fight and yanked it open in one swift pull—only to have his extremely startled wife issue a loud yelp as she tumbled towards the floor.

She'd had enough. After days of craving him and long, torturous nights where all she'd wanted to do was go and wrap herself around him, Willa had finally snapped. Dressed in nothing but her nightgown and slippers, she crept down the dark hallway in the direction of Leo's room like a thief in the night or a woman meeting her lover for a tryst, not a married lady in search of her own damn husband.

The cold night air, made cooler by the storm that had washed in unexpectedly, swirled beneath her cotton nightgown, prickling her skin and forcing the fine hair on her arms upright. She shivered and, wrapping her arms around her body, quietly approached Leo's bedroom.

She raised her hand to knock on the door. Paused. And lowered it again. 'What am I doing?' she mumbled. 'This is ridiculous. He's probably fast asleep.'

Her courage started to dwindle. Since the day after he had arrived, Leo hadn't as much as held her hand again. And although she longed for him, Willa, too self-conscious of her courses and too unused to asking for what she wanted, had not told him so.

In a lot of ways, it felt like a torturous game. If he looked at her too long, his eyes dark and intense, she felt herself heat with a pleasure blush—and then managed to convince herself that she had a stain on her dress that he was too embarrassed to tell her about. If he reached for her and then stopped, she would wish he hadn't—and then reminded herself that they were at breakfast, and he had probably been reaching for the salt.

At night when she left him to go to her bed and felt his eyes following her, she told herself that if that had been true he would have come to her. It was, after all, and in her experience, a husband's right to visit his wife when it suited him.

Now, she exhaled a frustrated breath and banged her head slightly on the door. She wanted him. She needed him. And she still could not just open her mouth and tell him.

'There's something wrong with me,' she muttered. She had never heard of a woman *needing* sexual gratification—and yet here she was, standing outside her husband's bedroom like a huzzy. She must have been born in sin. Or, maybe, there was some internal organ—a liver or a kidney, perhaps?—that had been constructed falsely in the womb? Something…

Any additional thoughts she might have given her failings were abruptly nullified as the door flew open and, Willa, who had been resting against it, toppled forward. She yelped and flailed as she fell, her arms waving wildly as she tried to counterbalance.

Leo caught her only a second before she hit the floor. His hand cinched around her upper arm, halting her downward trajectory, then hauled her back into the upright position. He steadied her on her feet, using both his hands, and Willa's momentary fright was immediately replaced with a hollow, spreading ache as his big palms smoothed over her arms.

'Willa,' he rasped, 'you scared the hell out of me. I thought someone was breaking into the house.'

'What?' she asked, confused. 'No. It's just me.'

Leo's laugh rumbled through his chest. He didn't release

her. Instead, he gently pulled her against him and wrapped his arms around her. 'I can see that, love.'

Willa sighed deeply, inhaling his scent. He was so warm and solid, so dependable and familiar.

Oh, how I've missed this.

She closed her eyes as she battled with a wave of pleasure so intense it made her tremble.

And, Leo, misreading her, crooned, 'Poor little love, did I scare you?'

His eyes raked over her as if he needed to see that she was fine for himself, and Willa saw the exact moment his attention caught on her aching nipples, the outline of which were visible through the thin cotton garment. His irises darkened perceptibly. His fists clenched at his sides. And, although he averted his gaze quickly, Willa saw his Adam's apple bob as he swallowed.

Encouraged by his obvious struggle, Willa took one small step forward. 'Yes,' she whispered.

'What is it?' he asked, his lust momentarily overridden by his concern. His brows came together. 'Are you ill?'

Willa nodded, even as her heart beat a frantic rhythm against her ribs. 'Yes.' She took a deep, steadying breath and, raising her hands, began on the small buttons at her throat.

Leo watched her warily as she slowly unbuttoned her nightgown. 'What is wrong?'

Willa's entire body was overheated, inflamed by his gaze. Lowering her hands, she gripped the flimsy cotton of her nightgown and lifted it up and over her head. She held it in front of her body, covering herself for a small moment before tossing it on to the floor. 'I have this ache,' she whispered. 'And it hurts.'

The breath left Leo's lungs in a ragged exhale. He lowered his head, momentarily undone, but when he raised his eyes to her again, Willa knew he felt it, too. She could see it in the tense set of his shoulders and in his pained expression. She could hear it in the winded sound of his breathing.

He didn't speak for a long moment, only absorbed the sight of her as she stood naked in front of him. It was only when she started to fidget with nerves that he seemed to recover. 'Show me where it hurts, love,' he demanded.

Willa blushed, but unwilling to cower after she'd come this far, she lowered her hand to hover in front of her aching core, half begging, half concealing. 'Here.'

The sound that left his throat was half-groan, half-growl. 'Willa, are you asking me to touch you?'

'No.' His head snapped up. Undeterred, Willa corrected, 'Leo, I'm *begging* you.'

Leo paled. 'Willa, I do not want you to *beg*. I only want you to be sure.'

'I am sure,' she replied immediately. 'Leo… I don't sleep when you're not with me. I can't. It…it feels wrong. As though I am adrift at sea without hope of ever reaching land. You…you anchor me. You make me feel safe, so that I can close my eyes and dream. Please…' she hurried on, her voice hoarse with emotion '…please come back to my bed. Indefinitely.'

He came to her then. Instead of kissing her as she'd hoped, he wrapped his arms around her and held her against his body as if he needed the contact after the days apart. His warm skin seeped through the fabric of his robe. 'Willa, I never wanted you out of my arms,' he whispered. 'I only wanted you to feel safe and free, to know that you are more than an available body for my pleasure and…' He laughed quietly. 'My wild girl, when you are close to me, it is hard for me to think of anything else. Lying next to you and not touching you is impossible for me. That is the only reason I have not shared your bed… Do you understand?'

Willa, who could feel his straining length against her stomach, rather thought she did.

'After everything that you have lived through, Wilhemina, I would hate myself if you ever felt that you didn't have a choice.'

'I don't want to have to *ask*,' she argued. 'It's so… difficult—to speak of such things.' She blushed just thinking about it.

'No, it's not. It's only me. And they are words I *long* to hear.' Raising both his hands, he cupped her face and looked into her eyes. 'I was made to love you, Willa. It is my greatest pleasure—and it always will be. All you have to do is reach out and take it.'

His lips hovered over hers, so close she felt as if there was an invisible force pulling them together. 'Leo…' Willa sighed dramatically when he only smiled. He was going to make her repeat it.

'Yes, love?' He leaned forward and nuzzled her throat.

'Touch me.'

'I am touching you,' he murmured and trailed the tip of his tongue lazily down her neck.

'No.' Willa reached for his hand and, gripping it in hers, lowered it between them.

Leo chuckled. 'So impatient. I—'

His words died as she brought him to her centre and pressed his fingers firmly against her so that he could feel how wet she was. '*Touch* me,' she commanded, bold in the face of her desperate need for him.

And he did.

His index and middle fingers slid through her damp curls, parting her heated flesh. He groaned loudly. He closed his eyes and grit his jaw against his own pleasure, but his fingers remained gently searching, each long, firm stroke coiling that heavy tension through her. His other hand found her breast, his nimble fingers teasing her nipple with small plucks and rolls until she was moaning.

She pressed herself more firmly against his hand in silent plea for more.

Leo cursed and withdrew, but before Willa could whimper in protest, he crushed his mouth to hers, silencing her. His lips and tongue wrung pleasure from her even as his hands moved to cup her bottom, and when he lifted her, Willa wrapped her legs around his waist, holding him to her as she angled her head and took the kiss deeper.

He carried her to the bed and, instead of releasing her as she'd expected, he sat down and slid his black nightgown from his shoulders while Willa untied the sash at his waist and greedily ran her hands over his bare chest.

He took a minute to steady her on his thighs and then he lay back on the bed so that she was straddling his hips. 'Come here,' he said quietly and, when she moved to climb off him, his large hand snaked out and gripped her knee, stopping her. He shook his head. 'Same position, love.' He grinned devilishly at her. 'Except I want you here—' he touched his lips '—so that I can taste you.'

Willa frowned, sure she had misunderstood. 'You want me to…?'

'I do.'

She tilted her head, trying to figure out the logistics of what he wanted before she moved, but Leo just laughed and, levering up, reached behind her, gripped her bottom with both hands, and dragged her up his torso as he lay back down.

He lifted her knees over his shoulders, positioning one

on each side of his neck, placing her directly in front of him, so that all he had to do was rise up and—

He licked her. Only once. But the slide of his tongue through her and the ensuing flash of sensation had Willa dropping her hands forward on to the bed to support herself. A ragged breath left her lips. 'I see,' she said, rather proud that her voice sounded unaffected.

Leo's dimples flashed when he smiled, but his eyes were almost black with lust. 'Shimmy forward a little,' he instructed and, when she did, angling herself almost directly over him, he growled his satisfaction.

Willa should have been humiliated—she knew that. He was looking directly at her… In a way that not even she had. But one look at her husband's face was enough to quell her embarrassment. He wanted her. He wanted *this*. And, though, she couldn't voice it, she wanted it, too. She wanted his mouth and tongue on her, licking her, sucking her—she wanted it all.

His shoulders flexed beneath her shins as he bent his elbows and his hands came back to grip her hips, supporting her weight. 'You can control the pressure.' He tugged her downwards until she felt his probing tongue, then gently pushed, forcing her away so that he could ask, 'Do you see?'

Willa nodded mutely.

'Good.' He tugged her forward again. 'Now, come here. Let me eat you.'

And Willa did. She slowly lowered herself down until his tongue worked between her folds, separating the halves of her with clever, quick strokes that flicked sparks of pleasure through her. She kept her hands on the bed, too afraid that she would lose her legs and collapse on him, and when he sucked her soft flesh into his mouth, she counterbalanced against the waves of sensation by mercilessly gripping the bed linens.

She panted his name when he penetrated her with his tongue. When he began teasing the bunch of nerves at her apex with flickering strokes, Willa couldn't stop her back from arching and her hips from moving in small thrusts as her body worked with him to reach completion.

She closed her eyes as her womb knotted and began to draw in. Her breath quickened to match each swirl of his tongue. And when Leo's large hands gripped the rounds of her bottom, spreading her wider as if he couldn't taste enough of her, she tensed her thigh muscles and found her release on a long moan.

Wave after wave of sensation rippled through her, each pulse of it sending a matching tremor down her unsteady legs, which suddenly felt too heavy and uncoordinated.

Leo chuckled and blew a cool stream of air against her sensitised flesh. 'So greedy, wild girl.'

'Yes,' she moaned.

'Tell me what you want, Willa,' he demanded. 'Tell me what you want and I'll give it to you. Anything.'

'Again,' she did not hesitate to reply, too desperate, too close to orgasming a second time to be self-conscious.

'Like this?' He slid his tongue through her wet heat, not stopping until he hit that same ball of nerves, which he mercilessly, slowly circled.

'Yes!'

He drew away again, teasing her. 'Ask me again, beautiful.'

Willa's eyes flew open. She looked down at him and felt a hard kick of love when he grinned at her.

Acting completely on impulse, she shimmied, crawling backwards inelegantly down his body until she felt his thick length beneath her open thighs. She gently lowered herself over him and then moved her hips back and forth, wetting him with her lust. 'I want you inside me,' she said clearly and, reaching down her hand, guided him to her aching centre.

Leo's hands found her thighs and gripped as she positioned the head of his sex at her entrance and, so slowly, began to slide down his steel shaft, taking him in one tiny bit at a time. His breath billowed from his lungs. And even as he twitched with the desire to thrust, he held back, letting her have complete control. 'You're so perfect for me, Willa,' he groaned. His face was red with the effort of holding himself back. 'Being inside you feels like coming home.'

Willa did not laugh. She understood what he meant perfectly: each inch of him had been flawlessly created to match each inch of her. And for the first time in her adult life, she realised that home was not a place, but a person.

Epilogue

London—1845,
two years later

'What in God's name is taking so long?' Leo demanded as he paced outside the bedroom. Given that it was potentially the hundredth time that he had asked the same question, nobody replied. The Countess of Heather smiled and took a sip of the brandy that Greyson had left for Leo over an hour before. Willa's mother, Lady Russell, didn't even raise her eyes from her book.

Though Willa had slowly started communicating with her family, beginning with Jameson and her mother, six months after they'd married, things were still tense between her, Lord Russell and Greyson, who, in her eyes, had been responsible for her diabolical marriage to Windhurst. It didn't matter how many times Grey apologised, or how many times Willa said she'd forgiven him, Leo knew it would take his wife a long time to truly trust her brother again. He didn't worry about it either, knowing that Willa deserved to take as long as she needed.

But despite their differences, when Leo had sent word that Willa's labours had started over eight hours earlier, every single Russell had hurried over and piled into the house to await the arrival of their new nephew or niece.

And now, while everybody else seemed perfectly calm and patient, Leo was slowly going mad. Every time he heard Willa cry out, his heart stopped. And, worse, very time the room was silent, he wished she would cry out so that he knew she was still fighting.

He had wanted to be in there with her, holding her hand and promising her that it would all be okay. Instead, he had been exiled to the hallway when, after one of Willa's particularly painful contractions, he'd asked Dr Taylor—rather politely, he thought—if he knew what the hell he was doing. The doctor had maintained that he couldn't work with Leo hovering over him. Mary and Isabelle had quickly agreed with him, deciding that perhaps it was best for Willa if he took his nervous energy outside.

That had been four hours ago, and every second since had been hell. The silence from the bedroom was deafening just then and Leo stopped his pacing to rest his forehead against the door, exhausted from worry.

'This is all normal, my boy,' the Countess assured him quietly.

Leo peeled himself off the door to run both hands through his hair.

Normal? Normal? There was nothing normal about this!

'Why don't you go drink with the men, my lord?' Lady Russell suggested kindly. 'You look as though you could use it.'

Leo ignored his mother-in-law and resumed his pacing, walking up and down the short hallway like a battle-lost soldier. When this was over, he vowed he would never touch Willa again. They would live out their lives in blissful celibacy, perfectly content with one child irrespective of whether it was a boy or girl.

The hysterical promises he was making to himself died suddenly as the door opened and Mary popped her head out. 'Leo, we need you.'

Leo didn't pause, or even stop to consider the scene he'd be walking into. He hurried to the door and entered the room, pulling up short when he saw Willa lying on the end of the bed, her knees raised beneath a sheet that was dappled with large rust-covered splotches. His typically healthy wife looked so tiny. Her hair was slicked with sweat and plastered to her face. And her face was almost as pale as the bed sheets beneath her.

'Willa,' he murmured, unable to approach.

Isabelle came to him. 'There were some complications,' she whispered, 'and though Dr Taylor has managed to turn the baby, Willa's too tired to push.' Her face was grave. 'Leo, you need to help her through this—and quickly.'

Leo swallowed the fear clogging his throat when he saw Isabelle's thinly concealed panic. He approached the bed, his heart racing in his chest when Willa's unfocused gaze turned to him. She tried to smile, but the attempt melted into tears almost immediately. 'I—I can't,' she panted.

'Yes,' he countered immediately. 'You can, my love.' She shook her head, but he didn't let her argue. He lay his upper body across the bed, brushing back her hair from her face. 'You are the fiercest, bravest woman I know.'

She grappled for his hand and Leo linked their fingers, only briefly wondering in the back of his mind if it was him or her sweating so profusely. His entire body was ablaze with fear and urgency and, when Willa moaned loudly, he looked to Dr Taylor.

'Push,' he mouthed.

'All right, wild girl.' He gripped Willa's lax hand in his, forcing her to return the pressure. 'We're going to count to three and then you're going to push one last time, all right?' She shook her head. 'You need to do this for me, Willa,' he urged.

Willa's tears ran freely down her face, but she moistened her chapped lips and nodded tiredly. 'One,' he started and her hand tightened on his, crushing his fingers. 'Two.' She panted, inhaling a few short breaths, and when he said, 'Three!' Willa bore down and pushed.

Leo didn't dare look at the doctor or at Mary and Isabelle, both of whom had moved to help. He kept his eyes locked on Willa's, whispering blind encouragements repeatedly. Things like, 'Good girl' and 'you're almost there,' words that were lost in Willa's high, keening wail.

Still, he knew the moment the baby was out; Willa's face slackened, and she collapsed back on to the bed. She lay completely still, her eyes closed, the rapid rise and fall of her chest the only sign that she was still alive. Terrified beyond explanation, Leo squeezed her hand, his heart settling into a steadier rhythm when she returned it weakly.

'I'm so tired,' she murmured quietly, her eyelashes fluttering.

'Sleep, my love.'

'I can't,' she argued weakly. 'The baby…' In her confused state, her tears turned to sobs. 'Leo, the baby.'

Leo gently brushed his thumb over her cheek, trying to soothe her. 'Shh, my love,' he whispered.

He turned back right as an almighty wail rent the air. His eyes found Mary, who held the screaming baby in her arms, her pale face mapped with relief. 'A boy,' she said, her own eyes filling with exhausted tears.

'A boy,' he repeated to his wife dazedly. 'We have a boy.'

Willa half laughed, half sobbed.

And Leo, unable to leave his wife just then, buried her thin hand between both of his and pressed their joined fingers to his forehead. He couldn't believe that women did this—and more than once, too. And Willa… 'You were amazing, my love,' he rasped, too overcome with emotion to say what he really thought—that amazing didn't begin to describe her, that she was extraordinary and that he would spend the rest of his life worshipping her and her incredible body.

Willa managed to pry open her eyes in an attempt to see her son, but the first thing that filled her vision was Leo, his head bowed over their linked hands, his eyes closed, his day-old stubble making him look unkempt. His clothes were wrinkled and dishevelled, his waistcoat and cravat both undone. And yet somehow he was still impossibly handsome.

She gently disentangled their hands so that she could run her palm through his sweat-slicked hair. Leo pressed his head more firmly into the caress, like a barely tame lion who needed reassurance, and when he raised his eyes to hers a moment later, she was shocked to see them brimming with tears. 'What's wrong?' she asked, her eyes immediately finding the baby, who was being coddled by his aunties.

'Nothing,' he replied quickly. 'You're perfect. I'm just…' He raised both his hands in front of them to show her how he trembled. 'You are incredible, Willa. So brave. *Fierce.*'

Willa, understanding that he was simply overwhelmed, smiled tiredly. Beneath the exhaustion, she was overcome, too, numb with pain and confusion, but also strangely euphoric.

Mary carried the baby to Leo. 'Would you like to hold your son, my lord?'

Leo paled. He turned to Willa, his eyes wide with fear. 'Do you want—?'

'No. You take him for now,' she said, looking pointedly to where the doctor worked beneath the sheets. And although her arms ached to hold her baby and her heart yearned to see his face for the first time, she wanted Leo to take his reassurance first, knowing that once her son was finally in her arms, she would have a hard time letting him go.

Leo took the bundled infant with impossible care, his movements almost comically slow. He cradled their son in his huge hands, the baby's body completely supported by the breadth of his palms. Leo was completely silent, completely still, as he stared down into their son's tiny face. He blinked rapidly as a wondering awe spread over his features and a ragged exhale left his lips.

'Leo?' Willa reached out a hand to touch him, to reassure him.

He leaned closer without delay, making it easier for her to reach him. 'He's perfect, love.'

'I know,' she said without having to look at the baby. For how could he be anything but? Their son was born of a love that had transcended suffering and pain, a love that had been born of a second marriage that, for both Leo and Willa, felt oddly like the only. But because she thought she might cry at the beauty of it all, she forced a mocking smile and drawled, 'He is yours, after all. It's only fitting that he look like you after I did all the work.'

Leo's quiet chuckle wrapped around her. 'Oh, but he doesn't, wild girl.' And he gently passed her the baby who, even after one glance and with his eyes closed, was clearly more Russell than Vickery.

Willa's heart constricted with a strange jolt that was oddly resonant of a seizure as their son's weight was transferred to her arms. A rush of warbled nonsense left her lips as the baby shifted and opened his little mouth. His perfect eyelashes fluttered over his closed eyes. His lips already worked in a silent, instinctual rhythm.

Leo climbed fully on to the bed, boots and all. He cradled the back of her head with one huge hand and gently kissed her forehead. 'Are you going to finally pick a name?' he asked quietly, having heard her change her list of top ten boys' and girls' names repeatedly over the last months.

'Wilder,' she replied immediately, not knowing where the name came from or why she had never considered it before. 'Wilder James Vickery.'

She looked up at Leo for a small moment, wanting to make sure he agreed, but her husband wasn't looking at her at all. He was watching their son, his blue eyes glazed with shock and love, his lips moving as he whispered, 'Wilder.'

* * * * *

If you enjoyed this story, be sure to read the first book in Maggie Weston's Widows of West End miniseries

One Night with the Duchess

And look out for the next book in Maggie Weston's Widows of West End miniseries, coming soon!